ANTONY MELVILLE-ROSS started his career in submarines in 1941 and left them in 1947. In two years he rose from the most junior officer aboard to a command of his own, and took part in the sinking of twenty-five enemy vessels in the Mediterranean, off Norway, and in the Java Sea. He was mentioned in despatches and won the DSC.

After the Second World War he became involved in Intelligence activities and subsequently worked as an oil company executive in the Middle East, New York and South America. He is married, and now lives near Lewes in Sussex.

Many of the characters who established themselves in *Trigger* and *Talon*, the first two highly praised novels in his submarine series, reappear in *Shadow*.

Available in Fontana by the same author

Trigger
Talon

ANTONY MELVILLE-ROSS

Shadow

FONTANA/Collins

First published by William Collins Sons & Co. Ltd 1984
First issued in Fontana Paperbacks 1985

Copyright © Antony Melville-Ross, 1984

Made and printed in Great Britain by
William Collins Sons & Co. Ltd, Glasgow

Bad form it may be, but I dedicate this book to my friend and editor Richard Ollard

Chapter 1

The dim blue light hanging from the submarine's jumping wire jerked fretfully at the thrust of the gale gusting in from the North Sea, illuminating a small area of driving rain like bright hair-lines caught in a swaying bubble. A stronger squall set the lamp swinging violently, alternately revealing and concealing the figure of the sailor on sentry duty huddled against the conning tower. His arms were hugging his chest, his sou'-wester was pulled low over his eyes and his oilskin glistened wetly.

It was very cold, close to snow the young officer thought. He was standing, rocking slightly in the wind, on the jetty ten feet above the moored vessel, watching it surge and strain against the mooring wires in the swiftly running ebb tide, seeing a water-logged baulk of timber butting against the sharp bows for a moment before sliding aft along the main ballast tanks and out of his field of view. A strong sense of anti-climax took hold of him. In whatever conditions he had imagined joining his first submarine none had approached such a depressing reality as that presented by Rosyth on a streaming February night. After long seconds he breathed in deeply, picked up his suitcase and moved to the top of the steps leading down to the floating wooden platform against which his new home lay.

'You down there!' he shouted. 'Is this HMS *Shadow*?' He was almost certain it was because there was no other warship in sight, but it seemed best to be sure.

The man on the casing pushed back his sou'wester and peered questioningly up towards the jetty, unable to distinguish anything with the light shining into his eyes.

'Halt,' he called uncertainly. 'Who goes there?'

'It's a bit late for that,' the officer replied. 'I've already shot you and dropped half a dozen grenades down the conning tower hatch. Is this *Shadow*?'

'Yes,' the man said, 'this is *Shadow*.' Then, deciding that the voice coming from the darkness sounded like an officer's, added the word 'sir'.

'Right, I'm coming aboard.'

The officer stepped onto the casing seconds later, returned the man's salute and walked towards the fore hatch. Before he reached it he set down his suitcase and reversed direction.

'What's your name?'

'Prentiss, sir. Able Seaman, sir.'

'Well, Prentiss, don't you want to know who I am? Are you just going to let me go below and chuck some more grenades around?'

'No, sir,' Prentiss said. 'Identify yourself please sir.'

'That's better. I'm Sub-Lieutenant Harding, the new navigating officer. Here's my identity card.'

Protecting it from the rain with his hand Prentiss looked at the card under the blue lamp and gave it back. 'Thank you, sir. I'll take your bag to the wardroom, sir.'

He reached down for it, but straightened again when the officer spoke his name.

'Sir?'

'There are several things you don't seem to have got quite right, Prentiss. First, you're a sentry, not a porter, and you don't leave the deck until somebody relieves you. Second, when the tide's out you keep watch from the bridge. You can't see what the hell's going on on the quay from down here. Third, when you challenge somebody take that gun you're wearing out of its holster. The damn thing's there for a purpose. Fourth, don't get impressed by the sight of an officer's cap badge. Anybody can get hold of one. Make him tell you who he is and make him prove it. All right?'

'Yes, sir. Are you – are you putting me on a charge, sir?'

Sub-Lieutenant Peter Harding looked at the sailor curiously. It had been a strange question and there had seemed to be real trepidation in the voice.

'What would I want to do a thing like that for?' he asked. 'As nobody else appears to have done it I'm telling you how to do your job, that's all.'

Immediate relief visible on Prentiss's face, even in the feeble illumination. Walking thoughtfully away Harding picked up his case again and clambered down the ladder to the torpedo stowage compartment. There he paused, squinting in the bright light, then nodded to a group playing cards at the far end. One of the group said 'sir' quietly. None of the others spoke. Harding stripped off his dripping coat, turned aft and made his way along the narrow corridor separating him from the wardroom. Men seated in the messes to his right watched him pass, their expressions blank. At the wardroom he drew the curtain aside and stepped in. A lieutenant was sitting at the table reading a book.

'Harding, sir. I've come aboard to join.' The standard phraseology sounded silly in his ears as though on some other occasion he might be required to say that he had come aboard to split, like an amoeba.

'Oh, hello,' the lieutenant said. 'Glad you got here at last. We were expecting you yesterday.'

'Yes, I'm sorry, sir. Bloody awful train ride from London. Nearly forty hours. Diversions, troop movements and all that sort of thing.'

'Christ, you must be shagged out. Have you eaten?'

'Not since York last night, sir.'

'Christ,' the lieutenant said again. 'Press the tit there. Ford will fix you something. He's the wardroom steward.'

The bell push was hanging by a cord from the deckhead beside a lampshade covered in cut-outs of the strip-cartoon character 'Jane' and other partly dressed girls. Harding pressed it and as though impelled by the completion of the electric circuit a head appeared through the gap in the curtains.

'Sir?'

'Ah, Ford. This is the new navigating officer, Sub-Lieutenant Harding. He hasn't eaten for about six months. See what you can do about it, will you?'

'Yessir. Scrambled eggs and spuds do you, sir?' Ford raised

his eyebrows enquiringly at Harding. Harding nodded, smiling, and the head disappeared.

'Sit down and have a gin while you're waiting.'

'Thank you, sir.'

'Oh, you needn't keep calling me "sir",' the lieutenant said. 'I'm only the gunnery and torpedo officer. Name's Michael Lynd.' His face clouded then and he added, 'Well, perhaps you'd better, in public at least. We haven't had a sub-lieutenant aboard before and I don't know what the Old Man will want.'

'Bit of a stickler, is he?' Harding asked.

The other handed him a gin and stared at the table for a long time before saying, 'Commander Cheaver is a very difficult man to get along with and that's putting it mildly. I'd step softly when he's around if I were you.' Lynd hesitated, then went on, 'That sounds pretty disloyal, but it's only fair that you should be warned. The reason you're here at all is that your predecessor couldn't take any more of him. He's left submarines now and gone back to General Service.'

Harding remembered Prentiss's reaction to his words of a few minutes before and his subsequent thankfulness when he had realized that what he had taken to be a reprimand was no more than instruction. He remembered too the guarded faces of the card players and the other people he had passed. Now this. The evidence was no more than circumstantial but, unpleasantly, it fitted.

'Oh dear,' he said.

'Yes, oh dear it is. I'll give you one tip though. Stand up to him. It'll bring fire and brimstone down on your head, but he reacts marginally better to a challenge than to subservience.'

It occurred to Harding that Lynd, however bad the situation, was talking far too readily to a stranger about their mutual commanding officer. Recognizing that as further proof of an unhappy ship didn't make him like him any the more for it, but he contented himself with saying only, 'I'll bear that in mind.'

Much of his hunger had deserted him by the time Ford had produced the steaming plate of food, but he forced himself to eat it because he didn't want to be the cause of further friction however slight. Before he had finished, the ship's first lieutenant and engineer officer returned from shore together and were introduced as Lieutenants Bradbury and Wright. Later he was to learn that they were known collectively as 'the long and the short of it'. Bradbury with his tall, gangling frame and the stocky, round-faced engineer with tufts of black hair growing out of his cheek bones were inseparable shore-going companions. At first they were cheerfully tipsy, but minutes after coming aboard they quietened and their eyes grew watchful.

'The Old Man will be back soon,' Bradbury said.

'The Old Man is back already and wants to know why he was not received aboard correctly.'

They all got to their feet and looked at the man with three gold bands on his sleeves standing by the curtain. He was about the same height as Harding's five foot ten, had similar mousey brown hair and the same pale blue eyes, but the likeness ended there. Whereas Harding's expression was diffident, a little withdrawn, Commander Cheaver's face with its hooked nose and a chin which seemed to curl up to meet it was almost theatrically aggressive.

'I don't understand, sir,' the first lieutenant said.

'That's par for your particular course, Number One. I want to know why I was not afforded the customary courtesy of being met at the top of the gangway at least by my sentry if my officer of the day is too lax to come on deck himself. That bloody man Prentiss is standing on the bridge. Why?'

His voice held carefully level to conceal the nervousness in it, 'Because I ordered him to stand there, sir,' Harding told him.

The Punch-like face jerked towards him. 'And who the hell might you be?'

'Harding, sir. Sub-Lieutenant. I'm the new navigating officer, sir.'

'Yes, I can see you're a sub-lieutenant. You make this officers' mess look like a bloody gunroom. As to being the new navigating officer, you'll be that when I say you are and not a second sooner. Do you understand?'

'Yes, sir.'

'Good. That puts you one up on the First Lieutenant. Now perhaps you'll have the goodness to tell me who gave you the authority to order my crew around.'

They were all looking at him now and Harding could feel the colour glowing in his cheeks. 'Nobody, sir,' he said, wanting to add, 'Except Flag Officer Submarines whose orders I have in my pocket,' not adding it because regardless of what Lynd had recommended he do there *were* limits.

'So?'

'Sir, I just saw that a sailor on sentry duty had failed to notice my approach for the simple reason that with the tide out he couldn't see me from where he was. He was below the level of the jetty and the gangway light was in his eyes. I told him to go to the bridge so that he could see to do the job he was supposed to be doing. What if I had been a German agent, sir?'

The captain yawned as though he had suddenly lost interest in the subject. He sat down and spoke indifferently. 'I expect they would have stopped you at the main gate.'

There was more than a streak of stubbornness behind Harding's unassuming facade and it showed when he replied, 'If they hadn't, nobody would have stopped me sabotaging your ship, sir.'

'By Christ, you do carry on!' Cheaver was standing again, head thrust forward like a bird of prey. 'If you felt so strongly about it why didn't you put Prentiss in the First Lieutenant's report? We have a short way with defaulters aboard here.'

'I can believe that,' Harding thought before saying aloud, 'For all I knew, sir, he was simply carrying out his orders. I couldn't very well run him in for that.'

'Orders you disagreed with?'

'Under the circumstances and in tonight's conditions – yes, sir.'

'Very well, as you're so full of yourself let's hear what you've got to back it with. What class certificate did you get in navigation?'

Harding wanted to deny that he was full of himself, but knowing it to be pointless restricted himself to replying. 'First, sir.'

'Gunnery?'

'First, sir. Er – I got a "first" in everything.'

'Did you now? Where did you come in your submarine training course?'

'Fourth, sir.'

'Out of four?'

'Out of thirty-seven, sir.'

'Well, well. You do enjoy parading your self-satisfaction, don't you?'

'I'm only answering your questions, sir.'

'Then answer this one. Are this ship's charts corrected up to date for wrecks, minefields and everything else?'

Rattled and reckless now, 'I haven't the remotest idea, sir,' Harding told him. 'I'm not the navigator and I have *your* authority for saying that!'

He was answered by a short, barking laugh and a grin, but there was no humour in the laugh and no friendliness in the display of teeth.

'You are now, Harding. Be seated everybody and we'll drink to the health of our latest young genius.'

Harding remained standing. 'If you'll excuse me, sir, I'll go and see to the chart corrections.' He could hear the tautness in his own voice.

'I told you to sit down,' his captain said. 'We're not going anywhere tomorrow. You can do them in the morning.'

The long train journey from London had tired Harding and the absurd confrontation with the man who had almost total control of his destiny had drained him completely. Lying in an upper bunk, hearing faint snores coming from the one below him, not even the three whiskies he had not wanted but had felt obliged to drink had succeeded either in bringing sleep to him or holding his depression at bay. That had firm hold of him and he felt bemused too for, in all his short naval career, he had never encountered an officer, senior or junior, remotely like Cheaver, least of all amongst the submarine captains he had met on his training course. The bulk of those, although they fell into no set pattern, he had mentally placed in two rough categories at either end of the spectrum. There were the bearded extroverts after the Elizabethan tradition and the quiet, shy men with an almost mystical sense of purpose. Of these two extremes he had enjoyed listening to the former, felt emotionally closer to the latter, and now wished fervently that someone of either type would miraculously replace a man he considered to be not only mannerless but stupid with it.

Shadow moved restlessly at her moorings and Harding did the same within the confines of his curtained bunk, searching his mind for something to be thankful for, finding only the fact that the captain had elected to leave the ship and sleep at the base so that, for a few hours, he was free of him. The future would have been marginally brighter, he thought, had this been one of the larger T-class boats where Cheaver would have had a cabin of his own, thus sparing his officers his proximity for some part of each day, whereas in this tiny wardroom ... Harding groaned and turned over again. So much for a decision which had appeared to hold out so much promise.

1939 had dragged towards its close in an endless succession of gales and four-hour watches constantly repeated while the light cruiser to which he had been appointed pitched and rolled along her lonely pattern of courses between Iceland and the Faeroe Isles. When one pattern had been completed she would steam another and another and another. It had made him think of Penelope awaiting the return of Odysseus and the web she wove by day and unravelled at night, never to complete it. The long hours on the heaving bridge, the lack of sleep, the indifferent meals and the clothes that were never quite dry, all that he had withstood stoically as had everyone else in the crew. It was the grinding monotony of the existence that got to him and he began to envy the six midshipmen in his charge. They at least had the entertaining task of leading boarding parties onto intercepted neutral ships and conducting them to Kirkwall in the Orkneys to be searched for contraband.

That he had to find for himself a more positive role in a war which only the Navy seemed to be fighting became increasingly obvious to him and he reviewed the possibilities carefully.

There had been requests for volunteers for 'special and hazardous service', but as the type of service was not specified and could not, for reasons of secrecy, be established that was too much like signing a blank cheque for Harding. Then there was the Fleet Air Arm. His father had owned a three-seater Avro Cadet during the last years of peace and had taught his son to fly it. After some thought he had discarded that option because it seemed obvious that flying aircraft was not, by a long way, the fastest route to command of a warship. Such a command had, he knew, to be his prime target and did not include anything as small as a motor torpedo-boat.

The realization of what the fastest route was, and the knowledge that its destination was where he had subconsciously wanted to arrive at for some time past, came to him simultaneously. Being by nature cautiously conservative he had examined his thought processes again as though constructing a syllogism, then, finding no fault, requested permission to see his captain.

The interview had been brief and, to his relief, pleasant. He had felt that his commanding officer, a gunnery specialist, would disapprove and had approached him timidly.

'I hardly think volunteering for submarines can be construed as disloyalty to me, Harding,' he had been told, 'so put that out of your mind. It's a very good idea for a young fellow like you. Let me have your official request on paper and I'll forward it with my recommendation as soon as we reach harbour.'

Things had happened fast after that and, within three days of the cruiser's return to Scapa Flow, Harding had found himself fearfully gripping the seat-belt of an RAF Anson transport plane as it soared, swooped and bumped its way south above the stormy waters of the Pentland Firth en route for Aberdeen. From there he had made his way by train to a coastal town called Blyth in Northumberland he had never heard of to begin his submarine course.

It had been a happy time. He felt at home immediately with pupils and instructors alike, the technicalities he was taught fascinated him and he absorbed them all readily because they were so logical. Only waiting his turn for a medical examination disturbed him because he thought that the rigours of life under water might require physical attributes of him which he didn't possess, but his worries had been groundless. The examination was not so much a formality as a joke.

'No, don't bother to undress,' the doctor had said. 'They wouldn't have sent you here if you weren't fit. Ever had piles or trouble with your ears?' At the shake of Harding's head, 'You will before you've finished with this lot,' he had added. 'Send in the next chap, please.' Too relieved even to wonder what the doctor had meant, he jerked a thumb at the next in line on the way out.

He hadn't even minded when he and all his class-mates were confined to the base for a week because some of their number had climbed the face of the 'Roxy' cinema in the town and sawn the leg from the 'R' of the illuminated sign there, turning it into a 'P', to show what they thought of the place. It had been fun, the seriousness and the childishness and the anticipation of the future, but now it had all curdled as quickly as milk in a thunder-storm. This was no band of brothers he had joined, no happy few. It was nothing more than a small group of officers filled with dislike for their captain and suspicion of each other. Even the bond of friendship he had observed between first lieutenant and engineer officer had withered in Cheaver's presence. Morosely he wondered how deep was the disaffection he had already sensed in the crew, an alienation which could have its source only in the wardroom.

It was after four in the morning when he fell asleep. Aware of the exhausting train ride from London he had undergone the others let him lie when they got up for breakfast and he was awakened at eight by an already detested voice demanding to be told why the bloody sub-lieutenant wasn't working on the charts. As he clambered from his bunk Harding added his own quota to the atmosphere of mutual suspicion by assuming that his new mess-mates had deliberately failed to call him to deflect the captain's sarcasm from themselves. Fear fingered him slyly but he struck its hand away with the grim resolve that within a week nobody would be able to fault him on the workings of the ship and his job in it. Determination born of dislike blended with his natural stubbornness to form a quiet fanaticism.

Chapter 2

The grey water of the North Atlantic heaved sullenly for thirty metres around the U-boat. Beyond that there was only the mist, opaque, motionless in the still air, menacing in its passivity because of the hazards it concealed. Moisture gathered, clung, then surrendered to gravity in trickling streams meandering down vertical surfaces of the ship and the foul-weather gear of the men on the conning tower.

Kapitanleutnant Lothar Bruning swore softly to himself, dabbing at the moisture on his face with irritable flicks of his finger-tips as though removing some noxious substance. The droplets reformed at once.

'Come down to dead slow,' he said.

'*Jawohl, Herr Kaleu,*' the officer standing beside him answered and relayed the order.

Bruning frowned. 'I wish,' he said, then closed his mouth firmly, the sentence unfinished. He had been going to say that he preferred to be addressed by his full title, not its abbreviation, but guessed that he would be considered odd, even nervous, if he raised such a petty point at a time like this. He *was* nervous, and disappointed too. Nervous because he was lost and disappointed for the reason that the appalling weather of the last four weeks which had caused him to lose himself had also prevented any contact with the English.

'What, *Herr Kaleu?*'

'Nothing.'

The U-boat ghosted on, diesels rumbling idly, with only the constant tortured wailing of sea birds to tell him that land was near, and enemy land at that. So much, at least, he was sure of for his dead reckoning could not be so far out that he was approaching the Norwegian coast. No, it had to be part of Scotland ahead, or the northern islands. But which part? Which islands?

'Stop engines,' he said.

Ears straining to catch the sound of surf, eyes watering with the effort of trying to pierce the grey blanket around him, but there was nothing but the soft surge of the sea against the pressure hull. And the fog. And the crying of the gulls.'

'Too risky,' Bruning muttered to himself. 'Much too risky.' Then aloud to the watch officer, 'Slow ahead. Come left onto a reverse course. We'll put out to sea until the visibility improves.'

It had been a bad month. Twenty-seven days of storm-force winds urging the sea into waves of such size that diving and surfacing had been dangerous and depth-keeping almost impossible. Eventually he had decided to remain on the surface and ride it out. Even given an enemy ship to fire at he doubted that his torpedoes would run true in such conditions. There had been no enemy ship in all that time, just the storm clouds skidding across the sky depriving him of the sun by day and the stars by night from which he could have calculated his position on the empty ocean. On the twenty-eighth day the wind had dropped, but the overcast had stayed stubbornly where it was. Then the fog had come.

A zephyr touching his cheek and the watch officer's shout came simultaneously.

'Land on the starboard bow, *Herr Kaleu*! Close! Very close!'

'Hard a'port. Full ahead starboard. Full astern port. Crew to collision stations.' Bruning had spoken calmly. It was expected of him and there was nothing to be gained by speaking any other way in the near silence, but he didn't feel calm.

For a fleeting second he glimpsed the towering crags himself, on the starboard beam now, then the greyness swallowed them again. Minutes later with the ship moving away from the land, 'It would be nice if we knew where that was,' he said.

'It was Saint Kilda, *Herr Kaleu*.'

'What? Are you sure?'

The other nodded. 'Absolutely. It's very distinctive and I got a good look at it while you were giving emergency manoeuvring orders.'

'I'll be damned,' Bruning said. 'Well done, Frisch. Steer 025. At last we know where we are.'

It had been little short of a miracle to have chanced upon that desolate outpost of Scotland rising from the sea some sixty kilometres from the Outer Hebrides and he took it as a sign. Throughout the blank mission his frustration had grown until it was barely containable and he had searched his mind ceaselessly for some way to strike at the enemy. Embarrassment and envy had both goaded him. Embarrassment at the thought of the polite nods of understanding from his superiors when he returned to Kiel with his quota of torpedoes intact and not a shell fired. Envy because his class-mate *Kapitanleutnant* Gunther Prien had broken into the enemy's main base of Scapa Flow, sunk the battleship *Royal Oak* and now wore the coveted *Ritterkreuz* at his neck. *There* was something to emulate, but not at Scapa Flow. The enemy would not let that happen twice.

It was dream more than plan when he had begun to consider his chances of penetrating the defences of the naval base at Rosyth. The English mine-sweepers clearing the swept channel would show him the way in if he could remain undetected for long enough to plot their course, if the visibility was good enough to do so, if he had sufficient fuel remaining after this abortive patrol to carry out the operation, if those *Luftwaffe* idiots didn't mine the channel again before he could get in and out. A lot of 'ifs'. With fuel running short and his whereabouts unknown he had dismissed the possibility from his mind. Then Saint Kilda had revealed itself fleetingly to tell him within a few metres where he was on the world's surface. The sign.

Bruning went below to chart his course around the north of the Shetland Islands and down the east coast of Scotland to the Firth of Forth and its naval base of Rosyth. With luck it would not be necessary to explain why he had returned to Kiel with all his torpedoes. With luck the English would remember his visit with dismay as, no doubt, they remembered Gunther Prien's.

Why he always thought of the British as the English he didn't know. Perhaps it was because he disliked the English more than the other people in the United Kingdom. He shrugged and set to work with pencil and parallel ruler at the chart table.

Two hundred kilometres to the south and west of Saint Kilda *Kapitanleutnant* Otto Rademacher raised the attack periscope precisely in time to see the last torpedo of his final salvo strike the corvette near its stern. The result was devastating, the explosion of the torpedo warhead totally lost in the fury of the sympathetic detonation of the corvette's depth-charges. The little escort vessel disintegrated.

Not far from it the three thousand ton freighter it had been escorting lay stopped, listing heavily, members of the crew sliding down the sharply canted deck into the water. A straggler from the Liverpool-bound convoy he had attacked the day before which the corvette had gone back to protect Rademacher guessed. It capsized and sank as he watched, dragging most of its crew with it. Slowly he turned the periscope in a full circle, but there was nothing left to look at across the tossing waves. It was choppy, exactly right for a submarine attack, nothing more than the fringe of the storm the weather reports said was raging to the north of him and he was very glad about that for it had enabled him to carry out a most productive patrol. Two tankers, one large, one small, sunk, one big merchantman damaged, and now this smaller one and its escort sent to the bottom.

'We'll go up and try to identify the targets,' Rademacher said.

The U-boat reared to the surface seconds later and with water still pouring from her bridge moved towards the area of debris which minutes before had been two ships. There were men there too, seven of them, three swimming weakly, aimlessly, four clinging to an upturned life-boat. In every case their eyes gleamed whitely from oil-blackened faces.

'Close on that boat.'

'*Sofort, Herr Kaleu!*'

Rademacher rather liked being called '*Herr Kaleu*'. There was something both comradely and respectful about it, something a little devil-may-care as well which he thought suited his character.

When the boat was within hailing distance he raised a megaphone to his mouth and shouted, 'What ships are you chaps from?' For two years before the war he had studied at Cambridge University and his English was fluent and colloquial.

The faces watched his approach in silence.

Sixty metres from them he ordered the engines stopped and called, 'I was wondering if any of you blokes would care to tell me what ship or ships you are from.'

The U-boat had come to a stop close to the group before one of the faces said, 'Get fucked, you stinking Hun bastard.' There was more resignation than venom in the words.

Rademacher smiled and said, 'That's precisely what I intend to do as soon as we get home, my friend,' then to the officer beside him, 'Nudge that boat over, Willi, and let's see if there's a ship's name painted on the side.'

That was his first mistake.

The wallowing boat rolled when the submarine's bows rode over it, scattering the four men, then it disappeared from sight.

'SS *Amber* of Cardiff, *Herr Kaleu*.'

'Thank you.'

Looking astern Rademacher saw that the faces had vanished and all that remained of the life-boat was a few planks of wood. It didn't occur to him that the blades of his propellors could have come into contact with the boat's engine block.

That was his second mistake.

Two minutes after diving the man on duty in the 'sound' room reported a constant singing noise from astern. Rademacher ordered both propellors stopped in turn and the 'sound' man told him that the noise was coming from the starboard one.

It was the end of a successful cruise, all his torpedoes had been expended, and Rademacher was anxious to be on his way back to Germany. Without much thought, 'Well, there's nothing we can do about it now,' he said. It was as though saying it had made it so and it didn't occur to him that there *was* something to be done about it, that he should have forbidden the use of that propellor when submerged until the nicked blade had been repaired in dock.

That was his third mistake.

Chapter 3

'All hands on board, ship ready for sea, sir,' the first lieutenant said. Cheaver nodded an acknowledgement, his expression without apparent interest, his fingers beating a monotonous tattoo on the rail in front of him like the sound of a galloping horse.

'Obey telegraphs, sir?'

'Yes.'

Shadow's little bridge was crowded and more men were moving in orderly confusion on the casing, both in front of the conning tower and behind it, stowing away wires and fenders.

From the jetty somebody in the berthing party shouted, 'Good luck, Harry!' and a sailor on the casing replied, 'See yer, Fred.'

'Have that damned chattering stopped, Number One,' Cheaver said.

'Aye aye, sir.'

Harding listened to the first lieutenant delivering a reluctant reprimand to anyone who was listening, then looked drearily around him. He looked at the dreary wind-swept jetty with its rows of cranes like long-legged wading birds. Well then, like cranes. Make it herons to avoid confusion, he told himself, but found no humour in the laboured joke he had contrived. He looked at the dreary buildings of the town, at the oily, garbage-bearing water sliding past to seaward, and at the diamond-shaped spans of the Forth Bridge like something assembled from a gigantic Meccano set. That looked dreary too. When he had looked at all that he glanced at his captain and met the now familiar unfriendly show of teeth.

'Right, Mr "first class certificate" Harding, let's see you take the ship to sea as a good little navigator should.'

Harding had been expecting something of the sort and had worked out what he would do if he was told to do it, but the order still increased his pulse rate unpleasantly because the largest powered craft he had ever handled had been of wooden construction and less than thirty feet in length. Now he was faced with the immediate task of manoeuvring over two hundred feet of steel warship.

'Aye aye, sir,' he said.

The tide was ebbing as it had been when he had first seen *Shadow* almost three days before and the pressure of water between jetty and hull was forcing her outwards against her mooring ropes.

'Let go for'ard,' Harding ordered, saw the line slacken and the bows begin to swing out into the stream. 'Let go aft. Half ahead port,' he added, making his voice sound as firm as he could, trying unsuccessfully to subdue the fluttering of his heart. *Shadow* appeared to move sideways from the quay, then began to forge slowly ahead. When the stern rope was clear of the water and the starboard propellor clear of other obstructions, 'Half ahead starboard, port fifteen,' came with reasonable steadiness from between lips which felt as stiff as if a dentist had given him an injection. Men from the casing, their work finished, clambered up the side of the bridge and disappeared down the conning tower hatch. The traffic distracted him, but he forced himself to concentrate on the now simple task of facing the submarine down the Firth of Forth and towards the North Sea. That done, he turned to the captain.

'Main engines, sir?'

'I hadn't intended to go all the way to Skagerrak on the batteries, Harding.'

One after the other Harding had the electric motors stopped and the engine clutches engaged. Diesel smoke eddied and

Shadow began to move more quickly through the scummy water, her bow wave building higher at the stem and swirling aft along the ballast tanks. Cheaver lit a pipe, shielding the flame of a succession of matches against the wind and driving rain until the tobacco caught. Apart from an oblique answer to a single question he hadn't spoken throughout the departure. It was to take Harding some time to realize that that constituted a compliment. Now he was simply thankful that nothing had gone wrong, that he could relax a little and look around him once more. Ahead there wasn't much shipping to be seen, what there was keeping carefully to the correct side of the channel except for a small tug, towing an improbably massive barge upstream against the ebb tide, which was having difficulty in keeping itself anywhere. To either side the shores of the Firth were receding, fading into a blur of distance and rain. Astern the Forth Bridge loomed massively. Harding found it less dreary to look at now because he was wondering when he would see it again, if he would ever see it again. Had there been anyone to tell him that he would be seeing it in less than forty-eight hours he would have found that difficult to believe.

The first lieutenant took the first two-hour watch after the crew had secured from harbour stations and the Isle of May was in clear sight on the port bow when Harding, followed by his captain, climbed the two vertical brass ladders connecting control room and bridge to relieve him. The winter afternoon was sliding rapidly towards evening, but visibility had increased with a watery sun glinting periodically through breaks in the overcast. As Harding watched it sent down a shaft which lit up the horizon astern like a pale searchlight beam.

'Are you nearly ready to take over the watch, Harding? I hate to hurry you, but Number One would like to go below if it's all right by you.'

Harding swung round to face Cheaver. 'I'm extremely sorry, sir. I thought you were taking over.'

'Oh I am, sonny. I am. But it would be an immense relief to all of us if we knew that *you* were fully *au fait* with the situation. Things like the ship's course and speed, it's position in relation to trivial hazards like rocks and minefields. Tedious, but you know how it is.'

'Yes, sir,' Harding said.

He had felt no resentment when told that he would stand watch with the captain, who normally kept no watch at all, until he was adjudged fit to do it by himself. To have left him on his own in his unproved state would have been foolhardy and personally alarming for him. For all that, he had been very far from looking forward to the experience and, because he had done nothing more than pause to follow the natural course of checking the weather conditions while the light lasted, he bitterly resented Cheaver's uncalled for sarcasm. Harding felt suddenly physically sick and the sensation had nothing to do with the submarine's jerky pitching and rolling motion.

'I'm sure you do,' Cheaver told him. 'Now, I expect that the First Lieutenant wants to explain to us that that is the Isle of May ahead there, that the course is 080, speed 12 knots and that when South Ness is abeam we should come to 010, thus enabling us to follow the swept channel all the way to Bell Rock. Is that right, Number One?'

'That's right, sir. A battle-wagon and two destroyers crossed about six miles ahead heading south down the other channel half an hour ago. I think she was the *Barham*. Apart from that its been all coastal traffic, pretty dense too, and some trawlers.'

When Bradbury had gone below the captain took his pipe from the pocket of his oilskin, but *Shadow* moved out of the lee of the peninsula of Fife at that moment and the north-easterly wind and swell struck her, sending repeated dollops of thick spray flying about their heads. He muttered to himself and put the pipe back in his pocket. By the time the Isle of May provided them with a new lee, and the plunging motion had eased, the daylight had faded too far for it to be safe to strike matches on the bridge with *Luftwaffe* mine-laying aircraft likely to appear with the coming of night.

Stooping over the compass binnacle, aligning the prismatic sight on the dimly seen unlit lighthouse, 'South Ness abeam to port, sir,' Harding said.

'Very well. You know what to do.'

Harding bent to the voice-pipe. 'Port ten, steer 010,' he told it and heard his order acknowledged. *Shadow* swung towards the north and steadied ten degrees to the east of it. The only shipping in sight was astern of them now.

'I'm going below for a smoke,' Cheaver said. 'Call me at once if you sight anything at all, or hear aircraft.'

'Aye aye, sir.'

Much as he disliked him, Harding felt very lonely on the bridge without his captain, lonely and anxious with only the silent figures of the four look-outs for company, four men he would have been unable to name even if duffel coat hoods and binoculars had not been obscuring their faces. There was, he supposed, little danger. Visibility was adequate to the west where the last rays of a sun already set brushed the underside of some bank of cloud with faint luminscence. To the east it was very dark, but the great mine barrier stretching from Scotland to the Thames lay there and nothing, except aircraft which would not be able to see them, need be expected from that direction. Cheaver, he supposed, had chosen this moment to give him his first taste of responsibility before *Shadow* passed through the swept channel in the mine-fields and entered the real war zone on their far side.

Harding had completed his first slow sweep of the horizon and was wiping spray from the lenses of his binoculars with a wad of tissue before starting another when the port after look-out shouted, 'Submarine surfacing on Red 145, sir!'

Jerking round to face the bearing, his feelings a mixture of disbelief and dismay, he found his line of sight blocked by the forward periscope standard. Side-stepping, he bumped heavily into the port forward look-out, said 'Sorry' out of automatic politeness, and raised his binoculars to his eyes. The western horizon still visible as a hard line rising and falling in and out of his field of view as *Shadow* rolled. Nothing! Two seconds wasted! Train further right! The blackness of the Isle of May excluding all light. Train left! Four seconds gone, but something, something dark which hadn't been there before! He whirled for the voice-pipe, bending at the same time, catching his head a glancing blow on the side of the bridge.

'Control room! Hard a'port! Cap'n on the bridge! Sound the alarm! Stand by all tubes! Full ahead together!'

Acknowledgements, urgent but faint, reaching his ears as he straightened, raising the heavy binoculars to his eyes again, his thoughts racing, tumbling over each other. No friendly submarines in the area. Fact. A black object against the slightly paler sea. Fact. Only a buoy torn from its moorings, drifting? Don't think so. Too big. The sudden sharp hissing of air in the conning tower as an ascending body impeded its flow to the racing diesels. The captain coming! Oh God! If he had flooded six torpedoes in their tubes for nothing, they would all have to be drawn back into the ship for overhaul and . . .

'That look-out! Are you sure it's a submarine?'

'Yessir. Saw the water pouring off the bows and conning tower when she come up. Weren't nothing there before. Opposite course to us, sir.'

The squat shape of what might well be a conning tower clear in the field of his binoculars and the smudge of a hull below it, a hull foreshortened by perspective with broken water at its base. On the port beam now, seeming to move forward as *Shadow* swung towards it. Hissing of air from the conning tower abruptly cut off. A figure half seen out of the corner of his eye cannoning into him.

'What the bloody hell's going on, Harding?'

Suddenly, miraculously not flustered anymore, 'U-boat, sir. Bearing Red 50. Heading about south.'

'A U-boat? In here?'

Without replying Harding bent to the voice-pipe. 'Control room, steady on 180 and come down to slow ahead together.'

'Steer 180 and slow ahead together, aye aye, sir.' The 'ting' of the engine room telegraphs faintly heard, then the voice-pipe saying, 'All tubes standing by, sir.'

Beside him Cheaver saying, 'I see it. Open bow caps.'

Relaying the order it occurred briefly to Harding that his assessment had been tacitly upheld, but there was not time to take pleasure in the assumption. Too many impressions crowding in on him, too much happening. *Shadow* swinging more slowly now, the vibration dropping away with the decrease in speed. Diesel fumes blowing around his head carried on the following wind. The black blob almost directly ahead appearing to rise and fall prodigiously, not really doing it, just the exaggeration of magnification through the binoculars and his own ship pitching. The voice-pipe telling him, 'Steady on 180, sir.'

Cheaver speaking for only the second time without a sneer in his voice. 'Come three degrees to starboard, Cox'n, and do your utmost to hold her on 183. I'm attacking a U-boat from dead astern, so there isn't much to aim at. You'll find it difficult because the swell is coming from astern too, so twist the rudder off her if you have to. Understood?'

'Understood, sir.'

'Right. Ask the Gunnery and Torpedo Officer to speak to me.'

'I'm here, sir.'

'Listen, Lynd, I'll be firing a full salvo of six fish. No spread, no aim off, no nothing. All aimed to hit. One of them should do that, given luck. I'll try to anticipate the swing of our bows and you hit the firing button the very second you get the word. Stand by.'

'Standing by, sir.'

'Give me a touch more speed, Harding. Make it easier for the Cox'n to hold her steady.'

'Half ahead together,' Harding told the voice-pipe and *Shadow* began to move more purposefully, outdistancing the following swell, beginning to close on the black blob.

Peering through binoculars clipped to the torpedo night sight Cheaver muttering inaudible things to himself, then calling, 'Fire One!' Several seconds pause before, 'Fire Two!' A shorter period and 'Fire Three!' The bows had swung quickly back on target Harding supposed. After half a minute they had all gone and he stood, bracing himself against the awkward movement of the deck under his feet, picturing the torpedoes arrowing through the water faster than any ship, willing them to strike their target, not wanting to watch the black blob anymore in case they did not, but watching it all the same.

Time stretching. Would the enemy, if it was the enemy, sight the pursuing ship and take evasive action? What was the running time of the torpedoes? Stupid! Unanswerable without knowing the range. Would they run true? Had Cheaver . . .

A tall pale phantom rising above the blob, towering for seconds, then fading as though exorcised. A dull boom carried away on the wind. The first lieutenant shouting excitedly up the voice-pipe, 'Bridge! Sharp under-water explosion! Could have been a torpedo hit!' The blob diminishing in size, vanishing. Cheaver saying. 'Get the signalman up with an Aldis lamp.'

Shadow vibrating at full power, running in towards the site of the sinking, her progress pathetically slow compared with that of the torpedoes she had sent ahead of her. The stench of diesel oil growing in strength. The beam of the Aldis pin-pointing floating debris in the darkness. The signalman saying, 'Two blokes in the water over 'ere, sir.'

Shadow lying stopped, Lieutenant Lynd and three men on the fore casing, life-jacketed, holding heaving-lines. Able Seaman Prentiss in the sea, one line about himself, tying the ends of the others around the two men. The men being dragged aboard, one conscious, the other not. The conscious man being helped along the casing, up the side of the conning tower and onto the bridge. Cheaver saying, 'Who are you?' and the shivering, dripping figure replying, '*Kapitanleutnant* Lothar Bruning,' with a break in his voice.

'Sling that signal pad over here,' Cheaver said.

Harding slid it across the wardroom table and watched him write 'Most immediate. Surfaced U-boat torpedoed and sunk five miles east Isle of May. Captain and navigator recovered but latter died within minutes of being brought aboard. Returning harbour to disembark prisoner and body and to replenish torpedoes'.

Cheaver pushed the pad back to Harding. 'Cipher that and have it transmitted.'

'Aye aye, sir.'

He had almost finished converting the message into five-number groups when the petty officer telegraphist appeared with a signal form in his hand, said, 'Urgent for us, sir,' put the paper on the table and departed. Harding set the first signal aside and began to decipher the incoming one. When he had finished it read. 'Enemy heavy unit provisionally identified as *Gneisnau* reported preparing depart Wilhelmshaven. Disregard previous order and proceed at best speed to vicinity Heligoland. You will be given precise patrol instructions in due course. Acknowledge.'

Leaning his body sideways into the passage Cheaver called, 'Who's on the wheel?'

'Ford, sir.'

'Ford, tell the officer of the watch to turn back to o1o for the swept channel again.'

'Aye aye, sir.'

'Harding.'

'Sir?'

'Delete the last sentence of that signal of mine and substitute "Now proceeding in accordance your 192".'

The message enciphered Harding took it to the radio room. On his way back the coxswain stopped him.

'We've dried off the Jerry officer, sir, and kitted 'im out with some of your clothes like you said. What shall we do with 'im now?'

'Bring him along to the wardroom, Cox'n. The Captain will want to question him.'

'Aye aye, sir.'

Kapitanleutnant Lothar Bruning sat at the wardroom table, his hands resting on it. He was very pale and still shivering slightly. Harding guessed that the shaking was caused by shock rather than fear.

'Sorry about your ship, Captain,' Cheaver said.

'*Danke.*'

'Would you like a drink?'

'*Nein danke*. Already I am rum having.'

'What was the number of your submarine, Captain?'

The German compressed his lips and shrugged.

Cheaver nodded. 'Quite. I wouldn't tell me that either, but

they'll probably persuade you to tell them when we put you ashore. Which reminds me. We are going on patrol now and I'm afraid that you have to come with us. I'm also afraid that I must put you under guard. It would be nice to accept your parole, but as a qualified submarine officer you're too potentially dangerous to be allowed to wander around. I'm sure you'll understand.'

For several seconds Bruning stared at him, frowning in concentration, then shook his head. 'Again, please. At English I am not so very good.'

Patiently Cheaver explained, using simpler words and Bruning smiled briefly, without humour.

'You are right, Captain,' he said. 'I would very much enjoy to sink your ship.'

'Don't blame you,' Cheaver told him and astonishment grew in Harding that his captain could be so pleasant to this enemy officer and so consistently awful to his own.

Cheaver might have been reading his thoughts when he turned to him and barked, 'Harding!'

'Sir?'

'Never again do I want to hear you give the order "Hard a'port", or "Hard a'starboard" for that matter. It may sound very fine to you, but if the helmsman is fool enough to take you literally there's a chance he'll jam the steering. Say "Port 30" or "Starboard 30" as the case may be. Thirty degrees of wheel is ample, even if it doesn't sound so dramatic!'

'I'll remember that, sir.'

'Kindly do,' Cheaver said. 'The last thing I need is my ship going round in bloody circles with a jammed rudder!'

It was like a blow in the face. Harding had been growing in confidence, feeling pleased almost to the point of complacency, following his successful manoeuvring on leaving harbour and the way in which he had placed *Shadow* in position for the attack on the U-boat. Now this, and in front of a prisoner of war too! He got up slowly and left the wardroom, imagining the rictus-like grin following his departure.

In the control room he stood for a long time staring down at the chart, not seeing it, his mind jumping from one to another of the events of the day, a negative sense of purpose growing in him that whatever else he might become in the Navy it would be nothing resembling Cheaver. The sense of purpose took on a more positive slant when he reached the decision that now was as good a time as any to start not being like him. He went in search of the coxswain and found him in the petty officers' mess.

'No, please don't get up,' he said to the four men playing Ludo there. 'I just wanted a quick word with you, Cox'n. Do you happen to know who was port after look-out when we attacked the U-boat?'

The chief petty officer thought for a moment before saying, 'Let's see now, sir. That watch was Lloyd, Mungo, Price and – and Michaelson, but I dunno who was look-out for which sector. 'Ang on a tick, sir, and I'll find out.'

'Thanks, Cox'n. Ask him to report to me in the control room, will you?'

'Right, sir.'

Harding went back and leant on the chart table until a sailor approached and said, 'Able Seaman Mungo, sir. You wanted to see me, sir?' He looked and sounded defensive.

'Yes, Mungo. You had the port after sector on the bridge tonight, didn't you?'

'Yes, sir.'

'I'm sorry for calling you "That look-out". I haven't been aboard long enough to learn everybody's name yet.'

Mungo looked confused, then half-smiled and said, 'Oh, that's all right, sir. Bit bloody dark to recognize anyone even if you did know who they was, I reckon.'

'That's what I wanted to see you about,' Harding told him, 'to congratulate you on sighting the U-boat in that visibility. It was a first class bit of work.'

Mungo's confusion intensified, producing a surge of bright colour in his face. 'Oh. Yessir. Thank you, sir. Is that all, sir?'

'That's all, Mungo, except that I'll see to it that your sighting is officially recorded. Carry on.'

Watching the man walk away towards his accommodation in the torpedo stowage compartment Harding was wondering how many valuable contributions to the war effort had gone unrecognized in this very peculiar ship. Not a lot, he supposed, because the only two war patrols before the present one had both drawn blank and the U-boat had been *Shadow*'s first sinking. The further thought that there had been no previous successes because the atmosphere on board precluded enthusiasm was a tempting one to follow up, but he dismissed it for lack of evidence in that there could genuinely have been no targets to attack. Not having been there he was in no position to know and his fellow officers were uncommunicative on the subject.

Eastward bound through the mine-free channel leading from Bell Rock to open water it was too rough to allow anyone onto the casing and the little ceremony was held on the bridge. Cheaver recited the words for burials at sea and, at his invitation, *Kapitanleutnant* Bruning spoke a few sentences in German, then the facsimile of the Nazi naval ensign Cheaver had had made in case it should be usable as a *ruse de guerre* was removed from the canvas-wrapped body of the U-boat's navigating officer. Three sailors lifted the corpse, pushing it sharply outwards in an attempt to prevent it striking the main ballast tanks on its way down, the two commanding officers saluted and it was all over.

'*Danke schön, Herr Kapitan*,' Bruning said.

Cheaver nodded and spread his hands in a gesture of helplessness, then realizing that the indication of sympathy would be unseen in the darkness murmured, 'Pity about that. Please go below now.' He reinforced the request by pushing Bruning gently towards the conning tower hatch. A Webley .45 revolver in his hand Harding was waiting for him at the bottom of the ladder in the control room.

It was Chief Engine Room Artificer Archer who had solved the problem of where to find a length of chain by dismantling one of purchases used for lifting pistons from the main engines. With one end of it padlocked round his waist and the other secured to the table leg Bruning could lie in the bunk behind him or sit at the table as he wished. Speaking slowly and distinctly the first lieutenant explained to him that if he wanted to go to the 'heads' he only had to ask and that the only piece of mechanical equipment within his reach was the brass wheel of a low pressure master blowing valve protruding from the deckhead. He was welcome, Bradbury told him, to turn that to his heart's content because it wouldn't do anything without the blower running. The curtness with which the German acknowledged the information indicated that he had already guessed the valve's function and had no intention of bothering to tamper with it.

When a second radio transmission was received he was ordered into his bunk and had the curtain drawn on him while it was deciphered. The signal stated that the *Gneisenau* was steaming north-east under RAF attack heading for the Kiel Canal and, presumably, the Baltic. It cancelled the earlier communication numbered 192 and reinstated the original patrol area at the entrance to the Skagerrak. Muttering about making up their bloody minds Cheaver ordered the necessary alteration in course to the north of east.

Shadow was nearing the centre of the North Sea when she dived at dawn.

Chapter 4

With the six spare torpedoes, each twenty-two feet in length and twenty-one inches in diameter, loaded into the tubes to replace those fired at the U-boat there was much more space in the torpedo stowage compartment which also served as the seamen's mess. Three of the engine room staff had gone for'ard to join a group squatting on the steel deck for a game of poker. The playing of poker was strictly forbidden in view of the financial and personality problems it could lead to, but as this was *Shadow* and because any form of defiance against authority was better than none they played it, with a man keeping watch at the water-tight door leading to the senior ratings' messes.

'Three Kings,' said Mungo and turned his cards face up.

'Well, fuck that for a lark,' Lloyd replied without any particular heat and tossed his hand onto the discard pile. 'Deal me out. I'm two and a half quid up the creek.'

'Yeah, me likewise.'

'Me too. I'm going to get me 'ead down. Mungo's been markin' the cards again.'

'I've got to be on sonar watch in fifteen minutes,' Able Seaman Dunsmore said.

Mungo grinned at them. 'Yellow bastards. What shall we do then? Talk about women?'

'Not likely,' one of them replied. 'Leave that until the end of the patrol when I can try to cash in on your bleeding imagination.'

Shrugging, Mungo patted the cards together, put them to one side and said, 'I like the Subbie.'

'Who? Harding?'

'Who else? He's the only sub-lieutenant aboard, ain't he?'

Prentiss nodded. 'Seems like a nice enough bloke. Chewed me out that first night he came aboard, but very polite about it he was and he didn't put me in the rattle neither. Then the cox'n says it was him who ordered rum for me and the Jerry officer after we had that little swim together yesterday.'

'He's not bad for a "pig",' Lloyd agreed.

Had Harding heard the conversation he might have been mildly flattered, but had he been in submarines longer he would have been more than simply concerned at the use of the word 'pig' to describe any officer. It was in fairly common usage in the surface fleet, but a rarity amongst submarine crews who worked and lived at close quarters in an atmosphere of mutual respect.

Able Seaman Dunsmore was the first to hear it, a rhythmic pulsing hiss such as a rope makes when repeatedly swung in a circle.

'Hydrophone effect bearing Red 35, sir,' he said.

The first lieutenant gestured for the forward periscope to be raised, watched it slide upwards out of its well, jerked the handles into a horizontal position, then turned it through three hundred and sixty degrees before settling on the bearing he had been given. It was twenty seconds before he spoke.

'I can't see anything.'

'Well, there's something there, sir.'

'What's it sound like? Turbine? Reciprocating engine?'

'No, not like them, sir. It sounds strange.'

'Down periscope,' the first lieutenant said. 'Here, let me listen to it.' He stood for half a minute, pressing the earphones of the sonar set to his ears, frowning in concentration, then whispered 'Very odd,' before saying in a louder voice, 'Ask the Captain to come to the control room. Up periscope.'

The wet, squally weather had moved away to the south of them leaving behind it a clear winter's day with almost extreme visibility, but there was nothing to be seen on Red 35 except broken water.

'What have you got, Number One?' Cheaver asked.

The first lieutenant told him, still staring into the binocular eye-pieces of the periscope.

'Well then, get out of the way and let me look.'

Cheaver looked and saw nothing but the small waves between him and an empty horizon. He listened to the swishing sound coming from the earphones and looked through the periscope again. Still nothing.

'What's the bearing now, Dunsmore?'

'Steady on Red 35, sir.'

'Louder or softer?'

'Louder I think, sir. Hard to tell.'

'Louder and on a steady bearing. That means we're on a collision course and . . .' Cheaver stiffened visibly and ended the sentence with, 'It can't be!'

'Can't be what, sir?'

The captain ignored his second-in-command's question and spoke rapidly, tensely. 'Send somebody for Lynd, Harding and the Cox'n. No, go yourself. I'll take over the watch. Hurry and be quiet about it.' Then to the helmsman, 'Starboard twenty, steer 180.'

The two officers and the chief petty officer arrived in the control room almost simultaneously with the first lieutenant behind them and they all stood in an arc facing the captain. 'Sir?' Lynd said, but it was to the coxswain that Cheaver turned.

'Cox'n, get some cotton waste and scarves or something. Take two big men, jump the German officer, gag him and secure him to his bunk so that he can't move an inch. Knock him out if you have to. If he makes a single squawk or manages to hammer his heels on anything I'll have you court-martialled. Get on with it!'

'Aye aye, sir.'

'Lynd, go aft and order dead silence throughout the boat, shoes to be removed and the crew to move quietly to action stations. Harding, you do the same for'ard. Number One, all orders to be passed by word of mouth and on no account is the Tannoy to be used, or the telegraphs.'

As Harding left the control room, tiptoeing on stockinged feet, he heard the first lieutenant say, 'Destroyer, sir?' and Cheaver's muted snarl, 'An invisible destroyer? I appear to be served by cretins. It's a submerged U-boat, you young fool.' From the wardroom a muffled gasp, a brief scuffle followed by silence, then the coxswain reporting the prisoner secure.

Leading Seaman Topham, chief sonar operator, had replaced Able Seaman Dunsmore at the set when Harding got back to the control room.

'Bearing's about Red 90, sir.' he said. The captain nodded and ordered the helmsman to hold the present course, then looked at Harding.

'Well, Harding? Are you just going to stand there like a wet week-end, or could I persuade you to start working on the plot?'

'Sorry, sir,' Harding said, moved to the chart table, marked

Shadow's position and began to lay off the bearings of the sound as Leading Seaman Topham called them out. He was to continue doing it for nearly eighty minutes, the strangest, most nerve-racking minutes of his life.

'We're heavy aft, sir,' the first lieutenant announced. 'Permission to move some men for'ard and balance the boat? I don't want to use the ballast pump.'

'You run the pump and it'll be the last thing you ever do,' Cheaver told him. 'I'll see to that even if the enemy doesn't.'

Bradbury took that as permission to move the men and moments later three of the engine room staff walked silently through the control room on their way towards the torpedo stowage compartment. *Shadow*'s stern rose fractionally, steadied.

'Bearing Red 95, sir.'

'Very well.'

Two minutes passed. Three.

'Bearing Red 100. Fading a bit.'

'Come ten degrees to port,' Cheaver said.

There was little for Harding to do beyond plot his ship's advance, its alterations in course and the changing direction of the hydrophone effect. No pattern had emerged yet that he could usefully report on and he spent long minutes standing, listening to the silence, a silence so intense that the breathing of the men around him sounded loud in his ears and he imagined that he could detect the surge of blood through his veins. He was sweating with tension, expecting from each second to the next that Leading Seaman Topham would report the scream of engines as the U-boat loosed torpedoes towards them and he started violently when the sonar operator next spoke.

'Enemy's pumping ballast, sir. It's loud. In fact it's very loud.' Topham removed his head-set, held it up and a faint whine was clearly audible coming from the ear-pieces. The sound cut off abruptly.

'Enemy's stopped pumping, sir.'

'Any idea how close, Topham?'

The sonar operator shrugged. 'Impossible to say, sir. Depends on the water conditions and how noisy their pump is.'

'Bloody hell! We don't know anything,' Cheaver said.

Harding looked round at him. 'We know one thing now, sir. We know they don't know we're here or they wouldn't have run that pump.'

Cheaver didn't spare him a glance.

'Topham, if they were to range on us with one solitary sonar transmission would you know what it was?'

'Yes, I would, sir, and if you want my advice I wouldn't try anything like that on them if that's what you're thinking.'

'Never you mind what I'm thinking and, as it happens, I don't want your advice, just your information.' The bird of prey forward thrust of the head directed at the sonar operator, then turning to take in the rest of the people in the control room. Suspicion hardened to conviction in Harding that his captain was at least partially mad.

'Aye aye, sir,' Topham said.

'How long since you did an all round sweep, Topham?'

'I'm doing them all the time, sir. Not a sound from anywhere except the port beam.'

'Just as well,' Cheaver announced to nobody in particular. 'I can't afford to go deep and I can't use the periscope in case we find ourselves staring down each other's throats.'

Shadow moved ever forward, slowly, blindly, like a grey ghost beneath the surface of the North Sea. No sound came from her electric motors, her idling propellors, or the hydraulic systems which controlled her rudder and hydroplanes. Even the gentle susurration of the ventilating system had been silenced. Pausing only to check the enemy's bearing at each revolution her electronic ear circled endlessly.

'Enemy's speeding up, sir! Increased revolutions on Red 92.'

Harding felt his nerves tauten again and a bead of sweat release itself from his hair line to trickle towards his eye. Almost furtively he brushed it away then, feeling ashamed, glanced around him. It brought him very small relief to see other faces glistening damply. Bleakly he pictured the long shape of the U-boat swinging onto an attacking course, hearing

41

in his imagination the harsh German vowel sounds which would send the torpedoes on their way. With grim self-control he drew the compass equivalent of Red 92 on the plot.

'Revolutions slowed again, sir. Back like they were before.'

Just a short burst of speed to maintain depth Harding thought and let his muscles relax.

Of the four officers in the control room only Lynd had nothing at all to do. He was standing by the new-fangled torpedo data computer known as the 'Fruit Machine', but the electro-mechanical contraption required more than bearings to produce a jack-pot. It needed ranges, speeds and angles on the bow too. Not one of those things was yet available and Lynd continued to stand, yawning repeatedly in nervous boredom.

'Bearing's Red 98 about, sir.'

'Decrease speed by five revolutions,' Cheaver said and the words were whispered from mouth to ear along the length of the ship from control to motor room.

Six minutes later, 'Bearing seems to be constant now, sir. Possibly fading very slightly,' Topham said.

Shadow made another small course alteration, another slight variation in speed, then did it three more times. At last, 'Bearing steady on Red 100, sir. Sound volume remaining constant too,' Topham announced.

There was still nothing useful that Harding could say. The two submarines were running parallel at two and a half knots on a course of 157 degrees with the U-boat at an unknown range ten degrees abaft *Shadow*'s port beam, but the captain knew all that, so he didn't say anything.

'Well? Are you going to tell me the situation, Harding?'

Harding reported the obvious and ended with the words, 'This course leads to Cuxhaven, sir.'

Cheaver nodded absently, then speaking as though to himself, 'Can't afford to keep this up for another five hours until they surface for the night. Might lose them in the darkness, or they might detect us before then. No, this is the best we'll get.' He stood staring at the deck for a moment before jerking his head up and saying incisively, 'Lynd, go for'ard and angle all torpedoes ninety left and set them to run at thirty-five feet.

When that's done stand by all tubes, open bow caps and report back here. Everything to be done in total silence. Off you go.'

When Lynd had gone to supervise the settings of the torpedoes in the tube space in the bows of the ship Cheaver appeared to draw back into himself again. 'Got to assume they're at periscope depth,' he said, nodded and added, 'No logical reason why they should be deeper than that.' Obviously no comment was called for and nobody made one.

Harding engrossed himself in a visual examination of the control room, the twin brass pillars of the periscopes, the twin hydroplane wheels, the depth gauges, the single steering wheel and above his head the maze of pipes and electric leads. After that he looked at the diving panel with its complex array of levers, valves and dials. He was trying not to think of the clicks of metal on metal as the angle and depth was set on the torpedoes, of the sound of sea-water flooding into the tubes, of the creak of the bow caps covering the ends of the torpedo tubes as they were wound open, noises an alert German sonar operator could detect. Try as he might he still thought of them and their possible consequences, his muscles taut again.

It was a relief when Leading Seaman Topham said, 'Bearing still steady on Red 100. Noise level constant,' and he could draw another line on the plot.

Gliding forward in broad echelon formation with an enemy nobody aboard had ever seen *Shadow* seemed to Harding to be stretching time by her motion and his nerves with it. He found the message of his watch that less than two minutes had passed when Lynd reappeared soundlessly in the control room difficult to believe.

'All tubes standing by, sir. Bow caps open.'

'Any change, Topham?' Cheaver asked.

'None, sir.'

'Stand by.'

Lynd put his thumb on the firing button. 'Ready, sir.'

'Fire one!' Cheaver said. 'Port twenty! Group up! Full ahead together!' He had spoken loudly. It made no difference now, Harding knew, because the torpedo leaping from its tube and angling towards the U-boat would be making a noise like a dive-bomber, but after the long tomb-like hush the effect was startling. *Shadow* had jolted slightly at the torpedo's departure as though she had run into some small obstruction, then had come the little increase in pressure on the ear-drums as the air which had expelled it vented back into the ship. Several voices now, repeating the captain's orders, confirming that they had been carried, the clang of the telegraphs, Topham saying, 'Torpedo running.'

'Fire two!'

Shadow vibrating as the speed built up, beginning to turn, providing the spread for the torpedoes which the parallel courses and equal speeds of the two ships would not have done.

'Fire three!'

The first lieutenant saying, 'Flood "Q". Vent "Q" inboard.' Water gushing into the emergency quick-diving tank to hold the submarine down against the temporary increase of buoyancy caused by the loss of the torpedoes' weight. Pressure on the ears increasing as the air from the tank adds its force to that of the torpedo firings.

'Fire four!'

Vibration heavier, water hissing past the hull, Cheaver calling, 'Wheel a'midships, starboard ten, steady as you go. Fire five!'

The submarine dropping deeper from the weight of water in the emergency tank, the first lieutenant ordering, 'Blow "Q",' and the roar of the released high-pressure air.

'Fire six!'

It was, Harding calculated, about three seconds after the final torpedo had left its tube that the stunning explosion shook *Shadow*, making the lighting flicker and bringing cork insulation showering like light hail from the deckhead. It was followed by another, six seconds later.

'Group down. Slow ahead together. Up periscope,' Cheaver said, then added, 'For Christ's sake get us back to periscope depth, Number One!' but there was nothing for him to look at when the upper lens rose clear of the water.

'Hydrophone effect has ceased, sir.' Topham's voice. It seemed a somewhat inadequate epitaph to Harding.

Moments later *Shadow* surfaced and Harding followed his captain onto the bridge, hearing him mutter, 'Wasted the last two fish. Pity.' There was nothing spectacular to look at even then. Just an expanse of diesel oil spreading across the surface of the sea, flattening the small waves, tainting the air. Here and there unidentifiable objects bobbed in it and a few bubbles formed lethargically under the sticky layer, then burst. *Shadow* dived again.

Back in the control room, 'Who do you suppose that was?' Cheaver asked, but received no reply. Nobody present had ever heard of *Kapitanleutnant* Otto Rademacher with his grasp of colloquial English and penchant for ramming lifeboats.

To everybody's embarrassment *Kapitanleutnant* Bruning burst into tears when the reason for his forcible restraint was explained to him. Lynd patted him sympathetically on the shoulder. Cheaver gave him a glass of brandy, then he was ordered into his bunk so that Harding could encipher the signal 'Second U-boat torpedoed and sunk 56 degrees 48 minutes north 2 degrees 5 minutes east + all torpedoes expended + returning harbour by reverse of outward route'. It was transmitted as soon as *Shadow* surfaced for the night and the reply was received forty minutes later. Harding decoded it and handed it to the captain.

'Happy birthday 2 U,
Happy birthday 2 U,
Happy birthday dear *Shadow*,
2 U-boats 2 U'.

'Stupid fools,' Cheaver said. 'Do they think we have nothing better to do than decipher that sort of crap?'

Again nobody answered him.

Chapter 5

'I wish you would stop saying "I just got into a fight with this pongo" like a bloody parrot and tell me how it happened and why,' Harding said. 'You're facing very serious charges and the Navy is almost certain to add to them when the civil authorities have finished with you. Won't you try to give me something that might help to get you out of here before you go up in front of the magistrate on Monday? It'll be too late after that.'

He was standing in a cell at a police station in Bethnal Green, London, looking at the battered and obstinate face of Able Seaman Mungo. Two of the sailor's front teeth were missing, one eye was closed and his nose was broken.

Mungo shook his head. 'I can't, sir. It's private, like I already told you.' It came lispingly from the damaged mouth.

'I'll be back to see you later,' Harding told him and asked the constable at the door to let him out.

The presence of acid in the sump of one of *Shadow*'s battery tanks had led to the discovery of cracks in five cells caused, it was assumed, by the explosion of the torpedoes which had destroyed the submerged U-boat. It had been much closer to them than had been expected and although the detonations had been heavy they were not thought to have been severe enough to have caused such damage. Prudence indicated the desirability of replacing the more than a hundred giant cells in that battery tank in case they had come from a defective batch and half the crew had been given forty-eight hour passes while this was being done. Mungo had gone to London and it had taken two policemen and a passer-by to break up the fight between the sailor and soldier outside the pub in the Bethnal Green street. The soldier had been taken to hospital with a suspected fractured skull and other injuries. Mungo was taken in charge and *Shadow*'s duty officer informed by telephone.

That was when Cheaver had ordered Harding to London to try to sort the mess out and get Mungo back for the Navy to deal with in its own way.

Harding visited the pub next, but nobody could say whether or not a sailor answering to Mungo's description had been there. The bar had been full of servicemen and there had been no particular trouble that night.

At the hospital he was told that the soldier was out of danger but not well enough to receive visitors, let alone undergo an interrogation and he went back to the police station.

'May I make a reversed charge call to Rosyth?'

'Help yourself, sir,' the desk sergeant said and pushed the telephone towards him.

It took nearly fifteen minutes to locate the coxswain, a chief petty officer named Ryland. Ryland had joined *Shadow* only a day or so before Harding. Six years the elder he was still young to be a ship's senior non-commissioned officer and this was his first appointment in that position. A man of little education who ignored the existence of the letter 'H' at the beginning of words and rarely bothered to sound a 'G' at the end of a lot of them he appeared to Harding, even on such short acquaintance, to be an excellent individual. Over a number of years together as shipmates Harding was never to have cause to reverse his initial impression.

'Ryland 'ere.'

'Hello, Cox'n. This is Sub-lieutenant Harding.'

' 'Ello, sir. What can I do for you?'

'It's about Mungo, Cox'n. I'm not getting anywhere with him, or with anybody else for that matter. The only thing I'm reasonably sure about is that he's hiding something, so I thought I'd have a word with his next of kin to try to find out a little of his background. Can you tell me who they are?'

' 'Ang on, sir. I'll get me book.'

A minute later, 'There's 'is wife, sir. Might be worth chattin' to 'er.'

'Oh, it hadn't occurred to me that he might be married. Have you got her address?'

Ryland read it out to him.

'Well I'll be damned,' Harding said.

'Got somethin', sir.'

'I think I may have. Thank you very much, Cox'n.'

Harding made his way to the pub again, glanced at it and around him at the grimy street, then rang the bell of the house next door.

'Yes?'

'I'm looking for Mrs Mungo,' he told the old woman who opened the door to him.

'Third floor front,' she said and sniffed.

The room was small, uncared for, with a bed in one corner, a gas cooker in another, two chairs and a small table. The bathroom and lavatory were on the landing outside.

He stood in the middle of the cheap felt carpet, watching the sharp-faced girl with dyed blonde hair and too much make-up badly applied, listening to her saying, '. . . so I wasn't expecting him back inside three weeks, was I? Then in he walks and finds me in bed with Jimmy, doesn't he? Fat's in the fire, isn't it? Wasn't half a laugh.'

'It must have been very amusing. What happened then, Mrs Mungo?'

'Well, Charlie tells Jimmy to get up and get dressed, kind of icy like. Then he drags him outside and throws him down the stairs and goes leaping down after him and before you know it they're both out in the road fighting like cats and these two coppers and some other bloke come along and jumps them. Just like the pictures it was. 'Ere! You're not going already, are you?'

A quarter of an hour later Superintendent Micklethwaite said, 'That does put rather a different complexion on it. The arresting officers thought it had started as a pub brawl. I think we had better have a talk with that young lady. Her withholding information when her husband is facing a charge of causing grievous bodily harm and him down in the cells keeping his face shut to protect her leaves a nasty taste in the mouth, doesn't it?'

Harding nodded. 'Can you release him into my custody, Superintendent?'

'Bit difficult to do that, Mr Harding, and it's not really necessary. If you tell your story, even if we can't get the girl to confirm it, the magistrate will let him off with a talking to and all Mungo will have suffered will be three nights in the cells.'

Harding nodded again, but his expression was worried and he was frowning. 'The trouble is,' he said, 'that it's not quite so simple as that from the Navy's point of view. If he's held here to be taken before the magistrate on Monday he will be technically adrift over the two days leave he was given. That's a punishable offence and the fact that he could not return to his ship because he was in police custody won't help him at all. It will simply be said that he shouldn't have got himself into police hands in the first place.'

Finding that he had picked up the Superintendent's pencil and drawn a row of three rabbits on the blotter Harding apologized and went on, 'Then if the ship sails before he returns, which it almost certainly will, there'll be a much more serious charge against him. Missing your ship is a very grave matter and carries a heavy penalty. Missing it in time of war can even be construed as desertion under certain circumstances and knowing my commanding officer as I do he'll do his best to make it sound like desertion in the face of the enemy. He's not a particularly logical man and if he exercises his unquestionable power to the full it could go very badly with Mungo.'

The superintendent picked up his pencil and carefully blocked in one of Harding's rabbits, then he looked at him and smiled.

'You should have been a barrister, Mr Harding. All right. It's no part of the police's duty to administer justice but, equally, it's no part of our duty to contribute to its miscarriage. I'll fudge the books somehow if you'll get hold of a naval escort to conduct Mungo out of Bethnal Green and back to Scotland. I don't want to take the risk of his breaking away from you and doing something regrettable about his wife. He'll probably have cooled down after he's been back at sea for a bit.'

'I'll get in touch with the naval police, Superintendent,' Harding said, 'And thank you very much indeed.'

49

Almost as though she had been waiting for them, *Shadow* sailed less than two hours after Harding and Mungo returned on board. For a man whose world had fallen apart about him, and who faced the certainty of having his next period of leave replaced by exhausting days of extra work and enforced exercise for the trouble he had caused the Navy, the able seaman was comparatively at peace with himself. Charlie Mungo had already decided that he would not kill Edna after all.

Harding's second mission in *Shadow* was a period of tension, boredom and frustration, followed by more tension, more boredom, more frustration, for almost everybody. As long as the captain was paying him no attention Harding didn't mind. He was quickly entrusted with lone watch-keeping duties, both surfaced and submerged. His spare time he used well, tracing the hydraulic telemotor system from bow to stern until he could close his eyes and recite the function of every foot of tubing, every valve, every gauge, to himself. Then he did the same thing with the electrical system and the high and low pressure air lines, the internal ballast arrangements and the equipment for firing torpedoes. Inevitably he got to know the crew, a crew intrigued by the young officer who wanted to know who everyone was, what they did and how they did it. The only department he did not examine minutely was the engine room. On top of everything else that was too much to take in in three weeks and he said as much to the chief engine room artificer. 'Don't you worry, sir,' he had been told. 'When you've got a day or two spare in harbour I'll give you a course in diesel engineering. I hear you've just about got the rest of it wrapped up.'

Shadow spent those weeks probing the perilously shallow waters of the Kattegat, searching for German warships which might choose that route to break out into the Atlantic. She found none. Twice she sighted what were undoubtedly German merchantmen returning to the Baltic, but Cheaver's orders, and those of every other British submarine commander, were firm on the point that these vessels must not be attacked without warning. Both times *Shadow* surfaced, manned her 3-inch gun and signalled 'K', the International Code letter meaning 'Stop instantly'. On the first occasion she lost sight of her target almost immediately in driving rain squalls and never found it again. A week later the second ship, a fine modern banana boat, disregarded the signal, ignored a shot across her bows, turned her stern to *Shadow* and steamed out of range at a speed the submarine could not match.

Cheaver became morose, almost totally withdrawn except for those occasions when his need for release vented itself in gratuitous sarcasm. Lieutenant Lynd became the main objective of these verbal assaults.

'Are we or are we not meant to be fighting a war?' Cheaver asked the wardroom the day before *Shadow*'s recall signal was received. 'Am I not right when I say that the bloody Huns have been sinking unarmed merchant ships since the day war broke out?'

His officers had long since learned to ignore his rhetorical questions but, pushed beyond endurance, Lynd said, 'You need an echo chamber more than an audience, let alone a conversation.'

The remark, the explosion of rage it engendered and the subsequent entry of Lynd's name in the ship's log for impertinence towards a superior officer were to have far-reaching effects for *Shadow* in general and Harding in particular.

'It's begun, you two.'

Harding and his mother looked towards the middle-aged man standing in the doorway.

'What's begun, Dad?'

'The war, Peter. Germany has invaded Denmark and Norway. It came over the wireless just now.'

'Well,' Harding's mother said, 'whatever Germany may have done, that remark of yours really takes the cake for tactlessness, Jonathan. I had formed the distinct impression that Peter has been fighting a war for the last eight months.'

Her husband grinned sheepishly. 'Sorry. You're right, of

course, but there'll be a heck of a lot more people helping him to do it now.'

'Troopships,' Harding murmured. 'Tankers. Supply ships. There won't be any nonsense about not sinking those without warning.' He threw his newspaper aside and stood up. 'I must go back at once.'

'But, Peter, you said you had four days leave!'

He stooped and kissed her cheek. 'I've had two of them, Mum. That's better than nothing. Dad, call this number for me while I change and tell the duty officer I'm on my way, will you please?'

Twenty minutes later, wearing uniform and with his suitcase beside him on the back seat of the London taxi, he waved to his parents until they were out of sight. He was never to see them again.

'There's been a bit of a bust up,' Lieutenant Wright said. 'It happened the day you went on leave.'

Harding looked curiously at the pleasant round face of *Shadow*'s engineer officer, an embarrassed face now.

'Oh? What sort of bust up?'

'Apparently Michael Lynd went for the Old Man in a big way. I don't know any details. It's a sort of taboo subject.'

'Bloody hell! What's happened about it? Is Lynd under arrest or something?'

Wright shook his head. 'No, they've both been sent on leave pending reappointment. I imagine that means back to General Service for both of them. One suspects the "brass" are trying to avoid official action.'

Sitting, staring down at the top of *Shadow*'s wardroom table Harding digested the news. When his first flood of elation at Cheaver's departure had settled to more moderate thankfulness he found himself feeling mildly sorry for him. Why that should be he had no very clear idea, but the feeling persisted. For Lynd, although he hadn't liked him much, he felt more positively sorry, possibly, he thought, because he owed him a debt of gratitude for bringing an intolerable situation to a head.

'But for the grace of God,' he muttered to himself.

'What, Peter?'

'Nothing, Chief.'

'Oh. Well, Captain Submarines wanted to see you as soon as you got back, so as you are back you'd better go and see him, hadn't you?'

'Me? What's he want to see me for?'

'I'm not allowed to say, but I'd be prepared for some more surprises if I were you,' the engineer officer told him.

Harding stood, put on his cap and stepped out of the wardroom.

'Peter.'

'Yes, Chief?'

'If you decide to do what he wants, it's all right with me.'

'Cryptic,' Harding said. 'Extremely cryptic.' He had spoken lightly, but his thoughts were in turmoil as he left the ship and walked along the jetty towards the base. The opening words of the big four-stripe captain he had never seen before whose office he was shown into did nothing to ease his confusion.

'You're improperly dressed, Harding.'

An automatic glance downwards, checking his jacket, his trousers, his shoes. A hand fingering his tie then, almost in desperation, his trouser buttons.

'Am I, sir. In what way?'

The merest flicker of a smile and, 'You've been recommended for accelerated promotion to lieutenant and Their Lordships, in their wisdom, have ordered that it shall be so. I took the liberty of having one of your jackets altered while you were on leave. It's on that bench behind you. You'd better change into it.'

'Oh. Thank you, sir,' Harding said, not sure whether he was expressing gratitude for his promotion or for the trouble the flotilla captain had gone to in arranging for a second gold band to be stitched to the sleeves of one of his spare jackets. He took off the one he was wearing, put on the other, then began transferring the contents of his pockets.

'Sit down, Harding. I take it that you've heard that Commander Cheaver and Lieutenant Lynd are being replaced.'

'Yes, sir. The Chief, er, I mean our engineer officer told me, sir.'

'Right. Did he tell you that Lieutenant Bradbury is leaving too?'

'What, sir? No, sir.'

'Well, he is. He's going on his commanding officer's qualifying course and I want you to take over as First Lieutenant.'

Harding sat stunned, staring at the big man across the desk from him, unable to speak for long seconds. Then, 'But that's absurd, sir! I've only done one patrol and a bit!'

'Yes, but it was quite a bit, wasn't it? Two U-boats sunk in under eighteen hours. That and your last patrol must have taught you a lot.'

'Yes, sir but – Sir?'

'Go on, Harding.'

'Sir, may I ask who suggested this appointment to you?'

'Commander Cheaver. Who else?'

'I see, sir,' Harding said slowly. 'In that case I must respectfully submit that you ignore his suggestion. I don't consider Commander Cheaver a compet . . .'

'Harding!'

'Sir?'

'I can't imagine what you were going to say, but suggest that you steer clear of insubordination, in the unlikely event that such was in your mind. In addition, it would be a relief if you did not leave me with the impression that you are a precocious little brat. I am well aware that Commander Cheaver has a personality problem. I am also aware of the tragic family reasons for it. That is no longer our business. In all other respects Commander Cheaver was an efficient submarine officer and it is on the basis of that efficiency that I am prepared to accept his recommendation.'

After a brief pause, 'I beg your pardon, sir,' Harding said.

'Very well. Now, what do you say?'

'I don't think I've got the self-confidence yet, sir, and I doubt if I've got anybody else's really. That makes for a pretty poor starting-off point.'

The flotilla captain nodded, took a piece of paper from a

folder in front of him and tore off the top few lines. The remainder of the page he pushed across the desk. Harding picked it up and began to read.

'A most promising young officer who has been at pains to learn the ship inside out. He reacts instinctively and effectively to emergencies. In fact it would be no exaggeration to say that his prompt handling of the situation on the sighting of the first U-boat left me with little to do except order the torpedoes fired. This is one of my reasons for recommending his advancement to Lieutenant, a course which would be more advantageous to him and the Navy than a Mention in Despatches as is the case of Able Seaman Mungo for his excellent sighting (see below).

'Further, he is trusted by the crew and takes great trouble with his men both aboard ship and ashore. In the latter regard please see attached highly complimentary letter to me from a Superintendent V. H. Micklethwaite of the Metropolitan Police. Harding should do well as a First Lieutenant and I would submit for your consideration that . . .'

The page ended there and Harding put it carefully on the desk.

'Surprised?'

'Astounded, sir.'

'Well, not all impossible people are unfair. Just don't get a swollen head about it and let's have a little less about lack of confidence out of you. Do you want to go away and think about it?'

'Yes please, sir.'

'All right. Report back to me after dinner tonight.'

'Aye aye, sir. Thank you, sir.' Harding said, stood up and walked towards the door.

'Harding.'

'Sir?'

'You're forgetting your other jacket.'

He had followed a circuitous route through the base, crossing his own track several times, then stopped beside a red-brick building. Men passing in and out saluted him and he returned their salutes absently, automatically, deep in his own thoughts. Suddenly Wright's words came back to him. 'If you decide to do what he wants, it's all right with me.' So the engineer officer had known and, Harding thought, it had been nice of him to have provided advance encouragement, to have said, in effect, that he was prepared to accept him as *Shadow*'s second-in-command. But still Harding wavered. It really had been such a short time ago that he had been a junior watch-keeping officer in a cruiser. Now, out of nowhere, *this*.

The building he had stopped beside housed the chief petty officers' mess and, as he walked towards its main door, Harding was wondering what had drawn him there.

'Can I help you, sir?'

'Do you happen to know if Chief Petty Officer Ryland's in the mess?'

'Soon find out, sir.'

A minute later Ryland appeared, saluted, looked at Harding's sleeve and said, 'Congratulations, sir.'

'Oh that. Yes. Thank you, Cox'n. Could you spare a few minutes?'

'Of course, sir.'

Harding began to walk slowly towards the docks. Ryland fell in beside him. They had covered fifty yards before Harding spoke again.

'Cox'n?'

'Sir?'

'I've been offered the job of First Lieutenant.'

'Thought you might be, sir.'

'Eh?' Harding said and immediately wondered if he had ever before uttered a more fatuous interrogative sound.

'Logical step. Stands to reason, don't it sir? The lads'll be pleased too.'

Harding stopped walking and looked at Ryland. 'Then the "lads" must be out of their collective mind.'

'Yessir. Me as well, sir.'

'Oh, to hell with you, Cox'n.'

'Aye aye, sir. When do I report there?' Ryland asked.

Smiling, Harding turned and walked rapidly away. He had his answer for the flotilla captain now.

Chapter 6

'Officer to see you, sir.'

'Oh, bugger!' Harding said. He was tired, filthy, after a long day of physical effort storing ship and embarking torpedoes returned from the workshops after routine maintenance. It was customary in the Submarine Service, he had found, for officers to get their hands as dirty as anyone else and he had not spared himself in handling crates and urging recalcitrant torpedoes into spaces barely large enough to accept them. Now he was sitting coatless in *Shadow*'s wardroom working on a depressingly large pile of papers.

'All right, Mungo. Wheel him along.'

'I've already been wheeled,' a voice announced from behind the able seaman and Mungo stepped aside to make room for a small rain-coated figure. The officer's cap under its arm had no gold leaves on the peak. 'Name's Bulstrode,' the small man said, 'but it gets worse than that.'

'It does?'

'Yes, it does.'

'What can I do for you?' Harding asked.

'How about giving me a gin for a start?'

'Look, I'm awfully busy,' Harding told him. 'What do you want aboard here? Apart from a gin, I mean.'

'Well, I want to assume command, but not until I've had that drink. I take it the signal hasn't reached you yet. Here, I picked a copy up at the office on the way down from the base.'

Harding took the flimsy sheet of pink signal paper from him and read aloud, 'Lieutenant-Commander W. G. de Vere Charnley-Bulstrode appointed to HMS/M *Shadow* in command vice Commander M. J. Cheaver with immediate effect.'

'I told you it got worse,' the new captain said. 'It's bad enough being born a Bulstrode, but it's the absolute end having a wealthy de Vere Charnley aunt who says she'll cut you out of her will unless you latch her name onto yours.'

Smiling, Harding stood up. 'Welcome aboard, sir. My name's Harding. May I see your orders and your identity card, please?'

'Certainly, Number One.'

Harding raised an eyebrow. So he was already known to this man. He took the proffered documents, glanced at them and handed them back.

'Thank you, sir. Won't you take your coat off?'

'I thought you'd never ask,' Bulstrode said, and did so chanting, 'Slowly, sensuously, the raincoat slipped down, revealing a shoulder, an elegant arm, then laying bare the gleamingly golden two and a half stripes at its end.' He looked admiringly at his braid for a moment before adding, 'Look bloody good, don't they? I only achieved them the day before yesterday.'

Still smiling, but a little anxiously now for fear that fate had sent him a commanding officer as crazy, in a different way, as Cheaver, 'That's a coincidence, sir,' Harding said. 'That was the day I put up my second stripe. I think you should know that straight away. I'm pretty green.'

The other nodded. 'Yes, I did know that, but thanks for telling me anyway and don't worry about being green. We'll both be sere and yellow leaves before we know it. Now, how about that gin?'

For twenty minutes they sat, sipping their drinks with Harding, at Bulstrode's request, describing the attacks on the two U-boats, then Bulstrode said, 'Interesting. Now, why don't you wash that grease off your face, change your shirt and come on up to the mess?'

Harding glanced at the pile of papers before replying uncertainly, 'If you'd excuse me, sir, I really ought to go through this lot. There's only the Chief and me here and I'm getting a bit behind, what with one thing and another.'

The captain shook his head. 'Sorry, Number One. That was my first order, and don't worry about that correspondence. I read copies of it all up at the base and the only interesting thing in it is the signal about my arrival.' He grinned and Harding grinned back at him.

Walking along the jetty, 'Tell me. Why the sudden departure of Commander Cheaver and Lieutenant Lynd?' Bulstrode said.

They walked on in silence for several paces before Harding began to speak, doing it carefully, choosing his words. 'Commander Cheaver was released under the submarine "too old at thirty-five" rule I believe, sir. I understand that exceptions are never made to it. Lynd apparently developed claustrophobic tendencies and asked to be returned to General Service.'

'Did Captain Submarines tell you to say that, Number One?'

Harding looked down at the small figure at his side. 'I don't know what you mean, sir.'

'Well done,' Bulstrode said. 'I'll stick to the same yarn.'

It occurred to Harding that he had just passed a loyalty test, but he decided to treat his captain's apparent approval and friendliness with caution until he knew him a great deal better. The acquisition of that knowledge began as soon as they had dined when Bulstrode led the way to two arm-chairs in a quiet corner of the mess and they talked for three hours about *Shadow* and her ship's company. At the end of that time it was obvious to Harding that Bulstrode knew his job very well.

'I'm sorry for taking up your whole evening, Number One,' the new captain told him. 'I had to satisfy myself that you knew your job. Obviously you do. Very well, I'd say.'

It was as though the words, applied in the opposite direction, had been plucked from inside his skull. Although Harding was not conscious of it then, an affinity was born at that moment, an affinity which was to vary hardly at all throughout a year and a half of war, a similarity of thought which, in time to come, he would experience between himself and his own second-in-command.

'How does it look, sir?'

Bulstrode ordered the periscope lowered, then glanced at Harding standing behind the two hydroplane operators, watching the depth, watching the angle of the planes, watching the inclinometer bubble in the big, curved spirit level which showed the submarine's angle in relation to the horizontal.

'It looks revolting, Number One, but that probably isn't what you meant. Had you asked me what it looked like, I would have replied that it resembles a *Roederer Maas*-class destroyer coming in our direction with possible evil intent. I suggest that we sink down into the Stygian depths which, fable has it, exist at one hundred and twenty feet. Up periscope.'

'One hundred and twenty feet, Cox'n,' Harding said, then took the Tannoy public address microphone from its hook, pressed the button on its stem and added, 'Shut off for depth-charging. Shut off for depth-charging. Total silence throughout the boat. Total silence throughout the boat.' He replaced the microphone.

'Pity you put in that last bit, Number One. I was going to suggest that we all hummed the "Horst Wessel" song in case they're listening to us. Down periscope.'

'We don't know the tune, sir.'

'Oh, don't be so limited,' Bulstrode said. '"*Deutschland uber alles*" would have done. I particularly like the verse which opens with "Aunty Mabel has just farted". It's sonorous and moving, one might say. Can you hear anything yet, Topham?'

The chief sonar operator, with one receiver of his head-set pressed to an ear, stifled a giggle and replied, 'Can't hear nothing, sir, but it's a bit difficult in the circumstances.'

'What circumstances?'

'Well, sir, you, sir.'

'All right, I'll shut up. She's bearing Green 15, steering almost due north and should cross our bows from starboard to port at a range of a couple of miles. Tell me when you get the first whisper of sound.'

'Aye aye, sir.'

It was ten days since Lieutenant-Commander W. G. de Vere Charnley-Bulstrode, all five foot four and a half of him, had assumed command of *Shadow*. For seven of those days she had been constantly at sea in protected waters close to the

Scottish coast, diving going ahead, diving going astern, surfacing normally, surfacing as for gun action, manoeuvring at all speeds and carrying out practice torpedo attacks, both surfaced and submerged, on any vessel which passed through the area. Sailing before dawn and returning to harbour long after dark Bulstrode worked his crew hard, exercising them in every possible emergency from man overboard, to fire in the motor room, to failure of the ship's entire hydraulic system when she was passing two hundred and fifty feet with a bow-down angle of twenty degrees. On the fourth day a shoot was carried out with the 3-inch gun and continued until the canvas target towed by a tug was in such tatters as to be barely visible. On the fifth Harding asked his captain if it wasn't about time they went on patrol and received the sharpest rebuke he was to get from Bulstrode, it's cutting-edge unconcealed by the blandness with which it was delivered.

'You've been straining at the leash ever since that "sink at sight" signal was despatched to submarines at sea, haven't you Number One?'

'Well, sir . . .'

'Quite. No more arsing about flashing silly instructions which are ignored, or firing warning shots. We just put to sea and blow the hell out of anything that floats as long as it isn't on our side. Right?'

Harding hadn't replied and Bulstrode said, 'May I ask you a question, Number One?'

'Of course, sir.'

'Thank you. You and the Chief are old hands now, so you're in a position to judge. Do you consider that the three new officers aboard constitute an effective attack team?'

'Three, sir?'

'Yes, three. Tollafield on the "Fruit Machine", Gascoigne at the plot and me at the periscope. Remember us?'

'I suppose you haven't had very long together, sir.'

'Oh, come on, Number One, do grow up. We've managed to fit in eleven practice attacks. In two of those we would certainly have alarmed the enemy with the sight of our torpedo tracks missing them, but in the other nine we would have had to wait for them to die of old age before we could claim any advantage.'

For several seconds Bulstrode had appeared to find interest in the scuffed appearance of his sea-boots, then looked up at Harding again. 'You know, there are only three things required of us. To proceed to our patrol area, to seek out and destroy the enemy, and to return to harbour. I'm satisfied that we could manage the first, I'm as keen as you to attempt the second, but I'm absolutely fanatical about achieving the third. Call me idiosyncratic if you wish, but a desire to stay alive is one of my foibles and we'll sail when I am reasonably certain that there is a good possibility of that whim being catered to. Do you get the general idea?'

'Yes, sir. I'm sorry, sir.'

'So I should bloody well hope.' A whimsical smile robbed the statement of any offence and Bulstrode turned away, then back again.

'Peter?' It was the first time he had used Harding's Christian name.'

'Sir?'

'There are lots of "does" and "don'ts" relevant to this war, but very high on the "don'ts" list I place "getting excited". Enthusiastic – yes. Excited – no. Leave that to the Latins. It's going to be a long war. Relax and enjoy it.' The smile came again and Bulstrode had walked away.

Now *Shadow* was off the Norwegian coast covering the approaches to Stavanger with a big German Fleet destroyer close to her.

'There it is, sir,' Leading Seaman Topham said. 'Hydrophone effect bearing Green 5. Fast turbine. Bearing dead ahead now, sir. Bearing changing very fast. Red 3 about. Red 5 – 7 – 10 . . .'

Bulstrode nodded. 'All right, Topham. She's passing ahead of us. No sonar transmissions?'

'None, sir.'

'Very well. Sweep between Green 10 and Green 70.'

Eyes slitted in concentration Topham twisted the knurled knob in front of him slowly to the right, then turned it back in the opposite direction. He repeated the process several times.

'Nothing, sir.'

'Okay, check on the destroyer.'

'Bearing Red 35 and fading, sir.'

'I see. Carry on with an all round sweep and let me know if the destroyer appears to make any radical alterations in either course or speed. Bring us back to periscope depth, Number One.'

Planing slowly upwards *Shadow* was passing seventy feet when, in a loud whisper as though he was afraid of being overheard, Topham said, 'I've got something here, sir. A lot of something, bearing between Green 20 and Green 80. Sort of jumbled it is, sir, and pretty faint, but I reckon there's turbines there.'

Bulstrode glanced at Harding 'Use speed, Number One. Not too much, but get me up there quickly.' Then to the chief sonar operator, 'Bless your heart and any other organs you consider vital, Topham. Keep the information coming.'

'Aye aye, sir. Can't isolate much yet, but I'm getting sonar transmissions. Several sets of 'em.'

At fifty feet Harding ordered the speed reduced and the captain gestured for the search periscope to be raised, then stood with eyes pressed to the binocular fitment waiting for the upper lens to break surface. At the 'Fruit Machine' Lieutenant Tollafield and at the plot, Sub-Lieutenant Gascoigne saw the sudden brilliance of refracted light strike at his eye-balls and heard him murmer, 'Sainted Aunt Agatha de Vere Charnley I love you.'

They were still wondering what he was talking about when he snapped, 'Start the attack! Bearing is that! I am thirty degrees on her port bow!'

A man standing behind him wiped grease away from the vertical line etched into the periscope column, noted where it passed through the azimuth ring on the deckhead and said, 'Green 67.' Bulstrode swung the periscope right, left again, then clicked the handles into the 'housed' position and watched as it sank down into its well before saying, 'Target is a German pocket-battleship. Set a masthead height as for the late unlamented *Graf Spee*. When you've done that I'll give you a range.' Almost inaudibly he added, 'This course will do fine for the moment.'

Muttering to himself Tollafield flicked the pages of a reference book, grunted and made an adjustment to the 'Fruit Machine'.

'Masthead height set, sir.'

'Up periscope. Bearing is that. I'm thirty-five degrees on the port bow and the range is – ' Carefully Bulstrode turned the stud of the range-finder, watching as the image of the big ship became two and the water-line of one rested on the topmost part of the other '– is that. Down periscope.'

The man behind him relayed the message of the azimuth ring and the range dial and Tollafield said, 'Range eight thousand four hundred yards, sir. Distance off track six thousand three hundred yards.'

'As much as that, eh? Group up, full ahead together, sixty feet, give me a course for a ninety track.'

He was given it, ordered it to be steered and *Shadow* began to bore through the water, vibration building up with the speed of her passage setting crockery clinking somewhere forward of the control room. Topham removed his ear-phones and put them on the sonar dial. There was nothing he could hear above the turbulence the submarine was creating.

'I think,' Bulstrode announced, 'the destroyer that crossed our bows was deliberately positioned to force any submarines in the path of the fleet to go deep. Probably didn't bother with sonar transmissions because at the rate they're travelling at they'd simply advertize their position without much hope of obtaining a submarine contact.'

'Did you say, "fleet", sir?'

'Well, it isn't exactly Admiral Scheer sailing to engage Jellicoe at the battle of Jutland, Number One, but it's quite crowded up there. The pocket-battleship's in the van, followed by a *Hipper*-class cruiser, then a *Köln*-class I think. Astern of that there's some sort of Fleet auxiliary. Big ship, but I don't know what it is. Oh, there's a destroyer screen too. I counted four, but there are probably more on the far flank.

Topham will be able to count the sonar transmission sources when we slow down.'

Three minutes later *Shadow* did so and returned to periscope depth. Except that the enemy ships were closer, finer on the submarine's bow, there was little change in the situation. Bulstrode could see five destroyers now and Topham counted transmissions from the same number. Ranges and bearings were taken before *Shadow* went deep and fast again.

'Plot suggests enemy course and speed 005 degrees at nineteen knots, sir,' Gascoigne said.

'Thank you. Use those figures. There's a destroyer bearing about Green 85 which looks as though it's going to pass close. Get onto it as soon as you can hear, Topham.'

'Aye aye, sir.'

There was little for anybody to do with the submarine running blind and deaf at full speed. Harding stood, staring at the depth gauges, their pointers steady on sixty feet, not seeing them because he was looking hard at himself, trying to judge the intensity of his nervousness. The only yard-stick available to him was the attack on the submerged U-boat. It had been the eeriness of that long silent hunt which had affected him then, the mental picture of the two dark shapes gliding beneath the sea like a pair of sharks each awaiting a second's lack of vigilance in the other before turning to rend it. Now there was the exhilaration of speed with the sound of water hissing past the hull clear in his ears, the excitement of the developing situation, the anticipation of striking a smashing blow at the enemy but, for all that, he concluded that he felt quite remarkably alarmed. The force they were about to attack was extremely formidable, the penalty for detection possibly, even probably, fatal and he found himself wishing wistfully that the target was one of the undefended merchant ships they were now authorized to sink at sight. Just one, he thought, would have been nice. Just one to make sure that everybody knew what to do and how to do it.

Colour flooded Harding's face at the recollection of urging his captain to put an end to practice and get on with the war.

Feeling very foolish, hoping that nobody had noticed, he waited for the blush to subside, then looked around the control room.

Bulstrode was standing near him, apparently deep in thought, twiddling the hairs in his left nostril between finger and thumb. Lieutenant Tollafield, built like a rugby forward, was glowering at the 'Fruit Machine' as though defying it to issue false information. The very tall figure of the very young Sub-Lieutenant Gascoigne was jack-knifed over the chart table, the one eye Harding could see wide with expectancy. Leading Seaman Topham was carefully wiping his ear-phones with a grimy handkerchief.

More men were behind Harding's other shoulder, but he didn't turn in their direction. That would be making his anxiety too public. Instead he looked at Able Seaman Mungo at the steering wheel. All he could see was the back of his head and he found himself wondering incongruously when the helmsman intended to have his front teeth replaced. It seemed a long time since the fight in the Bethnal Green street. It seemed a long way away too.

'Periscope depth, Number One.'

'Sir.'

There was no need to repeat the order, both Chief Petty Officer Ryland and his second coxswain had turned their hydroplane control wheels at the captain's words. Harding looked down at the tops of the heads of the two seated figures. The close-cropped scalps told him nothing, but their shoulders looked relaxed enough. He sighed softly to himself, wondering what the next periscope observation would reveal, wondering, too, how effective the enemy's sonar was and what it felt like to be depth-charged. His apprehensive questioning thoughts were to be answered very quickly.

'Bearing is that. Range is that. I am seventy degrees on her port bow. No destroyer closer than a mile. Down periscope. What's the Director Angle?'

'Green 14, sir,' Tollafield said.

'Right, I shall be firing a full salvo. Stand by all tubes.' Bulstrode turned to Harding and added, 'It's looking good,

Number One. They aren't even zig-zagging,' and that was when everything started to go wrong.

'Transmissions bearing Green 50 in contact, sir. Revolutions increasing.' Topham's voice.

'Up periscope.'

The thick brass tube seeming to rise so slowly, the captain snatching at the handles, jerking round onto the bearing looking to Harding to be moving in slow motion. With an effort he dragged his eyes away and concentrated on depth keeping.

'Down periscope. Ninety feet. Group up. Full ahead together. Shut off for depth-charging. Oh, you've already shut off, haven't you Number One?'

'Yes, sir.'

'Did you detect any change before we speeded up, Topham?'

'No, sir. Still in contact. Bearing steady. Attacking I think, sir.'

'Yes, she was pointing straight towards us. Another *Roederer Maas* – class by the look of it. Warn everybody that things may get a bit noisy in a minute or two, Number One.'

Harding took down the Tannoy microphone. 'We may be depth-charged shortly. Hold onto your hats,' he said, momentarily pleased with the steadiness of his voice, the bit about hats. Casual that, with nobody wearing one. Oh Christ! *Casual?*

Shadow gaining depth so slowly, only just passing forty feet as though surface tension were holding her up.

'Flood "Q", sir?'

'Not now, Number One. We've got a little time.'

The pointers moving faster, the angle of dive increasing so that Harding had to grasp hold of the control room ladder, the captain the periscope hoist wire and everybody else standing whatever there was to hold on to within their reach. Fifty feet, sixty, seventy. The flail-like sound of fast-turning propellors passing overhead clear above the racket of their own movement, then the waiting for the charges to sink down to the depth at which they had been set to explode. The hairs at the back of Harding's neck prickled and one part of his mind recorded the fact, vaguely intrigued by having a cliché come true.

Eighty feet, and a thunderous detonation shaking *Shadow* as if her main propulsion bearings had torn free, here and there light bulbs breaking, somebody saying, 'Fuck this!' the words indistinct because of singing in the ears. The second detonation appalling, Harding convinced that the hull had contracted under its savage assault. Total darkness, then the emergency lighting flickering into life. Water pouring in? Probably not. Just the ear-drums protesting, but better check. Two more explosions, laughably far away, like twenty yards or so, only rattling the teeth in his head, nothing like that second one. Laughable *Don't laugh! Steady!* Check, as you told yourself to do!

'All compartments report damage,' Harding said to the Tannoy microphone, realized that he hadn't pressed the transmit button, did so and said it again. The captain and two men sprawled on the deck, staggering to their feet now, apparently unhurt. One after the other different parts of the ship reporting slight leaks in the hull, min leaks from the high-pressure air system, no casualties.

'There appears to be no significant damage, sir.'

'Thank you, Number One,' Bulstrode said, 'but I really wish they wouldn't *do* that. It plays hell with my sinuses.' Topham giggled nervously, aloud this time.

'Open bow caps. Reduce speed to half ahead group down. Stay at this depth.'

Harding, his thoughts very far from aggression, blinked at the captain's order. *Shadow* was at fifty feet, blown up there by the expanding gases from the explosions, but the planesmen had halted the rise. He repeated the speed and depth and heard Tollafield ordering the torpedo tube bow caps opened. The control room looked sepulchral in the dim emergency lighting, but the thought that the Germans hadn't finished with them yet decided him against ordering broken bulbs replaced.

'What's the plan, sir?' he asked.

Bulstrode went back to twiddling the hairs in his nostril for a moment before saying, 'Points are these, Number One. I daren't go up and look. Too much risk of being rammed by a destroyer. Topham won't be able to hear a bloody thing until all the turbulence from the depth-charges has died down, so I can't fire by sonar. We haven't altered course since they attacked us, so as far as we're concerned the Director Angle remains the same and it should be coming onto the pocket battleship any moment now. On the other hand, unless they're stark staring bonkers, which I doubt, they'll have begun to alter course away from us as soon as that destroyer made contact, but very little time has elapsed, they're big ships, they'll turn slowly and there's a long line of them. Consequently, *faute de mieux*, I'm going to poop six fish costing two thousand five hundred quid each off into the blue in the hope of hitting something. I'll probably get my arse kicked from here to breakfast when we get home, but these targets are too valuable to let go without trying something. If you can call that a plan, that's it.'

The words had come rattling out of Bulstrode with no pause between the sentences. For a man, Harding thought, who had just been thrown to the deck by a series of savage explosions it was a remarkably concise and precise assessment of the situation. He was revising his thinking to include the fact that it wouldn't have been at all bad from a man sitting in an arm-chair at home when Bulstrode added, 'Tollafield, I want to get those fish away before they drop some more charges on us and blow the things back into their tubes. What's happening to the bow caps?'

'One, two, three and four open, sir.'

'Fire one,' Bulstrode said, 'and carry on firing at ten-second intervals. Hurry with those last two bow caps. Start us on our way down, Number One. Level off at two hundred and fifty feet, then go to silent running.'

When the last torpedo had leapt from its tube *Shadow*, still sinking downwards, began a ninety degree turn to starboard and there was a flurry of depth-charge explosions. Twenty-eight were counted, all were noisy, none was close. If any torpedo had found a target there was no way of telling in the uproar. Then suddenly there was silence.

'I've been thinking, Number One.'

'Yes, sir?'

'I could have bought a dozen houses with what I've just shot off into the blue.'

'Oh, I wouldn't invest in housing, sir,' Harding said. 'It's likely to get bombed. Feel free to pass that on to your aunt.'

Bulstrode smiled at him, then turned to the sonar operator. 'Don't suppose you can hear anything, Topham.'

'No, sir. The water's still churning around.'

'Depth is two hundred and fifty feet, sir,' Harding said. 'Ship running dead slow on one propellor. Do you want me to try for a "stopped" trim?'

'It's a thought. Ask the Engineer Officer to speak to me, please.'

Lieutenant Wright arrived in the control room looking hot, dirty and wet.

'Sir?'

'What's the form, Chief?'

'The high-pressure air system is okay again, sir. No fractured piping. Just had to tighten some joints, but we're leaking water through the starboard shaft stern gland and a bit through the engine room hatch. I think it must have jumped from its seating and not settled properly again. There's a fair amount of water sloshing around in the bilges.'

'I see,' Bulstrode said. 'Thank you, Chief.' Then to Harding, 'No "stopped" trim. You'd never hold it. It's time for us to fold our tents and steal away on our brothel creepers, or whatever the Arabs do.'

'Cap'n, sir?'

'Yes, Topham?'

'Sonar transmissions bearing Red 125, sweeping, sir.'

'Any hydrophone effect?'

'Yes, sir. Lots of it, stretching from the port quarter to the starboard quarter. Can't tell what they're doing yet exactly, but I think they've increased speed.'

'Gettin' a bit 'eavy aft, sir,' the coxswain said.

Harding could see it from the angle of the hydroplane indicators, from the position of the bubble in the inclinometer, even feel it beneath the soles of his shoes. He ordered the second propellor set to slow ahead. *Shadow* levelled, but began to sink below two hundred and fifty feet.

'We're bodily heavy, sir,' he told the captain. 'Do you want me to pump?'

'No, Number One. Just let her go down.'

It occurred to Harding that if Cheaver had said that he would have had no idea whether the words constituted an order or were sarcasm. With Bulstrode they were clearly an order. The ship had a long way to drop before she reached her tested diving depth and could go below that if necessary. Of course the leaking might get worse as the pressure increased, but on the other hand it might have the effect of sealing the leaks. Then there was the matter of the hull being compressed as it got deeper, which meant that it would displace a smaller volume and so become heavier in relation to the water around it which in turn . . Harding frowned worriedly, then relaxed his facial muscles. The captain would tell him what he wanted done.

'Sonar transmissions bearing Red 120 in contact, sir,' Topham said and Harding's muscles tightened again, but he managed to keep his face expressionless.

'This is the bit where I came in. I think I'll go home now,' somebody said and Bulstrode nodded, smiling.

'Speeding up, sir. Bearing steady. Transmissions shortening. Attacking sir.'

'Starboard thirty, group up, full ahead together, get us below three hundred feet, Number One. Warn the crew to . . .' Bulstrode stopped talking at the sound of a prolonged, rumbling explosion then asked, 'What the hell was that, Topham?'

'Dunno, sir. Wasn't no depth-charge, but – dammit, I can't hear now. We're making such a racket.'

'Can't hear what?'

'I'm not sure, sir, but just after the explosion and just before we speeded up I thought the destroyer's bearing was changing.'

'Stop both,' Bulstrode said and immediately *Shadow*'s vibrating died away.

'Yes, it is, sir,' Topham told the captain. 'Seems to have broken off the attack. Transmissions have stopped and she's bearing Red 145 – Red 150. Going very fast, sir. Red 160 – Red 165. Red . . . the same, sir. Sound beginning to fade a little like she was going away on that bearing. Yes, definitely fading.'

Staring at one of the depth-gauges as though it were a crystal ball Harding spoke slowly, softly. 'The inference being that, following the explosion, the destroyer was recalled or turned back on its own initiative to . . .'

'Render assistance, Number One?'

'Yes, sir. Otherwise why abandon a firm submarine contact? I think you may have hit something, probably something important.'

'May I mention somethin' else important, sir?' Chief Petty Officer Ryland asked.

Harding looked round at him. 'Of course, Cox'n. What is it?'

'The Cap'n mentioned somethin' called Stygian depths, whatever they are, bein' at a 'undred and twenty feet, then 'e tells you to get us below three 'undred. I don't know what they're called either, but if somebody don't start the motors soon we'll be passin' three 'undred and fifty which I calls bloody deep.'

'Half ahead together,' Bulstrode said, then gave a snorting laugh. 'Thank you, Cox'n. I'm glad somebody was looking after the ship while the First Lieutenant and I were indulging in wishful thinking. I'd completely forgotten I'd said "stop both". Topham's fault really. He wanted to listen to something. Come up to sixty feet, Number One, and we'll get rid of some of this excess ballast if it's safe to do so. Steer 210.'

Shadow was racing to the south of west across the surface of a choppy North Sea, spray from her bows exploding irregularly and with unexpected suddenness out of the darkness to sting the faces of the people on her bridge. Gascoigne had the watch, but Harding was standing it with him. 'Just until you know the ropes,' Bulstrode had told the Sub-Lieutenant, and Harding had thought that was rather funny in view of the very few days that had passed since he himself had been supervised by Cheaver.

With the totally unexpected and blessed departure of the destroyer, Harding had caught a reasonably satisfactory trim at sixty feet by ordering water pumped outboard and from aft to forward then, with only faint hydrophone effect audible fine on the port quarter, Bulstrode had had the ship brought to periscope depth. Only the mast, bridge and funnel tops of two destroyers had been visible to the north. They seemed to be moving very slowly, stopping entirely from time to time, and sonar transmissions were coming from them, probing beneath the surface of the sea in their vicinity. Then the bombers had come, two of them repeatedly criss-crossing the area at high speed and almost wave-top height, two more circling the destroyers' position at a greater altitude. Heinkel IIIs Bulstrode said they were and their presence had effectively prevented him from surfacing to transmit an enemy report. That had had to wait for the safety-curtain of darkness to settle around them and then its transmission had coincided with the receipt of a signal addressed to *Shadow*. Gascoigne had deciphered it.

'Enemy heavy units including pocket-battleship *Lützow* with *Hipper*-and *Köln*-class cruisers plus destroyer mother-ship approaching your area from Skagerrak + large destroyer escort + last position report 1445 today 20 miles due south Farsund course 340 degrees speed unknown + may be making for Stavanger +'

'Thanks for the memory,' Bulstrode had said and sent for the engineer officer.

Lieutenant Wright's report had been discouraging. It had proved impossible to re-seal the engine room hatch completely. Distortion of its hinges was suspected, but it was difficult to tell in the darkness. On top of that, the leak past the starboard shaft stern gland was no better, even with the ship on the surface.

'Then we'll have to go back to Rosyth,' Bulstrode had said.

'Write this down, cipher it and get it transmitted, Gascoigne.'

Now Harding was standing at the back of the bridge, the furthest he could distance himself from Gascoigne, trying to give the impression that he wasn't there at all. Half his attention was on what the sub-lieutenant said and did, not that there was much for him to do or say with the ship maintaining a straight course for Scotland. The battery charge had been completed before midnight and *Shadow*'s sole objective was to place as many miles as possible behind her, away from a coast becoming progressively more hostile as the Germans tightened their grip on it, before she had to pass the hours of day-light submerged in her damaged condition.

The rest of his thoughts were on the now abandoned patrol. Had he acquitted himself well or badly in Bulstrode's eyes? Had he been really afraid, or just normally nervous? It was difficult to be sure with most of the tension gone. Had they in fact damaged an enemy ship, as the evidence seemed to suggest? What, as second-in-command, would he have done had Bulstrode failed to rise from the deck after that initial accurate depth-charge attack? What if . . .

'It's beginning to get light, Number One. Should I dive the ship?' Gascoigne's voice from the front of the bridge.

Sounding very experienced indeed, 'No, I wouldn't do that if I were you,' Harding said. 'I think I'd tell the Captain.'

Chapter 7

'Finished with main engines,' Bulstrode told the voice-pipe, stepped to the conning tower hatch and began to lower himself into it.

'Cap'n, sir?'

'Yes, Number One?'

'I think that's Captain Submarines coming along the jetty towards us.'

Bulstrode pulled himself back out of the hatch. 'So it is. Come on. We'll meet him at the brow.'

Harding followed him over the side of the bridge, feeling for the foot and hand-holds in its side until he reached the casing, then both walked forward past the 3-inch gun to the ship's gangway. They saluted as the big man crossed it.

''Morning, Bulstrode. 'Morning, Harding. Sorry I'm late. Meant to be here to see you come alongside. Got caught on the blower.'

'Kind of you to come down, sir,' Bulstrode said. 'Particularly as I seem to have fucked it up.'

The flotilla captain glanced at the group of men still securing the berthing wires near them and jerked his head towards the bows. Bulstrode went with him and Harding joined them at the flotilla captain's gesture.

'On the contrary, Bulstrode. It looks very much as though you fucked *them* up. I've just been given an RAF reconnaissance report over the phone. That's what made me late. The *Lützow*'s in Stavanger and so is the *Hipper*-class cruiser. The *Köln*-class is there too, but her quarter-deck's under water and she's surrounded by salvage vessels. From what they told me it seems she won't be any use to them for at least a year. In addition to that, the pilot could see no sign of the destroyer depot ship at all, but we can't be certain she went down until his photographs have been developed.'

'Well, well. When will they have the pictures, sir?'

'In about a quarter of an hour they said. Come back to my office with me and you can listen in when they call through again.'

The big man and the very small one walked to the gangway together, then the flotilla captain turned back.

'Are you on the shore telephone yet, Harding?'

'It's being connected now, sir.'

'All right. Your captain and I are going to be busy for a while, but if we get confirmation I'll have my secretary call you so that you can tell your crew.'

'Thank you very much indeed, sir,' Harding said.

Twenty minutes later he replaced the telephone hand-set

and stood looking at it intently, trying not to allow his elation to show in his face. The strong emotion subsided slowly to be replaced by a glow of satisfaction and thankfulness that even if he had been frightened it hadn't been for nothing. Slowly he walked into the control room and took the Tannoy microphone from its hook then, changing his mind, put it back again. This was an opportunity not to be missed of observing the crew's bearing.

Harding found the coxswain in the petty officers' mess, talking to the torpedo gunner's mate.

'I'd like you to clear lower deck, Cox'n, and have the hands fall in on the jetty. It doesn't matter what they're wearing. This is quite informal.'

'Right away, sir,' Ryland said.

Minutes later Lieutenants Wright and Tollafield with Sub-Lieutenant Gascoigne followed Harding across the brow on to the jetty to stand beside him in front of Shadow's ship's company. The men were at attention in two lines their expressions curious, not watchful any longer.

'Stand them at ease please, Cox'n.'

Chief Petty Officer Ryland's answering bellow set gulls perched on Shadow's periscope standards reeling away in spirals of raucous flight.

Wincing slightly, 'Stand easy, everybody,' Harding said. 'I won't keep you long.'

Squared shoulders relaxed into more natural positions and feet shuffled, but all eyes were on Harding.

'I've just been authorized to tell you,' Harding went on, 'that in that attack when things got a bit noisy we sank a twelve thousand ton destroyer depot ship and hit a Köln-class cruiser. They got the cruiser into harbour, but her engine room at least is flooded and she'll be a write-off for many months. Well done all of you. Carry on please, Cox'n.'

For a moment there was silence, then a man shouted, 'Up yours, Adolph!' and another, 'Good for the Big Bad Bull!' General laughter spread along the ranks only to be silenced by another roar from Ryland. Satisfied that a group of resentful individuals had become a crew, Harding returned aboard wondering if he should tell his little captain of the soubriquet he had acquired. He decided to keep the information to himself for the time being.

'Seen your Skipper, Harding?'

Harding looked up from his chair in the wardroom of the submarine base at the lieutenant-commander who was operations staff officer to the flotilla captain.

'No, sir. Not since this afternoon. Do you want me to find him?'

'Glad if you would. Captain Submarines wants him, in a tearing hurry too.'

The cabin allocated to Bulstrode in the wing reserved for submarine officers between patrols was empty, so Harding telephoned the ship, but the captain was not on board. No, a sentry at the main gate told him, he hadn't noticed any very small officer leaving the base. 'I'll get the lads lookin' for 'im round the docks, sir,' Chief Petty Officer Ryland said. There were no other submarines in harbour, but two destroyers were moored along the quay. Bulstrode wasn't visiting either of them. Harding checked the cabin again. It was still empty.

Fourteen identical doors were ranged, seven a side along the gloomy passage, a fifteenth at the end led into a communal bathroom. Only the last door Harding tried was bolted and light was showing through the keyhole. Stooping, he found that the end of the bunk was just within his field of view and on it a pair of shoes pointed vertically at the ceiling.

'Cap'n, sir?'

There was no reply to the words or to the hammering of his fist on the thin wooden panel.

'Bloody hell,' Harding muttered and the flimsy bolt tore free of its fastenings at his first charge.

Bulstrode was deeply unconscious, breathing stertorously, his face flushed and his pulse rapid. 'Bloody hell,' Harding said again, picked up the empty gin bottle from the floor, found its cap under the bunk, walked quickly to his own cabin and thrust the damning court-martial evidence out of sight under the

77

mattress. Coffee, black coffee, gallons of black coffee. That was what you gave them, wasn't it? Ten to nine his watch told him and that meant that the wardroom pantry was shut. Couldn't go demanding a big jug of black coffee in any event. Make people curious. He went to the wardroom anyway, ambling seemingly aimlessly about, ignoring the officers there, pretending to look at the newspaper rack and the pictures on the walls until he reached the table in the corner where the silver cruets stood. Palming first a salt shaker then a mustard pot from their holder into his pocket he shook his head in feigned exasperation as though he had forgotten something and left the mess, moving rapidly. Three minutes to nine his watch said. At least it was unlikely that any officers would be going to their cabins for an hour or so.

It wasn't difficult to carry the little man into the bathroom, but getting him undressed was. The task took him several minutes and only when it was completed did he remember to lock the door.

Harding stripped off his own uniform, put his captain on the floor of a shower cabinet and turned the cold water full on. That done, he mixed salt and mustard in a glass of water, turned the shower off and, holding Bulstrode's nose, poured the mixture into his mouth. Bulstrode gagged, swallowed, choked and vomited violently. Harding turned the shower on again and began to smack his face, kept smacking it until Bulstrode said, 'For Pete's sake stop it, Number One!'

'I will when you pull yourself together, sir. Captain Submarines wants you urgently!'

It took another ten minutes to get Bulstrode upright, dry and dressed, the dressing quicker than the undressing because Bulstrode had begun to help. Harding took him to his cabin.

'Stay there, sir, until I find out where you've been.'

'What do you mean "where I've been"?' The captain asked, but Harding had gone.

Into the telephone at the end of the passage Harding said, 'Yes, yes, I know the last showing is nearly over. Just tell me the name of the film. All right, thank you.' He ran back along the passage.

'You've been seeing Anna May Wong in "Daughter of Fu Manchu", sir. I had your name flashed on the screen. Now, can you make it on your own?'

'Yes, I can make it,' Bulstrode said and Harding watched him walk fairly steadily away. He cleaned up the mess in the bathroom then, changed his shirt and underclothes, put on his uniform and telephoned Ryland to call off the search. That done, he took the gin bottle down to the jetty and threw it into the Firth of Forth, watching it bob away into the darkness. The salt and mustard containers could, he decided, await their return to the wardroom until there was nobody there to see him replace them. Harding went back to the cabin Bulstrode had borrowed. Feeling emotionally exhausted he tidied the bunk and began to screw the bolt back into place with a nail file.

The operations staff officer scowled at Bulstrode. 'Where the hell have you been, Bill? I say, are you all right?'

'I was,' Bulstrode told him, 'until my First Lieutenant had me dragged out of the local flea-pit. Now I'm frustrated. They're showing Anna May Wong in a black cheong-sam slit up to where you'd never believe. What's all the excitement about around here?'

'The Old Man wants to see you about that destroyer depot ship you sank. Come on.'

'Ah, Bulstrode,' the flotilla captain said. 'So they found you. Sit down. Hello, you're looking rather pale. Anything wrong?'

'Touch of flu, sir.'

'Really? Well, take care of yourself. Now, I want you to think very carefully and then give me an exact description of that depot ship you torpedoed. Take your time.'

'I hardly noticed the thing, sir. I was far more interested in the pocket-battleship and the cruisers.'

'But you saw it. You mentioned it in your enemy report.'

'Yes, I saw it, sir,' Bulstrode said. 'Wait a minute, will you?'

He closed his eyes, conscious of the clamminess of his skin, feeling nausea churning in his stomach, praying fervently that he wasn't going to be sick again. Slowly the sensations eased

79

and he began to concentrate on the line of ships. The pocket-battleship and the two cruisers were clear enough in his mind, but then he was familiar with them from photographs and the identification silhouettes. The depot ship . . .

'Single upright funnel, sir, with one of those fancy black cowls the Germans like to fit to make their ships look sinister.'

'Go on.'

'Bridge and two masts. Well-deck for'ard. Don't remember any armament. Raked bow, cruiser stern.'

'Any lifting equipment?'

Bulstrode sat silent for almost half a minute staring at the inside of his own eye-lids before saying, 'Yes, sir. A sort of big gantry thing over the well-deck.'

'Sure?'

'Certain, sir,' Bulstrode said and opened his eyes.

'Well done,' the flotilla captain said, reached for the telephone and asked for a number.

'Lycett? Mansergh here. It *was* the *Magdeburg*.' 'Yes, the submarine's captain described her more or less exactly. Quite different to the *Plauen*. What?' 'Oh yes, Excellent news, isn't it? 'Bye.'

'May one ask what that was all about, sir?'

'Certainly, Bill,' Captain Mansergh said. 'Two depot ships sailed with the squadron from Stettin, the *Magdeburg* and the *Plauen*. One of them put into Kristiansand we believe, but we haven't got a photograph of her yet because the weather down there has been too bad for the RAF to get one. The other went on with the *Lützow* and company, making for Stavanger. What you heard was a ship blowing up and it wasn't the *Köln*-class cruiser because they got her into harbour somehow, so it must have been the *Magdeburg*.'

'And that's interesting, sir?'

Captain Mansergh nodded, smiling. 'It is rather, Bill. The Intelligence boys tell me that she was carrying the entire German General Staff for the occupation of Norway.'

Bulstrode didn't feel well enough to do more than smile weakly back at him.

'Not a very edifying experience for you, Number One,' Bulstrode said. 'What are you going to do about it?' He was sitting on the end of Harding's bunk, short legs dangling. Harding pulled himself more nearly upright and rearranged the pillows behind his shoulders.

'There's nothing more *to* do, sir. I think I've tied up all the loose ends.'

'So I gather from you, every last one, but that wasn't what I meant. Drinking oneself unconscious is inclined to be frowned upon in this man's Navy and drinking on base anywhere but in the wardroom is a court-martial offence. There'll have to be some official action.'

Tired, troubled and embarrassed Harding let irritation show in his voice when he said, 'Oh, for Christ's sake! I don't usually spend my evenings rushing around like a chicken with its head off, stealing salt and mustard and chucking bottles into rivers if I intend to let things get official.'

Bulstrode smiled faintly. 'No, I don't suppose you do, but that was just a decent automatic reaction to prevent a brother officer ruining his career. Since then you'll have had time to consider the implications, the implications for you and *Shadow* generally.'

'Okay. In that case, sir, you'd better tell me how often it happens. I know you never drink at sea.'

'No, I'd never do that, Number One,' Bulstrode said. 'It happens just once, immediately after I get back from patrol. Silly, but it seems to provide some sort of emotional catharsis, clear away all the tensions.' He paused, then went on, 'What would do the job much better would be a large armful of warm woman, but the kind that I find attractive don't go much for sawn-off little runts like me.' He paused, then added, 'Ironic, isn't it? If the bloody German General Staff had taken a bloody aeroplane ride to Norway instead of deciding on a boat trip I wouldn't have been found out.'

The reference to women had brought blood to Harding's face. He thought they were the most wonderful things in creation, things to be worshipped. Probably for that reason he had never slept with one, that and lack of opportunity. The idea that they might be used for some purpose other than romance was unthinkable to him and he sought frantically for something to say before his shyness was noticed. He didn't find it, but neither did Bulstrode look at him and as the colour drained slowly from his cheeks his thinking became more constructive.

At last, 'Don't mess things up now, sir. They're going so well.'

'Are they? What things?'

'Everything since you joined. That successful patrol and the crew, particularly the crew. They've changed completely since Commander Cheaver's time.'

Bulstrode didn't speak and Harding went on, 'They've started calling you the "Big Bad Bull" and they've thought up a ship's song. When I was down at the main gate this evening trying to find out if you had gone into the town, some of our chaps were coming in a bit pissed. I was in the guard house, so they couldn't see me and they were singing,

"Where the Bull strode there strode we
Far across the wild North Sea
To clobber the King's enemy.".'

Grunting impatiently Bulstrode slid off the bunk and stood looking sombrely down at Harding. 'Very touching, Number One, but surely you must realize that I've placed myself in an impossible position vis-a-vis you.'

'Then you'd better transfer me, if that's how you feel, and get yourself another First Lieutenant.'

The suggestion was dismissed by a negative jerk of Bulstrode's head and Harding said crossly, 'Well, if you're determined to make a big deal out of this I can't very well stop you, sir, but it'll simply mean that everybody loses and I think that's bloody selfish.'

For long seconds Bulstrode continued to stare at Harding, then he nodded. 'All right. I'll think about it.' He began to turn away, but stopped the movement. 'I haven't been making particularly appreciative noises about your part in this evening's performance, Number One. That doesn't mean I'm not grateful. I am. Very.'

82

Harding shrugged his shoulders. 'Why don't we just get on with the blasted war, sir?'

'Okay,' Bulstrode said and smiled openly. 'We'll get on with the blasted war.'

Chapter 8

For six and a half weeks of disastrous spring which was to see the German armies spread north to the Arctic Circle and south to the Pyrenees *Shadow* lay in dry-dock. Other submarines sailed for patrol and returned, their tallies of enemy ships torpedoed or sunk by gunfire mounting steadily. Some sailed and were never seen again. *Shadow* remained static, her hull a target for the assault of a horde of men bearing pneumatic tools and oxy-acetylene torches, lengths of piping, coils of cable, micrometers, avometers, voltmeters and things Harding had no very clear idea what they were for.

'Very lucky, you were,' the yard foreman told him and Bulstrode. 'Very lucky indeed.' The yard manager said the same thing and the following day a senior engineer officer sent up by the Admiralty provided them with an identical opinion. The depth-charge which had exploded closest had cracked the pressure hull in two places near the engine room hatch, distorted the hinges of the hatch itself and thrown the starboard propellor shaft out of alignment, causing related damage to its bearings and tail clutch.

'How long?' Bulstrode asked and nodded politely when he was told that it would be at least five weeks before his ship was seaworthy. Harding received the news with dismay. Able Seaman Mungo went to London on leave and beat up his wife.

'I'd be grateful if you would do it, Number One,' Bulstrode said. 'It's young Gascoigne's job really, but if Mungo is going to have an officer appear for him as a character witness it had better be somebody who knows him well and the Cox'n tells me you helped him before I joined the ship.'

'Of course I'll do it, sir,' Harding replied.

Sitting in the London train, a little apprehensive about the court appearance he would have to make on the following day, he was nevertheless thankful to be away from his captain at least for the time being. He had guessed that a certain degree of stiffness born of mutual embarrassment would exist between them for a period, but had satisfied himself that that would be washed away by the tide of war and the demands which stemming it would make on both of them. Then the survey of *Shadow* had revealed the extent of the damage she had suffered and for them the tide had ceased to flow. As Edinburgh slid away behind him he shifted uncomfortably in his seat at the memory of Bulstrode's small naked body curled in the shower cabinet with needle-jets of water striking and spraying from it in all directions.

All of Harding's barely adult life had been spent in the Navy and his conception of that Service, with its almost pompous display of outward rectitude, did not include such scenes, at least where officers were concerned. That, and a certain priggishness in his own nature, blinded him to the fact that he had set himself up as an arbiter of the conduct of a senior he hardly knew and of whose responsibilities he had only the smallest conception. He had been guilty of it when, partly for the good of the ship because his training had imbued him with an ever-growing professionalism, partly for his own peace of mind because he rated Bulstrode so far above Cheaver, he had magnanimously persuaded his new captain not to take action against himself. He was guilty of it now as he relived his petty feelings of revulsion. For a little while longer immaturity was to hide these facts from him and he was to squirm harder than present recollection was forcing him to do when they were revealed.

A clicking sound intruded on his thoughts and he looked up in time to see the girl sitting opposite him throw a cigarette lighter impatiently into her bag, the cigarette in her mouth unlit. Harding hadn't noticed her before and wondered why as she was attractive in a disdainful way which seemed to proclaim that she was uninterested in what people thought of her

84

appearance. Her eyes met his regard and passed on, register-
ing nothing.'

'Here,' Harding said. 'You put the end against the cord
where it's smouldering and suck.'

She leant forward, lit her cigarette and asked, 'What on
earth is it?' The words held little curiosity.

'It's just a length of slow-match with a wheel and flint
attachment.'

'What's a "slow-match"?'

'Slow-burning fuse.'

'Goodness! Will it explode?'

'No, it just smoulders. Jolly useful in a high wind. That
makes it burn harder instead of blowing it out.'

'Goodness,' she said again. 'Well, thanks for the light.'

Harding watched her turning the pages of a magazine,
occasionally puffing absently at her cigarette. He decided that
he liked the slender column of her neck, the arrogant tilt of her
chin and the way she had fastened her dark brown hair loosely at
the back of the head as though she hadn't been able to think of
anything else to do with it. She would have been very pretty, he
thought, but for the sulky droop of her mouth and a flatness about
her eyes which, with the rest of her expression, stated that if
there was anything worth looking at she had seen it before.
Her legs were good and he began to wonder what the body was
like under the mannish pale fawn riding-coat she was wearing.

The train had crossed the border into England before she
took another cigarette from a small gold case and looked
enquiringly at Harding. He lit her cigarette and told her to
keep the lighter.

'Oh, come now. I can hardly do that.'

'Of course you can. It didn't cost me anything. Our ERAs
make them.'

'Really? What's an ERA?'

'Engine Room Artificer. Skilled mechanic.'

'I see. Thank you very much. What do I fill it with?'

'You don't fill it with anything. You try to find another length
of slow-match when that bit's burned away.'

There was no dining car on the train and at York he went to

85

the station buffet and bought food and drink for both of them. The girl insisted on paying for her share and he didn't protest.'

'Are you on a battleship or something?'

Automatically, '*In* a ship, not *on* one, but I'm not anyway. I'm a submariner.'

'How very glamorous.' She made it sound as exciting as tea at the vicarage.

'What do you do?'

'Rich bitch,' she said. 'I don't do anything, but I suppose they'll conscript me into some dreary job before this silly war's over.'

Harding's face turned wooden as though it had undergone instant fossilization and, for the first time, the drooping corners of her mouth turned upwards in a smile.

'That got to you, submariner, didn't it?'

'Yes, if it gives you any satisfaction.'

The smile faded. 'No, it doesn't. Pretend I never said it. Which of the women's Services uniforms do you think would suit me best?'

They discussed that companionably while they ate and then she slept, or pretended to, for an hour. He was dozing himself when she asked, 'Where are you staying in London?'

'No idea. Some hotel in Bethnal Green. I imagine. That's where I have to be tomorrow morning. I usually stay with my parents, but they're away.'

'Oh.'

After that there was silence between them until the train began to slow in the north London suburbs and he lifted her two expensive cases from the rack.

'Don't bother with those,' she said. 'Pinsent will take them.'

He didn't ask who Pinsent was and felt no surprise when a uniformed chauffeur opened the carriage door almost as soon as the train stopped.

''Evening, Miss.'

'Good evening, Pinsent. Take these bags, please.'

She took his arm while they followed the chauffeur along the platform.

'What's your name?'

'Peter Harding.'

'I'm Stephanie.'

'Stephanie who?'

'Empson, unless Mummy's got married again while I've been in Scotland. It's hard to keep up.'

At the ticket barrier he disengaged his arm. 'Well, it's been nice talking to you, Miss Empson.'

Her eyes opened wide in comical astonishment, 'Do you mean to tell me that that lighter fuse contraption *isn't* for picking up girls? Now you see it. Now it's exploded and blown the buttons off your blouse. *That* sort of thing?'

'I hadn't thought of that,' Harding said uncomfortably, 'but it's a terrific idea.'

'Of course it is. Much better than "Didn't we meet at George's last week-end?" And there was me thinking I was fighting off your unbridled lust all the way from Scotland. Come on. Mummy's going to absolutely die when you give her one of your glances of barely suppressed passion.'

'Oh, look . . .'

'Oh, look yourself. Nobody, but nobody, ever stays in Bethnal Green, for heaven's sake. Mummy's got ten bedrooms. You can take your pick. Consider it our contribution to the war effort.'

A blurred impression of getting into the back of a big Daimler limousine, familiar streets slipping by scarcely noticed, the girl talking more readily now, his answers automatic but not recorded in his brain, a large house somewhere in Belgravia and a butler opening the door. 'Good evening, miss. Good evening, sir. Madam's in the first floor sitting room.' A thin middle-aged woman with scarlet nails and dyed hair wearing a black cocktail dress. 'How very nice of you to come, Lieutenant Harding.' A paunchy man wearing expensive tweeds and a Brigade of Guards tie. 'Ah, the Navy.' The girl putting a drink into his hand. The mother looking at him with what he didn't recognize as hunger in her eyes.

First clear impression – I don't like Mummy. The second – I bet that man isn't entitled to wear that tie. Don't like him either.

'Where *did* you get that ghastly dress, darling? Whatever will Lieutenant Harding think of us?' Not much of a dress. A shapeless creation of mauve wool, but why did it matter what he thought? Feeling of protectiveness towards the girl. 'I bought it to blend with the heather, Mummy. A female needs some natural protection up there. After Alastair, you of all people should know what Highlanders are like.' Obviously no protection needed. Mind wandering while the paunchy man recounted his exploits at the second battle of the Marne in 1918, wedging him into a corner. Perhaps he was entitled to his tie after all. Quick switch of direction to a diatribe against the Navy. Saying he had no idea what was being done to improve convoy protection because that wasn't his war and being told that he was typical of his generation in its failure to accept responsibility.

Momentarily rescued while his glass was refilled, then the man pouncing again. 'Do you shoot?' Suddenly fed up, hearing himself reply untypically, 'Yes, but I always let the other fellow draw first. I'm greased lightning with a .45.' The man's face suffusing and, blessedly, the butler announcing dinner. Stephanie taking his arm again and whispering, 'Hidden depths, Lieutenant Harding. I could kiss you for putting down that idiot Henry Paice.' Asking, 'Who?' and being told, 'The fat man. He never likes to be introduced. You're supposed to know that he's the Minister for something or other. By the way, don't let Mummy upset you. She's a tramp.'

Dinner excellent, two wines and brandy with the coffee. Whisky and soda after it. The mother flirtatious and making risqué remarks. Another instalment of the second battle of the Somme. No, it was the Marne, wasn't it? Nervously drinking everything offered to him.

Nearly midnight and the mother showing him to his room, turning down the covers, patting the pillows, fussing, lingering. 'Thank you for a pleasant evening, Mrs Empson.' The door closing on a ruefully amused glance. The bed seeming to sway and circle like a rudderless boat. Drunk much too much, dammit. Sleep descending on him like a dark veil.

'Don't jump, Peter. It's only me.'

Stephanie standing with her back to the closed door, the mauve dress gone, everything gone except for a pair of elegant shoes. Walking across the room towards him, her body as excellent as her legs. Not that he knew anything much of that, only that it was so. Thinking oh God it's going to happen to me! Thrilled or terrified? First one, then the other, then both. 'I'm sorry for putting you through that awful evening.' Blanket and sheet drawn from him, deft fingers loosening buttons and pyjama cord. 'Move over, darling.' The mouth, not sulky now, descending on him, the devastatingly gentle touch of silken skin and the increasing pressure of softness, her mouth and body engulfing him. Star-bursts and an exploding universe.

'Peter?'

A forefinger tracing the outline of his lips.

'Yes, Stephanie?'

'How many girls have you been to bed with?' Dawning anticipation in her voice.

'Well, I – I . . .'

'Dear God! How incredibly, utterly marvellous!'

It was nearly dawn when she left him.

'Congratulations,' Superintendent Micklethwaite said. 'A full lieutenant now, eh?'

'Oh, yes. Yes indeed. Thank you.' So tired, so distraught, so miserable.

'Well, I'm afraid it's going to take more than two gold stripes to get your chap Mungo off this time.'

'I thought as much,' Harding said. 'How long do you suppose he'll get?'

'Three months at a guess. I'll be surprised if they're easier on him than that. There is one thing to his advantage though. He'll be going up before Mr Ian Cranborne. He's very "pro" the fighting services and has a particularly soft spot for the Navy. Still, there are limits to what you can do to your wife even if she is a tart, particularly when the neighbours get involved and assaulted for their pains.'

'What time is his case likely to be heard?'

'About 1130, but you'd better be ready a bit before that.'

'I will be,' Harding said. 'Thank you once again, Superintendent.'

He sat on a bench in a gloomy anteroom reserved for witnesses, the confused emotions and physical sensations seeping away, dull self-disgust flowing in to fill the vacuum they left. He had eaten his breakfast alone. 'No, sir, nobody else,' the butler had told him. 'Mrs Empson breakfasts in her room and Miss Stephanie has had hers and gone out. She asked me to give you this.' An envelope with 'Lieutenant Harding' written on it in a bold scrawl and the end of a new-found world inside. With an inward tremor he took the letter from his pocket to read it for the fifth time.

'Peter, my sweet – I feel very badly about last night and I want you to go away and not come back. If you try to phone me I shall be "out" and if you call at the house you won't be admitted, so please don't do either of those things, or write to me. If this seems cruel to you, try to believe me when I say it's not. We're a rotten pair, Mummy and me, and I'm just as much a tramp as she is. We run with a rotten crowd too. Pinsent has orders to take you wherever you want to go – Stephanie'.

Harding had made his way to Bethnal Green alone without the assistance of Pinsent and the Daimler, battered by conflicting waves of feeling so strong that he was conscious of stumbling several times as though he were still drunk. Once he dropped his overnight bag. The ravening scarlet beast of the night, its fiery breath igniting sensation and charring thought out of existence, had left him wildly elated. Not even on waking had his old ideas of romance risen from the ashes of common-sense to trouble him. That he was in love was the only thing clear in his mind. Then he had read the letter.

'Able Seaman Mungo's case coming up next, sir.'

He thanked the constable, put the letter back in his pocket and walked into the court room. Mungo was being led in from the opposite direction, mouth hanging open in a gap-toothed look of near-idiocy. That annoyed Harding because the sailor, whatever else he might be, was far from idiotic. Harding was too concerned with self at that moment to recognize apprehension in another, too broken-hearted, as he believed, to recognize anything very much. It was only as the police evidence against Mungo began to mount in both quantity and gravity that he began to pull himself together, to remember why he was in London at all.

'The woman's a prostitute,' the old lady who owned the house said 'Men in her room day and night.' One point in Mungo's favour Harding thought.

'I live in the basement rooms,' a male tenant said. 'Didn't hear no screams until the landlady come and asked me to break it up. Heard them then all right, went upstairs and he knocked me cold. That was before the landlady calls the cops.' Assaulting a member of the public. Bloody fool.

'On attempting to intervene I received a blow to the left eye which felled me to the ground,' the arresting officer said. Harding almost smiled at the terminology. Almost. Endeavouring to resist arrest as well. Oh Christ!

'Severe bruising to the back and thighs inflicted with a heavy leather belt,' the police surgeon said. 'I estimate something between twenty and thirty strokes.' Did grievous bodily harm apply to married couples?

'Do you wish to give evidence on your own behalf, Mungo?'

'No, Your Worship.'

'Very well, but don't call me "Your Worship". I'm not the Mayor.'

'Sorry, sir.'

'I believe there is an officer in court prepared to make a statement regarding the accused's character.'

Harding took the stand and said the usual things – nothing but the most minor charges on the accused's naval conduct sheet – trustworthy – loyal member of the ship's company – no previous trouble with the civil authorities as far as the Navy was aware. That was a lie, but he had no intention of embarrassing Superintendent Micklethwaite after his kindness. It all sounded so standard, so formal, so feeble to his ears. He looked at the magistrate.

'Sir, for reasons of national security might I be permitted to set down a very brief statement on paper for the eyes of the Bench only?'

'It's irregular, but these are irregular times. I can allow you three minutes, Lieutenant Harding.'

'Thank you, sir. I'll be quicker than that.'

On the back of the envelope which had contained Stephanie's letter he wrote, 'Sir, I am second-in-command of one of His Majesty's submarines at present in dock for repair following depth-charge damage. Able Seaman Mungo is the ship's helmsman during submerged action stations and has to steer a course within one degree when torpedoes are fired. That takes training. He is not irreplaceable, but his loss to us could have a significant effect. We are due to sail four weeks from tomorrow.' He contemplated his second lie of the hearing for a moment, then added, 'Would it be possible for us to have him back before then?' Folding the paper he handed it to the clerk and watched as the man gave it to the magistrate, watched while his message was read, still watched while something was written on the front of the envelope. Then the paper was back in his hands.

'There are certain aspects of the law you appear to be unfamiliar with, young man,' he read. 'Destroy this utterly when you have left the court'.

He looked up and, for countable seconds, found his gaze held by eyes staring at him over the top of rimless spectacles. It was a relief when the magistrate turned from him to Mungo, but he was aware that he was chewing his lip as he listened to the calm voice reciting the list of Mungo's transgressions, underlining their extreme gravity and the consequences which would result from them. When the magistrate ended by saying, 'You will, therefore, go to prison for a period of twenty-one days,' he thought at first that he had misheard him.

'They told me I'd be lucky to get away with three months, sir!'

'Did they, Mungo?' It was difficult to meet the man's eyes with the black hole of the mouth grinning at him. Why didn't he get his front teeth fixed? There had been plenty of time.

'Yessir. What did you write on that piece of paper, sir?'

'It's none of your business, Mungo.'

'No, sir. Sorry, sir.'

Wishing that his head would ease its throbbing, Harding looked at the sailor standing a few feet from him across the little cell. Superintendent Micklethwaite had authorized immediate access for him. He liked Superintendent Micklethwaite.

'What gets into you, Mungo? Why do you do these things?' It was a silly question with the answer so obvious.

'Well, sir, she deserved part of it, sir, so I give it to her. Well, you know, sir. You remember what she done before and it's got a lot worse since then, so I let her have it.'

Harding nodded, then said, 'She deserved part of it, you say. What about the rest? You went a long way too far, didn't you?'

Mungo's eyes slid away from Harding's and he shuffled his feet. It was a quarter of a minute before he spoke again, his voice quiet, matter-of-fact.

'She liked it, sir. Kept yelling and pleading with me not to stop, then when she *did* want me to stop I was sort of seeing red, sir, and I couldn't.'

The cell faded and became a bedroom, like one scene merging into the next at the cinema. Lying face down, exhausted. Stephanie saying, 'Oh yes you can, Peter. Indeed you can. I shall make you!' and the explosion of pain across his buttocks. She had hit him three times before he wrested the hair-brush from her, but by then she had achieved her object. The cell reformed around him and he found that he was sitting on the bunk, head in hands, feeling deeply ashamed and physically sick.

Having scant knowledge of sadism or masochism and, consequently, the difference between them, from the shallow depths of his new-found experience, 'She's one of those, is she?' Harding said.

'Yes, sir. Seems like it, sir.'

'You don't have to answer this question if you don't want to, Mungo, but do you love her?'

'Yessir.' No hesitation at all.

In his mental turmoil lost for what to say next, 'Have you got cigarettes?' Harding asked.

'No, sir.'

'I'll have some sent in.'

'Thank you very much, sir.'

Harding stood up then. 'Look, Mungo, would it do any good if I went to see her?'

'She rather fancies you, sir.'

'That hardly answers my question.'

'Glad if you would have a chat, sir. Can't tell you what to say though.'

'Very well,' Harding said. 'I'll go round to your place now.'

A very subdued Edna Mungo immediately promised him that she would visit her husband in prison whenever that was permitted by the authorities. He thought that she was probably telling the truth, but did not venture into the realm of what she would be doing the rest of the time. Not due back at Rosyth until the following evening Harding caught the night train to Edinburgh anyway. Of only two things was he absolutely certain. He wanted to be out of London as quickly as possible and if Lieutenant-Commander William George de Vere Charnley-Bulstrode wanted to drink himself unconscious once after each patrol, never again would he feel revulsion towards his commanding officer on that score or, he guessed, on any other.

Chapter 9

Bulstrode had a habit of standing with his legs wide apart which made him look even shorter than he was. He was doing it now, hands on hips, staring up at Harding, his expression a mixture of faint amusement and mild vexation. His glass of gin and water was resting in the top pocket of his uniform. That was another of his habits.

'Why don't you take some leave, Number One? We're going to be here for another couple of weeks at least. There's no point in inventing work for yourself you know. The ship's organization is pretty well streamlined, isn't it?'

Harding sipped his own drink before saying, 'I'm not really inventing work, sir. It's a question of officer training actually. Well, the Chief's fine of course and the engine room isn't my part of ship anyway. Derek Tollafield isn't bad either, but John Gascoigne doesn't know whether it's Christmas or breakfast time. Not his fault. His only sea-going experience was as a midshipman, then he came straight to us from training class, so I'm instructing him. Tollafield too a bit. Then there's always the dockyard to chase. Lazy buggers, a lot of them. Finally, Able Seaman Mungo comes out of clink tomorrow and I'd like to be here to size him up when he rejoins.'

'All right. Then why not wait and see Mungo and push off after that? I can handle the rest of it for you.'

'Nice of you, sir,' Harding said, 'but my father's away on a lecture tour, mum's gone with him and I don't have anywhere else to go at the moment. I'd rather save the leave up.'

Bulstrode extracted his glass from his pocket, drank from it and put it back again. 'I'm not sure saving up leave is a very good idea. The way the war's going there's no telling when you'll get another opportunity to take any. Still, have it your own way, but do something for me, will you?'

'Of course, sir. What is it?'

'Go easy on the dockyard. I've been getting complaints from the yard manager.'

'Oh? What about?'

Harding regretted the question as soon as he had asked it. There was little doubt of what one of the complaints would have been about and from the rarely seen flicker of annoyance on Bulstrode's face it was obvious that his captain knew that he knew.

'About you, Number One. Let's put it this way. Next time you find three dockyard workmen playing cards in one of our tanks during working hours, there has to be a better way of persuading them to get on with whatever they're supposed to be doing than sealing the tank and connecting it to the high-pressure air supply. I'm sure you'll agree.'

'Yes, I suppose so, sir,' Harding said. 'It's just that I wanted to inspect that tank and when I asked them to get out of it they told me to fuck off. They got out fast enough when I unsealed the tank again. I think their ears may have been hurting a bit.'

Finding it difficult not to smile Bulstrode stopped trying. 'Okay, Peter, but call their foreman next time. We don't want the whole bloody yard out on strike. Let's have another gin.'

Harding accepted it gratefully, not because his treatment of the workmen had passed off without trouble, but because he had not been ordered to take leave. He was going through a phase of mentally relating absence from the ship to proximity with someone like Stephanie Empson. That he was in no mood to contemplate.

'Cox'n.'

'Sir?'

'Are you busy?'

'Not particularly, sir.'

'Then come for a stroll, will you? There's something I want to discuss with you and it's too public around here.'

Chief Petty Officer Ryland walked beside Harding along the jetty as once he had done before. Neither spoke until there was nobody within ear-shot then Harding said, 'What do you make of Mungo?'

'Generally, or since 'e come back, sir?'

'Both.'

'One of the best seamen we got, sir, and the best look-out, as you know. Never makes no trouble on board and the lads like 'im, I think.'

'That's what I thought. What's his attitude been like since they let him out of the cooler?'

'Well, 'e's only been back a few hours, sir, but I'd say cheerful from what I've seen. Told me 'is misses 'ad visited 'im often. Didn't see 'er after, of course, because 'e was brought back by escort. She's moved in with 'is mother now.'

'Has she, by George!' Harding said. 'I'm very glad to hear that. With her out of that frightful . . .' He snapped his mouth shut so abruptly that his teeth clicked, paused, then went on, 'I suppose the Officer of the Day has put him in my report for being adrift over leave.'

'Yes, sir, 'e 'as. Lieutenant Tollafield, sir.'

'Right. Now this is what I want you to do, Cox'n.'

What Harding wanted the coxswain to do was not revealed for another thirty paces, then he began to talk slowly.

'Bring Mungo up in front of me as a defaulter. I can't imagine that he will try to say anything in his own defence, but he just might and could screw things up for himself with witnesses present, so warn him beforehand to say nothing. I shall stop his leave for twenty-one days and you will record that fact in the usual way, but the dates of the leave stoppage are to run concurrently with his prison sentence.'

'Con-what, sir?'

'The dates are to be the same.'

'Ah, gotcher, sir. So 'e don't get punished no more.'

'That's right, Cox'n.' Harding glanced sideways at the burly chief petty officer before adding, 'He'll do a day's work like everybody else, but I can't think of any reason why he shouldn't be granted over-night passes at least until the ship comes out of dry-dock. He'll be needed for sentry duty then.'

There was a pause before Ryland said, 'I think I see, sir. We find a room for 'em and get 'er up 'ere. We might 'ave a whip round amongst the lads to raise some cash and . . .'

'No!'

'No, sir?'

Both men had stopped walking and stood facing each other.

'No, Cox'n. We're not giving him a bloody medal for beating up his wife, for God's sake, or for putting everybody to a lot of trouble. What I'm thinking of is giving him a chance to do something about his marriage, if that's what he wants. What he does is entirely up to him, but what worries me is that it may not have occurred to him that it's possible for him to do anything. You know what junior ratings are like. Always imagining that the system is specially designed to make life as difficult as possible for them.'

'Ryland nodded. 'I know what you mean, sir. What do we do?'

There was a place at the angle of Harding's jaw his razor had missed that morning. He rasped his nails back and forth across it and stared thoughtfully past the coxswain's shoulder for a moment before asking, 'Who's his closest chum on board?'

' 'Im and Prentiss is "oppos", sir.'

'All right, suppose you just happen to get into conversation with Prentiss and just happen to mention that people have been wondering why Mungo doesn't get his wife up here for a few days as they seem to have got over a bad spot. Make it a casual observation. Prentiss is certain to pass it on, then we wait and see if Mungo does anything. Listen out for any reaction and if there *is* a money problem I'll authorize an advance on Mungo's pay. He won't have anything else to spend it on once we get back to sea.'

'Gotcher, sir,' Chief Petty Officer Ryland said for the second time.

Making his way slowly back to the base Harding was wondering what on earth Mungo saw in his wife. The very thought of Edna Mungo depressed him profoundly and the knowledge that he was playing at being a marriage counsellor on her behalf seemed ludicrous in the extreme until, with an irritable shake of his shoulders, he reminded himself what he was doing it for. An unhappy sailor was a dangerous sailor, particularly so in a submarine. A picture formed in his mind, a picture of death approaching out of the darkness in the sector supposed to be covered by the ship's best look-out, its advance unseen because a man's mind was turned inwards onto a wife's infidelities. Harding quickened his pace. Short of transferring Mungo on the basis of no evidence he had done all he could.

'This will probably be your last Norwegian patrol, Bill.'

Bulstrode nodded from the depths of his chair, turning his head to follow the movements of the flotilla captain up and down the room. He felt better seated when Captain Mansergh was perambulating. It made the difference in their sizes less obvious and relieved him of the notion that he was in danger of being run down by a bus.

'The pickings aren't what they were,' Mansergh went on. 'With the entire coastline in their hands the enemy's shipping can stick to the Inner Leads inside all those thousands of islands and shoals. Bad submarine waters. The volume of traffic's dropped off anyway. Now they've got the railways running again they can use the short sea passage across the Skagerrak.' He stopped abruptly beside the big chart on the wall and banged it with his fist to show Bulstrode where the Skagerrak was, then jabbed a finger at the head of the Gulf of Bothnia. 'Port of Lulea's ice-free now too and they're shipping high-grade Swedish ore out of the place, but there's bugger-all we can do about it.'

Knowing all that, and in the knowledge that Mansergh was aware that he knew it, Bulstrode simply nodded again, wondering if this unnecessary preamble was a prelude to being told to do something particularly dangerous.

'Now that the focal point has shifted to the Bay of Biscay and the Channel approaches I know you'll be anxious to get down there, Bill,' Mansergh told him, 'but before you go south there's one tricky little delivery job that needs doing.'

'Ah,' Bulstrode said.

Five silent Norwegians, four middle-aged men and a woman older than they with iron-grey hair and a dumpy body, boarded *Shadow* three hours later. They came, escorted by a lieutenant Harding didn't know, out of the darkness of a jetty so deserted that it had obviously been deliberately cleared of people. The sailors waiting on the casing to stow away wires and fenders watched them curiously. Harding shook the guests' hands, said 'Peter Harding' five times and mumbled acknowledgement of five names he didn't catch. Then he led them to the fore hatch, gestured at the ladder and suggested without much hope of being understood that they take care on the way down.

'*Vaer forsiktig!*' one of the men told the group. That sounded like the German *Vorsicht* to Harding, which seemed about right and he asked the man if he spoke English.

'Understand much, but no so good for speaking,' he was told.

'Your friends too?'

'*Nei*. Some word only perhaps.'

The woman was half way down the ladder before it occurred to Harding that he should have ordered the sailors below to face forward as was customary. He shrugged mentally. It was too late now and, anyway, she didn't have the sort of legs it was worth staring up a skirt at.

'There's to be no communication with shore by anyone,' he said to Sub-Lieutenant Gascoigne. 'Not one word. We sail the moment the Captain comes aboard. That lieutenant on the jetty will cast off the wires for us.' Then he followed the Norwegians below.

In the wardroom he offered them drinks. The men accepted and the woman refused. Harding searched his brain for something to say, but found nothing. 'They don't seem to have much English but, be that as it may, they're not to be questioned about who they are, or what they're doing, by anybody at all,' Bulstrode had said to him on the telephone and that, he thought, was a most effective conversation inhibitor.

'Cheers!' he said and they answered with '*Skäl*,' drank and sat staring at him.

It was a relief to be told by a messenger that the captain was coming along the quay, to murmur his excuses to the sombre group and join him on the bridge, to feel *Shadow* come alive under his feet and watch the land fade until the darkness had swallowed it altogether.

The sky azure, decorated with cotton-wool puffs of cloud on the western horizon. The sea bluer than slate, greyer than cobalt, glassy. The island of Radöy wearing its summer green, seemingly deserted, peaceful. It was all very pretty Harding thought. Pretty but dangerous too because it was nearly nine o'clock at night and still the daylight had not begun to fade significantly nor, in these latitudes above sixty degrees north, would it do so enough to provide *Shadow* with a reliable cloak of invisibility when she surfaced, as surface she must, to recharge her batteries. Broken water and a heavy overcast would have been a great help and he felt resentment against the anticyclone which appeared to be stationary over Europe.

Immediately Harding chided himself for his limited thinking. The near-perfect weather of the end of May and early June had been a major factor in the successful withdrawal from Europe of three hundred thousand men through some place he had never heard of before called Dunkirk to the safety of England. Still, that was over now and he wished that the only disturbance on the surface of the water was not the ripple left by the periscope through which he was looking. Clicking the handles into the vertical position he watched the long brass column slide almost soundlessly down into the well beneath his feet. It was the second day at the rendezvous and there had been nothing to look at except the coast of Norway, the empty sea and patrolling German planes. No trawler had emerged from Fedje Fjord to relieve them of their mysterious passengers. He frowned.

'Give them time, Number One. They'll have to pick their moment carefully with Jerries crawling all over the place.'

Harding hadn't noticed his captain come into the control room and he grinned in quick embarrassment at having his thoughts read.

'I know, sir. I was just thinking about the battery.'

Bulstrode nodded. 'We'll surface about 2300 and lie stopped. With luck that will give you two or three hours with a standing charge on both engines. That's unless the trawler comes, of course.'

It came, immediately visible in the half light when it cleared the point of Radöy, at ten minutes after midnight and *Shadow* slid below the surface with her batteries still only partly charged. By 0100 the submarine lay on a parallel course to the trawler, ten miles from the coast and eight hundred yards on her starboard beam.

'Looks like it,' Bulstrode said. 'Can't make out the name, but there's a white letter "J" on the funnel and the life-boat is angled down by the bows a bit on the davits as they said it would be.'

'Plane up and show them our conning tower, sir?'

'Not yet, Number One. I want another opinion on this. Gascoigne, go and tell the Norwegians that I think we've found their onward transport and ask one of them to come and identify it.'

While he was waiting Bulstrode turned the periscope, searching sea and sky over a full circle, then concentrated on the trawler again.

To Harding's surprise it was the woman who came to the control room, stared through the binocular eye-pieces for long seconds, then nodded at Bulstrode and said, '*Ja.*'

Bulstrode passed the nod on to Harding. 'Now you may expose yourself, Number One.'

Harding smiled.

'Aye aye, sir. Half ahead together. Twenty feet, Cox'n.'

Shadow cruised slowly upwards until her periscope standards and bridge were clear of the surface, then sank down again after the captain had said, 'All right. They've seen us. Lamp signal XOF correct.' He had paused before adding, 'Stand by gun action. Machine-gunners to the control room. Boarding party assemble by the galley.' With the Tannoy microphone to his lips Harding repeated the orders.

The orderly confusion of many men moving to their action stations in very confined spaces lasted for twenty seconds, then all was silence. Harding looked at Tollafield and his gun's crew grouped in the entrance to the wardroom close to the gun tower, at the petty officer and three men, all wearing Webley .45s, waiting at the after end of the control room, at Able Seamen Prentiss and Mungo with the butts of their machine-guns resting on the deck near to him.

'Crew closed up at gun action stations, sir,' he said. 'Boarding party standing by. Ship ready to surface.'

'Thank you, Number One.' Bulstrode turned to Tollafield. 'Guns, the target is a trawler which will be five degrees on the port bow when we surface, range one thousand yards. The

3-inch gun is to be loaded and aimed, but fired only on my direct order. The same applies to you Mungo and you Prentiss with your machine-guns. Is that clear?'

The three told him that it was.

Two alterations in course and a burst of speed brought *Shadow* astern of the trawler. Harding winced at the thought of more power draining from the already depleted battery cells, but knew that the manoeuvre had been necessary to place them in a position from which they could not be rammed. Bulstrode was taking no chances.

'Open lower hatches. Man the gun tower,' the captain said.

The clang of metal, the scuff of leather soles on ladder rungs, a muffled curse, then, 'Surface!' and nothing to be heard but the roar of high-pressure air blasting water from the ballast tanks, destroying *Shadow*'s neutral buoyancy, driving her upwards. Bulstrode's little legs disappearing into the conning tower. Prentiss and Mungo following him awkwardly, hampered by the guns they carried. Harding calling out the depths as the ship rose, stopping doing it with the realization that the men in the towers couldn't hear him in the din, taking a whistle from his pocket and letting loose a high-pitched squeal through it when the gauges read twenty feet, shouting 'Stop blowing!' Instant silence except for the patter of sea-water on the control room deck as Bulstrode opened the upper conning tower hatch. Ears popping slightly with the inboard pressure equalizing with atmospheric, then the sound of water hissing past and *Shadow* pitching very gently for a moment from her rapid transition from one element to two. Another trickle of water as the voice-pipe cocks opened and the captain's voice saying, 'Control room? First Lieutenant please.'

'Speaking, sir.'

'Bring the ship to full buoyancy, Number One, and give me half ahead on both engines, just to save the battery. I'll be going back onto main motors as soon as we're closer.'

'Aye aye, sir.'

The diesels coughing, then rumbling into life, dragging a sweet, salt-smelling draught down the conning tower, *Shadow* beginning to vibrate, the coxswain saying, 'Permission to carry on smoking, sir?' Harding hearing himself reply, 'No, we'll wait,' and not knowing why.

He didn't hear the prolonged burst of automatic fire, the noise of the diesels covered that, but a wild scream, the sound of bullets striking steel and the whine of richochets was clear enough. So were the words 'Dive! Dive! Dive!' coming from the voice-pipe and the double squawking snarl of the klaxon when he jabbed the button with his thumb in instantaneous reflex. The note of the diesels died abruptly and the click of the main vents opening came to his ears, a machine-gun dropped to the deck, missing him narrowly, Able Seaman Prentiss fell through the conning tower hatch after it followed by Mungo and Gascoigne. Harding was vaguely aware of them disentangling themselves, but his attention was on the wardroom now. Men were tumbling from the gun tower there, spilling into the passageway, two of them supporting a third. Thuds and someone shouting, 'Gun tower hatches shut, sir!' From the conning tower the captain calling, 'One clip on! Group up! Full ahead together! Ninety feet! Shut off for depth-charging!'

For some seconds after that Harding was preoccupied with driving the ship fast and deep, but part of his mind recorded Bulstrode ordering the boarding party to assemble the Norwegians in the petty officer's mess and hold them there at gun-point. At ninety feet *Shadow* reduced speed to dead slow and a white-faced Bulstrode crossed the control room to stand by the chief sonar operator.

'Any sign of them, Topham?'

'Yes, sir. Loud hydrophone effect on Red 10. Reciprocating engine. No transmissions.'

'Right. Transmit yourself. I want a range and to know which way they're going.'

'Aye aye, sir.' Topham turned back to the sonar set, fingers moving rapidly, paused, then said, 'Range four hundred yards, sir, and Dopler's down so they're moving away from us.'

Still pale, Bulstrode faced Harding. 'Stand by gun action again, Number One, and come up to sixty feet. The bastards killed Tollafield and Ford. They hit Riley too.' He glanced over his shoulder and added, 'Go for'ard and find out how Riley is, Prentiss.'

Prentiss was back in less than a minute. 'Riley's not bad, sir. Shot through the shoulder and forearm, but the lady's patching him up in the torpedo stowage compartment.'

Bulstrode frowned. 'Well, I'm glad about Riley, but I thought I gave orders for the Norwegians to be confined to the petty officer's mess. She should be there with a gun in her ear.'

'Yes, sir,' Prentiss said. 'Petty Officer Proctor said you'd say that and told me to tell you that she told him not to be a silly boy and just walked out. He sent Kirk with her, sir, with a gun, sir. Not much else he could do with her being a woman like.'

'She spoke to him in English?'

'Yes, sir.'

'How very curious,' Bulstrode said. 'Topham, what's the situation?'

'Still going away on the same bearing, sir. Range seven hundred.

'Very well. Periscope depth. Who are the replacements for the gun's crew, Number One?'

'Amersham and Prentiss, sir, unless you want Prentiss on the bridge as a machine-gunner.'

His voice cold, Bulstrode said, 'No I don't want Prentiss on the bridge as a machine-gunner. I'm going to surface outside machine-gun range and blow the bastards to buggery and beyond.' Face set, voice still icy, he added as though it were all one sentence, 'Damned good alliteration that. Can you control the shoot, Gascoigne, or would you rather I did it?'

'I can do it, sir,' the tall sub-lieutenant replied. 'Number One put me through gun drill and a lot of other things *ad nauseam* last time we were in harbour.'

'So he did. Okay, but don't be too proud to be guided by your gun-layer if you get confused.'

'I won't, sir.'

Bulstrode gestured for the periscope, to be raised and stood with his eyes to the binocular viewer until the upward motion of the submarine lifted the upper lens above the water. When the range had opened to two thousand yards *Shadow* surfaced and began her bombardment. The fourth round hit the trawler. So did the seventh and ninth. A spreading glow of fire provided the gunners with an excellent point of aim from that time on and there were no more misses. Machine-guns answered them for a while, but had no effect at such a distance in the near-darkness, then fell silent. With the trawler a flaming beacon advancing the approach of day *Shadow* broke off the action, running fast to the west for half an hour before slowing to charge her batteries in a race against the sun and the hostile air and sea units it would bring with it.

Chapter 10

'The operation was blown before we left Scotland,' Bulstrode said, 'otherwise the Germans couldn't have taken over the trawler and set their trap for us.' He smiled rather bleakly at Harding and added, 'Forgive me for stating a proposition that is inherently self-evident, but I'm trying to get my thoughts straight. At the moment they're somewhat convoluted.'

Harding nodded, not speaking, and Bulstrode began again to tug at the hairs in his left nostril, an action he appeared to employ as an aid to concentration. The words 'By whom?' spoken softly a moment later did not seem to call for an answer, but from the opposite side of the wardroom table Wright asked, 'As you've placed our passengers under arrest, sir, would I be correct in thinking that you don't exclude the possibility of there being a traitor amongst them?'

The captain shrugged. 'That was a reflex action, Chief. I didn't want them wandering around when I didn't know what the hell was going on. They might have been part of a plan to take over the ship, although how an old woman and four unarmed men would have set about that I haven't the least idea. But you're right. I don't exclude the possibility. Still, not excluding it and being able to do anything about it are hardly the same thing. If we start cross-examining them now we'd probably prejudice their interrogation by professionals when we got home. We'll just keep them under guard.'

There was a long pause before Bulstrode began talking again. 'The only other obvious point which strikes me is that there was a very brave Norwegian aboard that trawler. The skipper probably. Anyway we certainly owe him our lives, or at least the ship.'

'I don't follow, sir,' Harding said.

'You weren't on the bridge, Number One, so you couldn't really. I didn't work it out myself until after we had dived. There was me lolloping along like a blasted puppy which can't wait to grab the piece of poisoned meat the nice man is holding out to him when this bloke opened up with a machine-gun at a range of a hundred yards firing very wide of us. I took the hint and ordered the bridge and gun cleared, but the Germans were quick enough to get Tollafield and Ford. Riley too. Yes, Mungo? What do you want?'

Harding and Wright followed the direction of Bulstrode's gaze and saw the able seaman peering diffidently through the gap in the wardroom curtain.

'Um – Permission to lay the table for breakfast, sir? I've taken over from Ford as wardroom steward, sir.'

'Not now, Mungo. Just bring us some coffee, will you? I'll let you know when we're ready for breakfast.'

'Aye aye, sir.'

Mungo disappeared and Bulstrode looked at Harding. 'Dear God, Number One. Did you inflict that gap-toothed grin on us?'

'Not me, sir. The Cox'n must have done it.'

'Ah well,' the captain said. 'We'll probably get used to it. Mungo thinks you're the cat's pyjamas, so I suspect he volunteered. Where was I?'

'The warning shots fired by the Norwegian, sir.'

'Oh yes. Well, the Germans must have been a trifle put out over that. All they had to do was wait until we were alongside them, gun down the people on deck, dangle a chain down the conning tower so we couldn't close the hatches, follow it with a grenade and wait for the survivors to surrender. Simple. They'd have done it too but for that chap.'

Harding sat staring at the top of the table, not seeing it, remembering the first time he had seen *Shadow* and his warning to Able Seaman Prentiss about hand-grenades. He hadn't thought of the chain trick to stop a submarine submerging and that annoyed him because he tried so hard to think of everything.

'Quite,' he said.

Mungo's head reappeared then and he addressed the captain.

'The foreign lady's asking to see you, sir.'

'She is, is she?'

'Yessir. Says it's very urgent, sir.'

'Okay, have her brought along.'

The woman arrived a moment later, escorted by an embarrassed Petty Officer Proctor trying to conceal a .45 revolver behind his back.

'All right, Proctor, you can push off,' Bulstrode said. 'Sit down, *Madame*, and explain why you didn't tell us that you speak English.'

She lowered herself carefully onto the chair Harding held for her before saying, 'For the same reason, Captain, that I do not tell you that I also speak Danish, Swedish, German and Dutch as well as Norwegian. It was not necessary for you to know, and knowing makes me easier to identify.'

'So why tell me about your other languages now?'

'Because you will wish to know much about us now if I am to persuade you to turn your boat round and point it back to Norway.' Her speech was accentless and only small grammatical errors revealed that she was not British.

'Out of the question,' Bulstrode told her. 'I'm not going to hazard my ship and its crew again just to take five Norwegians home. I've nearly lost it once already, your onward transport has been destroyed and you're all going back to Scotland. No doubt some other method of . . .'

'Captain! *Please* listen to me!'

'Well?'

'There are things you don't understand!'

Bulstrode nodded curtly. 'You can say that again, but don't bother to. I heard you the first time. I don't understand why I was ordered to take you to Norway. I don't understand how the enemy managed to hear about the mission and set a trap for us. I don't understand why you think it's such a good idea to go back there when they are obviously expecting you. As I have strict orders not to question you we are obviously at an impasse and I have only my own judgement to guide me. That judgement tells me to return to base which is what I am doing and shall continue to do unless I receive orders to the contrary in reply to a wireless signal I shall send when we surface for what passes for the night in these parts.'

'Surface and send your message now, Captain. Time is very short. You will be told to put us on the land by any means in your power.'

Extending an arm Bulstrode tapped the wardroom depth gauge as though it were a barometer. The pointer remained motionless on seventy feet.

'My officer of the watch has seen fit to take us down to this depth,' he said, 'to avoid detection by German air patrols which, presumably, he has sighted through the periscope. Had he gone deep for any other reason he would have told me. I have no intention of surfacing under a bomber for you or anybody else.'

'Then, Captain, you must return to Norway without orders.'

Bulstrode's arm reached out again, this time for the bell-push hanging near the lampshade with the pictures of semi-naked girls on it. Only a second passed before Mungo's head was back. It said, 'Sir?'

'Tell Petty Officer Proctor to come and take this lady away.'

'Please! No! Wait!' There was a desperate urgency about the words.

Mungo looked uncertainly at his captain, at the woman, and back at his captain.

'Belay that order, Mungo.'

'Aye aye, sir. Shall I bring the coffee, sir?'

'Go away, Mungo.'

'Yessir.'

'I'm waiting, *Madame*,' Bulstrode said.

Watching, Harding saw the old lady's head droop, saw her wring her hands, literally wring them. It occurred to him that he had read of the action often enough, but never seen it performed before. He felt obscurely sorry for her.

'Captain.'

'Yes?'

'Forgive me for telling you what you must do.'

She got an inclination of Bulstrode's head in reply, sighed softly and went on, 'As you say, you have orders not to question us, but your orders do not tell you that you may not listen to what I wish to say, to what I now *must* say. It is imperative that I do so because the importance of our mission is beyond your wildest imaginings!'

Harding was mentally recording the fact that the old lady's English was deteriorating under the stress clear in her face when Bulstrode yawned audibly and said, 'You don't credit me with much imagination, *Madame*.'

Her answer came in a near-wail. 'But it is true! A fantastic thing almost beyond human conception!'

'If you say so,' Bulstrode said, 'but please don't waste my time with Ibsen. I already know about Peer Gynt and the rest of his trolls. Scandinavian folk-lore I can do without just at the moment.'

The sarcasm seemed to steady the woman and she stared almost arrogantly at Bulstrode for a long moment before saying 'I am Doctor Helga Lindgren.'

Puzzled by the apparently total irrelevance of the sudden identification Bulstrode opened his eyes wide.

'That's nice to know, Doctor. It doesn't seem to make any difference to this peculiar conversation, but I'm grateful to you for looking after my wounded man.'

She shook her head angrily. 'I do that as a mother only. I am a physical doctor, not a medical one.'

Bulstrode looked at Harding and raised his eye-brows.

'A physicist, sir?' Harding ventured.

'*Ja*, physicist is right. You cannot move much in academic

circles or you would know of me, but no matter. Please ask your officers to leave, Captain. There is a secret question I must ask you.'

'No,' Bulstrode said. 'I'd prefer to have them as witnesses when I'm charged with insanity which I undoubtedly shall be after this.'

The ruling appeared to have been anticipated and accepted for without hesitation she asked, 'Do you know of deuterium oxide?'

'Yes,' the captain answered. 'I may not move much in academic circles, but I did go to school. It's heavy water.'

'Exactly. It is heavy water and it is believed that this substance may be part of a process which perhaps will win the war, or lose it, in one single day. Whole cities . . .' Doctor Lindgren stopped talking and bit her lip before going on, 'It is only theory yet and I must not speak further of it except to tell you that in my country there is a place where people work with deuterium oxide and I and my friends must seek employment there to establish what the Germans have discovered of its meaning. We are all five well qualified to do this. If it is proved that they understand what they have captured we shall send a message to London and the plant will be destroyed by British and Norwegian special soldiers. Commandos is the name for them I think.' She placed her hands palm down on the table and looked at them for a full fifteen seconds before adding, 'So please, Captain, do two things for me. Turn your boat round and forget everything I have said. I beg you not for me, but for the life of my country and your own.'

'Very moving, Doctor. You make me feel positively godlike.'

'Captain, you must not joke. Not over this.'

'No, I mustn't, and I apologize. I haven't got the remotest idea what you're talking about, but the fact remains that you must be here for some purpose, so I'll take your word for what that purpose is, even if I don't understand it. Having said that, we haven't progressed very far and all I can do for you is what I have already offered to do which is signal for instructions when we surface tonight. Now, if you'll excuse me, I have . . .'

'By tonight all will be too late.' There was defeat in the voice.

'The guides who were to lead us through the mountains will scatter far away when darkness comes to give them cover. With the trawler sunk they will have no reason to stay dangerously exposed as they are. Many weeks of planning by many people will have been wasted. Perhaps the world will be wasted too because it will take so long to organize another route to the heavy water plant.'

'Oh hell,' Bulstrode said. 'I really don't know who's running this ship anymore. Number One, tell Gascoigne to reverse course onto 035.'

The long cavern of the engine room was deserted except for two men watching the meters on the main motor switchboards at its far end. Harding squatted down on a tool box and looked at the engineer officer.

'Sorry to drag you away from dreams of breakfast, Chief, but I thought we should leave the Skipper alone to think.'

Wright nodded and sat down on another box. 'What do you suppose he's going to do?'

'Haven't a clue, but I can tell you what he's up against.'

'Tell away, O Second-in-Command. I'm only a simple plumber.'

'Okay, O Simple Plumber. No doubt you will have absorbed the fact that we had to sink the trawler which was to have carried our guests ashore last night because it had fallen into unfriendly hands.'

'I did hear a persistent loud banging noise which resembled the firing of an artillery piece. From that, and certain rumours which have been circulating through the ship, I was able to draw my own conclusions.'

Briefly the thought came to Harding that the tenor of the exchange which he himself had set was in remarkably poor taste with two shipmates drifting somewhere in the North Atlantic since *Shadow* had dived beneath their dead bodies, but he pushed it aside. It had not taken him long to become aware of the Submarine Service's custom of never openly mourning its dead. It wasn't callousness, but more a form of self-protection and a desire to spare others the embarrassment of mourning you if that time came.

'Well done,' he said. 'You will also have noticed from the recent conversation a curious fixation prevalent among certain Norwegians for deuterium chloride, whatever that is.'

'Oxide. Deuterium oxide.'

'All right, oxide then. Anyway, the bloody stuff has put the Skipper in one hell of a fix on several counts now he seems to have conceded that it's important.'

The bantering tone had gone from Harding's voice and Wright nodded again, saying nothing.

'Leave the security leak, or flood, or whatever, out of it,' Harding went on. 'There's no time to look into that even if we were competent to do it, so let's concentrate on the definite strikes against us. The trawler will have reported our presence by radio the moment we first showed them our conning tower, so the Germans ashore know we are, or were, in the area. They even had planes out looking for us, although that's tailing off now. Next we're closing the Norwegian coast with a battery that's only partly charged which means trouble of the worst kind if we meet enemy warships. Even if we don't get intercepted it'll be next to impossible to put on a proper charge in only half darkness so near to the land.'

Harding fell silent, gazing at the greasy steel deck of the engine room between his feet, then he frowned and raised his eyes to Wright's.

'On top of that, Chief, I bet that the Skipper would dearly love to know if the game's worth the candle. He could have established that by signalling tonight if we'd been miles out to sea as we should have been, but to transmit within spitting distance of the shore would bring the Jerries down on us like a ton of bricks as soon as their radio direction finders got a fix on us. None of which is too good, is it?'

'No, it isn't,' the engineer officer agreed. 'There's also the small matter of putting the Norwegians ashore. I can't see old Doctor Whatshername swimming it.'

'Ah, that's where you two have been lurking. Resigned from the war, have you?'

They both stood and faced Bulstrode leaning in the watertight doorway between engine and control room.

'Yes, sir,' Harding said. 'It's all much too complicated for us.'

'I know how you feel. Remind me, Number One, when you buried the navigating officer of that first U-boat, do I remember correctly from the patrol report that a German naval ensign was used?'

'That's right, sir.'

'Is it still aboard?'

'Yes, it is.'

'Get it out,' Bulstrode said. 'U-29 is about to enter harbour.'

Chapter 11

Harding looked around him at the shining day, at the mirror-surface of blue water marred only by *Shadow*'s idling progress across it and at the islands in bright green summer livery with their spectacular back-drop of mountains. Feathers of smoke drifting upwards from a group of stone cottages on the side of a hill told of people preparing their midday meal and below them a gathering of fishing-boats lay on their reflections. It was an idyllic scene, at the same time eye-catching and calmly soothing. He wondered if he had ever felt so exposed, so vulnerable, so nervously tense in his life, and decided that he had not. The pretty entrance to Hjelte Fjord ahead was like the final section of some complicated trap they were already in, the island its walls, the twin-engined bomber skimming towards them twenty feet above the sea the spring-loaded bar which would snap their spines.

'It's a Ju88, sir!'

'All right, Prentiss, don't stare at it. Lounge about everybody. We're the wolves of the Atlantic and we don't give a damn for those *Luftwaffe* creeps.' Bulstrode's voice.

Harding lounged, turning his back on the plane, watching the German naval ensign fluttering lazily from the flag-staff at the back of the bridge, listening to the growing roar of aircraft engines, feeling the sweat trickling from his armpits down the sides of his chest. A languid wave of his captain's hand caught by peripheral vision, the shock-wave of the bomber's passing a brief pressure on his ear-drums, the sight of its wings rocking in salute as it sped away towards the west. He found that he had been holding his breath and let it out slowly so that nobody should know.

'Well, we seem to have fooled him, sir.'

'I thought we would, Number One. Nobody's nutty enough to do what we're doing.'

'You're probably right at that, sir,' Harding said.

Only a few minutes earlier *Shadow* had risen sluggishly from her under-water refuge, conserving high-pressure air, conserving power, appearing unhurried. 'I'll want you on the bridge with me as soon as you're ready,' Bulstrode had told him. 'The crew is to remain at diving stations with Gascoigne in charge in the control room.' Harding had ordered the ship brought to full buoyancy, set the port engine the sole task of driving life back into the battery cells and the starboard to assisting it, as well as propelling the submarine, then he had clambered up the conning tower ladder to join his captain as he had been instructed to do. That was when the aircraft had been sighted. Now it was a speck on the horizon, its menace gone, but not its legacy of tension.

With three quarters of her engine capacity devoted to the battery charge *Shadow*'s forward momentum was slow, not more than six knots Harding estimated, and that added to his unease. It was an illogical emotion he knew, because the battery was the key to their ultimate safety, but speed would have lent a sense of purpose, of aggression.

'We could hardly look more innocent dawdling along like this,' Bulstrode said and, by no means for the first time, Harding felt that his captain had read his thoughts.

'That's true, sir, and I'm practically counting the amps as

they go back into the box, but I'm afraid it's going to be some hours before we're fully charged.'

'We've got all day as long as the *Kriegsmarine* doesn't show up.'

'Will you still try to bluff it out if they do, sir?'

'Oh come on, Number One. I'm not *that* nutty,' Bulstrode said. 'I shall endeavour to retire from the scene discreetly and with the utmost despatch. Or, to put it another way, fuck off a bit sharpish. Not in the best traditions of the Service possibly, but that's how I feel about it. I'll leave you and our Norwegian friends behind to bluff it out if you're really sold on the idea.'

'No thank you, sir. I think I'd rather ride back with you if that's all right.'

'I thought you'd see it my way.'

Harding grinned, feeling obscurely better, grateful to the small man and his ability to cheer people up under trying circumstances. For a moment he let himself wonder what the present mission would have been like with Cheaver in command, then stopped doing it because it didn't bear thinking about.

An hour and a half passed, ninety minutes of slow progress, ninety minutes of power flowing into the battery cells, ninety minutes of returning trepidation, then the point of Askøy was abeam to starboard and a long stretch of Hjelte Fjord opened up to their view. There was nothing of menace in it, but its placid high-summer beauty held malevolence for Harding. He thought of Circe and Odysseus and of the Lorelei, then immediately felt silly.

'That looks like the place Doctor Lindgren was talking about,' Bulstrode said. 'You'd better get the chap she recommended to interpret up here.'

Harding spoke into the voice-pipe, then stood staring through his binoculars at the little town with its small harbour four miles beyond *Shadow*'s bow. Three fishing boats were moored against the short stone jetty. Small houses marched up the sloping ground in tidy rows. Shops and a single larger building fronted the quay. There were no warships, no *Kriegsmarine*, but the great port of Bergen was very close. Destroyers, alerted by the pilot of the Ju88, could be closing fast on them now and . . .

The voice-pipe broke his train of thought.

'Permission for Mr – er, a Norwegian gentleman to come on the bridge, sir?'

'Yes,' he told it.

The unpractised ascent of the nameless passenger up the conning tower ladder was recorded by the prolonged angry hissing of the air demanded by the diesels his bulk was depriving them of. To Harding, very much aware of the likely necessity for submerging quickly, the man's slowness was another unwanted tautening of his nerve-strings and his imagination pictured the appalling confusion resulting from the four of them already on the bridge having to force their way below, driving the uncomprehending Norwegian down again with them. The image so occupied his mind that he was unaware that the sound had stopped until Bulstrode said, 'Stand over here by me, will you?' and a voice replied, 'Certainly, Captain.'

'I don't see any sign of the fresh-water barge.'

'It will be there, Captain, on the other side of the jetty. It is always there for ships with too great a draft to enter the harbour.'

Glancing sideways at him Harding remembered this same man in the darkness of a Scottish night saying, 'Understand much, but not so good for speaking.' He shrugged.

Shadow and the minutes crawled, minutes too full of seconds during any of which disaster could strike in a number of forms. It was, Harding knew, a desperately dangerous gamble that Bulstrode had agreed to take for the Norwegian scientists, a gamble based on the hoped for inability of the *Wehrmacht* to tell one submarine from another, coupled to the probable fact that such bald-faced effrontery on the part of their enemy would never occur to them. The range had shortened to less than a mile and a half when a light began to flash from the roof of the large building on the water-front. Dot-dash, dot-dash, dot-dash. The letter 'A' repeated, the international call-sign for 'What ship?'

Bulstrode took the Aldis lamp from its bracket with his right hand, rested it on his left forearm and sent, 'U-29. *Kapitan-leutnant* Hans Etterlin.' He transmitted it very fast, then turned to the Norwegian.

'Write on that pad the German for "Your failure to sight us sooner is highly reprehensible". Use capital letters, please.'

'Very well, Captain.'

'He's still sending "A", sir,' Harding broke in. 'You were probably a bit quick for him.'

'Good,' Bulstrode said. 'If they can't read Morse at that speed they're almost certainly army.' More slowly he repeated what he had already sent and added the words on the pad the Norwegian held up to him. That time he got an acknowledge-ment and a reply. He called the letters out as he read them and the Norwegian jotted them down on his pad before saying, 'Message reads "You were up-sun from us.".'

Bulstrode grinned. 'Write down in German "Remember what the English ships did to us at Narvik and stay awake.".'

When that had been transmitted he followed it with the already translated signal 'Am proceeding to Atlantic war but must first replace polluted fresh water. Send barge to meet me off harbour entrance'.

The answer 'Heil Hitler' he could read for himself.

Shadow was close enough to the little town now for their binoculars to show them a soldier abandon his signal lamp, lean over the balustrade and shout something at another sitting on a bollard near the jetty.

'So far, so good,' Bulstrode said.

The barge, long, low and flat, except for a ramshackle wheel-house at its stern, lay dead in the water two hundred yards from the harbour wall when Bulstrode brought his ship alongside it. There was one civilian at the wheel, a second standing ready to receive mooring lines, and a third unmilitary head protruding from a hatch above the engine room. Their faces wore a uniform expression of contempt, an expression which stiffened first into suspicion, then shocked amazement before settling finally into lines of grim satisfaction as they listened to their own language coming from the mouth of the man on the submarine's bridge.

Nine of *Shadow*'s crew, all without insignia, appeared on the casing and set industriously about the task of securing the vessels together, a task two could have accomplished with ease, but Bulstrode wanted the watching eyes ashore to grow accustomed to movement, to comings and goings which would mask the transfer of his passengers. On the conning tower Harding spoke quietly to the voice-pipe, giving the orders to the motor room which would keep the barge screened from the harbour. Aboard the barge a pump coughed into life and the contents of one of its tanks began to flow from a hose, the silver stream wasting itself in the fjord.

'They say it will take half an hour to lower the level enough for us to stand with our heads above water.'

Bulstrode looked at the Norwegian and said, 'I'm afraid you're all in for some cold, wet hours.'

'That's the least of our worries, Captain, and better now than in winter.'

'Yes, I suppose so, but I'm worried about your getting out of the tank and off the barge unseen. It'll never be properly dark tonight.'

'It shouldn't be difficult,' the man replied. 'The barge's crew will arrange with the town's people for a diversion at the other end of the harbour. That will draw the guard away from the jetty.'

'Yes, I suppose so,' Bulstrode said again.

The mere fact of lying alongside the water barge gave Harding a spurious sense of security as though it was proof of their right to be where they were. The soldiers in the harbour area and at the windows of the big building seemed to have lost interest in them too, but the half hour was still a long one. At its end he watched the Norwegians appear at sixty-second intervals from the gun tower hatch to be screened by sailors until they had reached the safety of the side of the conning tower away from the shore. From there they were helped to the barge and lowered through an access hatch into the water tank. Bulstrode was standing on the walk-way round the conning tower to wish each of them luck. The old lady came last to save her at least a few of the hundreds of minutes they must spend in darkness immersed up to their necks.

Harding looked down at them and heard Bulstrode say, 'God go with you, Doctor Lindgren.'

'And with you, little one,' she answered him, 'I shall always remember you with love for what you have done.' Then Harding saw his captain's face drawn into a bolster-like bosom to re-emerge flushed scarlet. Embarrassed he turned momentarily away. When he looked back Bulstrode, still blushing, was climbing the side of the conning tower.

'Let's start getting under way, Number One.'

'Aye aye, sir,' Harding said and glanced once more at the woman being led across a narrow plank to the barge by Able Seaman Prentiss. He had no way of knowing that he would see her again.

The town was dropping astern when the destroyers were sighted. There were three of them and came not from the direction of Bergen but from the Atlantic, steaming into the fjord in line ahead.

'Dive, dive, dive,' Bulstrode said into the voice-pipe and Harding moved to the upper conning tower hatch waiting for the look-outs to swing themselves through it, hearing the klaxon snarl and the rumble of diesels stop, seeing the lowering sun paint the spray thrown up from the main vents with rainbow colours. Then the way was clear and he was dropping fast down the ladder, aware of Bulstrode above him. His feet hit the control room deck hard. He winced at the shock to his ankles and said, 'All right, Pilot, I've got her.'

Gascoigne nodded and moved away from the first lieutenant's position behind the two hydroplane operators. Harding replaced him.

'Ninety feet, Cox'n.'

'Ninety feet, sir. Aye aye,' Chief Petty Officer Ryland answered.

'Upper lid shut.' The captain's voice from the top of the

tower. 'Go straight to ninety feet, Number One.'

'Yes, we're on our way there, sir,' Harding called up to him, then returned his attention to the depth gauges. The pointers, as they so often did, hovered around the twenty-five foot mark for a small eternity before resuming their movement round the dial. Next time in harbour, he told himself, he would have larger slits cut in the sides of the casing with an oxy-acetylene torch so that the buoyant air trapped there could escape more readily. If he could decrease the ship's submergence time bv as little as three seconds that could be vital. The press liked to write about 'crash dives', little knowing that the expression was never used in the Submarine Service because every dive was carried out as fast as possible and . . .

'Have you shut off for depth-charging, Number One?'

Furious with himself for his day-dreaming Harding snatch-ed down the Tannoy microphone and said, 'Shut off for depth-charging,' into it twice, then looked apologetically at the captain standing beside him, but Bulstrode was already talking again, apparently unconcerned by the lapse.

'Come down to dead slow as soon as we pass sixty feet so that Topham can hear. Gascoigne, let me see that chart.'

Shadow was dropping fast now.

'Group down. Stop starboard. Slow ahead port. Blow "Q",' Harding said, and air roared into the emergency quick-diving tank.

'Stop blowing. Vent "Q" inboard.' The roaring ceased, to be replaced by a loud hissing and pressure on the ear-drums. Then there was silence and the chief sonar operator looked up from his set.

'Sir?'

'Yes, Topham?'

'Hydrophone effect ahead, sir. Sort of,' Topham said, paused, and added, 'Well, that's a daft thing to say, sir, but it's sort of all over the place and possibly amplified. Were they close when we dived?'

'No, a considerable way off.'

'Then I think it's being reflected off the walls of this here ford, sir. Like a sound-box, sir.'

'Fjord. It's called a fjord, not a ford,' Bulstrode said, but he said it absently as though his mind was elsewhere and gave no sign of having heard Topham's, 'Sorry, sir. Fjord.'

After a moment, 'Topham?'

'Sir?'

'This sound-box effect will work both ways, won't it?'

'Yessir. We'll be quieter than them, but they'll likely hear us in these conditions, specially as they seem to be moving slow.'

'That's what I thought. No sonar transmissions?'

'None, sir.'

'Port 20. Half ahead together,' Bulstrode said and *Shadow* began her slow turn back the way she had come.

Harding caught the captain's eye, his expression enquiring, and Bulstrode spread his hands in a Gallic gesture of resignation.

'I've just been recalling the rule book, Number One. I know that it's a reliable publication because I wrote it myself and I can't remember a thing which says I have to tangle with three destroyers in enclosed waters. In fact it's all coming back to me now and it's quite strong on the undesirability of doing it anywhere, so we're going to sit quietly on the bottom until they've gone by.'

'It's terribly deep in these fjords, sir. Most of it far below our tested depth.'

'That's true, but I don't intend to bottom in *most* of it. The ten fathom line sticks out quite a distance into the main channel right by the town. Perhaps that's why the town's where it is. Come here a minute.'

Harding walked to the chart table and looked at the area on the chart indicated by Bulstrode's finger.

'That's about where we lay alongside the water barge, sir.'

'Right,' Bulstrode said, 'and that's where I want you to set her down. You'll have to do it without the echo-sounder too. Those destroyers would hear it at once. Be very clear about this, Number One, we must *not* be detected by them and we must *not* bounce off the bottom, break surface and be sighted by the troops in the town. They may or may not have noticed us dive. If they did they probably wouldn't find anything odd about it. Submarines are supposed to dive. But if we start porpoising around off a harbour we had left half an hour before, well, that would make even a *German* pongo think.' He raised an admonitory finger and added, 'One hint that we are not what we pretended to be, the merest suggestion that we're a hostile submarine, and those five people have no chance of making a successful break from the barge tonight. All right?'

'Yes of course, sir.'

'Very well. What's the situation, Topham?'

'Hard to say, sir. Still confused. A bit louder, but not a lot. Slow turbine by the sound of it. Can't distinguish how many, but the bearing's shifted to the starboard quarter since we turned.'

'I see,' Bulstrode said. 'Come up to periscope depth, Number One. I want a reliable fix.'

Harding watched intently as the depth gauge pointers crept slowly back round the dial, noting the angle shown by the hydroplane indicators and the position of the bubble in the inclinometer marking the ship's attitude in relation to the horizontal. At forty feet he ordered the speed reduced to slow.

Bulstrode moved to the thinner-topped after periscope, gestured for it to be raised and said, 'Wheel a'midships. Steer 145. Stand by for bearings, Gascoigne.'

He gave two very rapidly the moment the lens cleared the surface, jerked the periscope round to look at the destroyers, then ordered it lowered.

'The destroyers are almost directly astern, range about two miles,' he announced and then asked, 'How far is it to the ten fathom line?'

Tongue protruding, Gascoigne worked on the chart with parallel ruler and dividers, retracted his tongue and turned to the captain.

'We're running towards it at an angle of forty degrees, sir. If you come round to starboard we'll cross it in a hundred yards.'

'Starboard 15, steer 195, Mungo. Number one, you can start taking us down as soon as we're steady on the new course.'

Both men acknowledged and Harding spoke into the Tannoy microphone. 'We shall be putting the ship on the bottom in a few minutes, so hold on in case there's a bump. After we're down there's to be complete silence until further notice.'

The keel struck rock at a depth of sixty-eight feet, squealed in protest and lifted. Harding had never done anything like this before and he had to fight to keep the tenseness out of his voice when he said, 'Slow astern together.' The keel touched again, rebounded, and he could feel the hull oscillating throughout its length. Then it settled bumpily, its protests a diminishing harsh grating sound and he ordered both motors stopped and 'Q' tank flooded to provide negative buoyancy. With a five degree bow-up angle and the same amount of list to starboard *Shadow* lay still.

'Well done, Number One. You too, Cox'n,' Bulstrode said and both replied with a murmured 'Sir.' That was when Topham gave the first indication that a procession was in progress up the fjord.

'There's something else astern of them destroyers, sir. Can't tell you what yet.'

He and the captain listened to the destroyers go by, then the something else, something heavy from the slow thrashing of its big turbine-driven propellor. Topham was adamant that it was 'propellor', not 'propellors', Bulstrode with earphones pressed to the sides of his own head could find no reason to disagree with him and that made for an interesting situation. There were, as far as he knew, no big, single-screw turbine-propelled ships. Bearings taken at regular intervals as the vessel passed astern of them gave an estimated speed of less than six knots.

The captain looked at his second-in-command. 'Do you know what I think, Number One?'

Harding, sitting on the deck with his back against the control room ladder because, with *Shadow* lying on the sea-bed, there was nothing for him to do, replied, 'That it's a damaged ship, sir?'

'Precisely. I couldn't understand why those destroyers were moving so slowly. Now I believe they're escorting a heavy unit with a propeller shaft out of action. Hell and damnation! That could be the *Bismarck* up there limping into Bergen, and here we are lying around like a lot of tarts on their day off. Christ, it's frustrating!'

'I doubt if tarts get frustrated on their day off, sir.'

'You shut your face,' Bulstrode said amicably. 'I'm the one who makes the smart alec remarks aboard this war canoe.'

Topham giggled.

Five more ships followed at the same slow pace, two hours elapsing between their first detection and the time when the water carried no sounds other than its own secret whisperings. By then day had faded into half night, there was no proof that one of the warships was not lying stopped off the town, or possibly more than one, and Bulstrode made the decision to remain where he was until full periscope visibility was restored to him with the coming of dawn. Harding ordered a meal prepared for the crew and, to save air, instructed them to go to bed when they had eaten it. He, Wright and Gascoigne divided the night into three between them, sitting at the sonar set, listening to the sea, watching the depth gauges and the compass, feeling the strange deadness of the ship pressing on them.

At one in the morning Gascoigne woke Harding to tell him that *Shadow* had begun to swing with the change of the tide. Harding looked at the jerkily moving compass, listened to the faint rasping of steel on rock and ordered more water flooded into the internal ballast tanks. The motion ceased.

Three hours later, with the crew back at their stations, the submarine came alive again, pumps expelled the excess ballast water, 'Q' tank was blown clear and she lifted from the sea-bed, moving slowly forward and upward.

At the periscope, 'Clear all round,' Bulstrode said, then Harding saw the small body go rigid.

'Something wrong, sir?'

'The bastards. The bloody fucking bastards.' The whispered, unstressed words came faintly to Harding's ears. He didn't speak, didn't stop looking at his captain for countable seconds, then moved to his side in response to an abrupt hand gesture. Bulstrode made way for him.

With the periscope set at high power they looked close

enough to touch, the seven bodies hanging from the parapet of the big building on the waterfront. The old lady's was the one in the centre.

Through the fog of shocked disbelief clouding his brain Harding heard Bulstrode say, 'Four of ours and the barge's crew, if I'm not mistaken. Stand by gun action, Number One.'

Harding stepped back from the periscope.

'What are you going to do, sir?'

'I,' Bulstrode said, 'am going to kill some Germans and give our friends the nearest thing to a Viking funeral we can arrange. Call it a consolation prize for having to let that bunch go by last night. Call it reprisal. Call it what you damn well please.'

From his action station in the control room Harding saw nothing of the destruction of the building the *Wehrmacht* had taken over, but he had it described to him later by Gascoigne and a little by Bulstrode. The 3-inch calibre shells exploding against and inside a target so large and so close that it was impossible for them to miss. The masonry crumbling and the fires taking hold. The partly dressed German soldiers running from the main door and dropping from windows scythed down by Mungo until his machine-gun overheated and Prentiss replaced him with the spare from the mounting on the other side of the bridge. The people debouching from their homes into the streets, capering, waving, cheering, pressing danger-ously close to the now blazing building. The dangling corpses of the Norwegians charring, two of them falling as the ropes burned through. The whole structure collapsing in on itself, hurling a column of dust, smoke and flame skywards. Of all that he registered only the heavy slamming of the 3-inch and the ripping sound of machine-gun fire.

Suddenly the coxswain was turning the wheel furiously, shouting at the voice-pipe, 'Thirty degrees of starboard wheel on, sir!' and to him, 'Cap'n says emergency full astern star-board and shut water-tight doors, sir!'

Steel doors, thudding shut, vibration heavy from the oppos-ing thrust of the propellors, one driving ahead, the other astern, *Shadow* swinging fast to the right, the gunfire ceasing abruptly, then the order, 'Midships, stop starboard,' and the captain's voice calling him to the voice-pipe.

'Get us onto main engines right away, Number One, and tell the Chief to work up to full speed as soon as he can. I want to get as far down the fjord as possible before somebody forces us to dive. Oh, and you can open water-tight doors again. I'll tell you what that was about in a minute.'

When *Shadow* was racing towards the open sea, Bulstrode told him.

'We nearly bought it there. I was steering to pass close to the end of the stone jetty, but the end isn't the end, if you see what I mean. Amersham spotted that. The jetty extends for another fifty yards or so, just under water. Presumably rough weather broke up the missing bit at some time. Anyway, we had to alter course bloody quickly and it's entirely thanks to God and Amersham that we're still in one piece.'

Harding found himself sweating in retrospective alarm, picturing the broken-backed submarine impaled on the submerged section of the old jetty. Picturing, too, the massacre of its crew which would almost inevitably have followed. He was still doing it when the petty officer telegraphist touched him on the arm.

'Two "most immediate" signals for us, sir.'

'Ask the Engineer Officer to decipher them quickly, please,' he said.

Within minutes Wright handed him the results with the remark, 'Hardly worth telling the Skipper now.'

'Why?'

'Try reading them,' Wright suggested.

Harding did so. 'For *Shadow*. Two torpedo hits on pocket-battleship *Lützow* reported by *Stinger* thirty miles north your destination. Enemy now proceeding Bergen at greatly reduced speed under heavy escort. If your mission accomplished endeavour intercept and destroy, but mission has first repeat first priority'.

The second message stated, 'Intelligence suggest probability member your party named Harald Jorgensen Nazi sympathizer. Place under close arrest and bring him back with you'.

'Oh Christ,' Harding said. 'That's what went wrong. That's why they only hanged seven of them.'

That was when the Ju88s came, but that had been expected and Bulstrode had his ship under water almost before they had positioned themselves for a bombing run along the length of the fjord. The attack was noisy, but did little more than loose a light shower of cork insulation from the deckhead. Destroyers came too, their speed betraying their fury and minimizing their ability to hear moving under-water objects. For that, and the proximity of the walls of the fjord which confused the enemy's sonar, Bulstrode was thankful. By noon *Shadow* was back on the high seas.

When the daylight had faded as far as it ever would that night, *Shadow* was well out into the North Atlantic. She surfaced and a lengthy ciphered signal was transmitted in a number of short bursts to make radio detection more difficult for the Germans. It recorded the incident of the trawler, the reasons for continuing with the mission after the sinking, the failure of the operation and, in case anybody could still do anything about it, the passing of the damaged *Lützow* on her way to Bergen.

The reply was brief. 'Words quote heavy water and deuterium oxide unquote are never to be repeated. Destroy all copies your signal'.

Until that point on the homeward journey Bulstrode had been untypically subdued, almost monosyllabic, but the receipt of the message from Scotland, drew him out of his depressed state because it tacitly confirmed that whatever was going on had been important enough to justify the risk he had taken in putting the party ashore. Harding found the change reflected in the patrol report notes which, with Tollafield dead, he was helping to type.

That death and Ford's had been recorded factually, unemotionally, but the sighting of the hanged Norwegians was so sombrely described that Harding had taken it upon himself to edit the section until it more closely resembled what normally would have been written by his captain. It was a relief after that to read and type a straightforward account of the destruction of the building commandeered by the *Wehrmacht* giving the number of rounds fired and the estimated enemy casualties. The description of the end of the action made him grin.

'The realization,' Bulstrode had written, 'that we were fast approaching self-destruction in the form of this previously unnoticed under-water obstacle caused me consternation, not to say alarm. But by dint of tugging at the side of the bridge, twisting the torso, contorting the facial muscles and other well-proven methods of achieving a sharp alteration in course, I managed to avoid calamity.'

Had he been possessed of prescience Harding would have found nothing to grin at.

Chapter 12

It was a strange homecoming. Bulstrode brought his ship alongside at Rosyth at three o'clock in the afternoon of another lovely summer day. Captain Mansergh was waiting on the jetty beside a large black limousine, fifty yards from the mooring party, talking to a man wearing a city suit and a Homburg hat. His nod to the officers on *Shadow*'s conning tower was in marked contrast to his usual cheerful wave.

'Finished with main engines,' Bulstrode said as soon as the berthing wires had been secured, then clambered over the side of the bridge to greet the flotilla commander at the gangway.

'Come ashore, Bulstrode, and bring your officers with you,' were Captain Mansergh's only words.

They followed the naval captain and the civilian into the back of the car, Bulstrode, Harding and Wright. Gascoigne got in the front beside the driver. Nobody spoke to anybody on the short drive to the base. Wordlessly Bulstrode handed the top copy of his patrol report to Mansergh and was rewarded with another nod.

At the base they walked in Indian file to Mansergh's office. The captain gestured them in and left, closing the door behind him. The civilian removed his Homburg and said, 'Sit down, gentlemen, and tell me what you know about heavy water.'

They sat, all except Bulstrode who propped himself on one corner of the desk. His officers watched him, not speaking.

'It isn't really a question of weight,' Bulstrode began. 'It's a matter of density and volume. For example, when water freezes it expands and becomes ice. That means that it is occupying a greater volume of space without any increase in weight. That's why ice floats. It's an interesting contradiction that warm water rises when . . .'

'That's enough!' A hand was raised, palm forward, to reinforce the command.

'Oh. All right,' Bulstrode said. 'I'm sorry you don't like interesting contradictions. They fascinate me.'

The civilian surveyed him with distaste for a moment before saying, 'I asked you a simple question. Kindly answer it and address me as "sir" while you're doing so, *if* you don't mind.'

Bulstrode smiled at him. 'I don't mind at all, as long as you address me as Lieutenant-Commander de Vere Charnley-Bulstrode. I'll tell you one thing though. I bet you give up first.'

'That's the most insufferable thing I've ever . . .'

'I entirely agree with you but, you see, I have this very rich aunt who . . .'

A loud braying sound forced its way past Harding's clenched teeth. He cut it off by holding his breath, then began to turn slowly red.

Regarding him gravely Bulstrode said, 'Actually, Number One, it's not really all that funny. Please go and find Captain Mansergh and ask him if he'd mind coming here.'

Harding stood up and walked out, still holding his breath.

When he followed the big four-stripe captain back into the office he heard Bulstrode's 'Sir, I . . .' cut off by the civilian's 'Relax, Commander. You win. Mansergh, your boy has done very well. He's not about to tell me or anybody else anything about heavy water. Obviously he obeys orders. Would you mind temporarily lifting your ban on those words so that I can establish how far this thing has gone?'

'You may all talk freely to this gentleman,' Mansergh said. 'Bulstrode stay here when the meeting is over. I want a word with you.' He turned and left again. There had been anger in his voice and Bulstrode watched his retreating back thoughtfully, then moved to a chair and sat facing the civilian.

'Commander.'

'Sir?'

'Never mind the "sir". I was only trying to needle you into an indiscretion. Try to tell me as exactly as you can the words which passed between you and Doctor Lindgren.'

'Would you prefer Sub-Lieutenant Gascoigne to wait outside? He wasn't present during the conversation.'

'Ah. I didn't know that. Thank you. Would you be so good, Sub-Lieutenant?'

When Gascoigne had gone Bulstrode closed his eyes and spoke at length, then he opened them, looked at his two remaining officers and asked, 'Anything to alter or add, you chaps?'

Harding shook his head. 'That was word for word, as near as makes no difference, sir.'

'Thank you,' the civilian said again. 'What did you infer from Doctor Lindgren's unfinished remark about whole cities?'

'That she was referring to their destruction, or the deaths of their inhabitants.'

'By what means?'

'By a means beyond my wildest imaginings,' Bulstrode said and smiled a small sad smile, then added, 'Poor old lady. I shall remember her with affection and enormous admiration, but I haven't the remotest idea what she meant.'

The man with the Homburg hat resting on the desk in front of him stared at it suspiciously as though it might be a means of destroying entire cities before saying, 'I see. Who else might have overheard the words she used?'

Bulstrode turned to Harding. 'Able Seaman Mungo, Number One?'

Harding shook his head. 'No, sir. He wasn't eavesdropping. His main preoccupation seemed to be serving us breakfast or coffee. For the rest of the time he was out of earshot. I could see him from where I was sitting.'

'Who else saw the uncoded signal?' the man asked.

'Gascoigne ciphered it,' Bulstrode told him. 'That's the chap waiting outside.'

'All right. Let's have him back in.'

In turn, the four officers signed a document relating to official secrets, a document enjoining them to silence. It was Gascoigne who wanted to know what would happen to him if he talked in his sleep and learned that he would spend the next thirty years sleeping in the Tower of London where his nocturnal indiscretions could do no harm.

Bulstrode stayed in the office as he had been ordered to do. Wright and Gascoigne went back to the ship. Harding turned to his left outside the building to call on the paymaster commander's staff about money for the ship's company. He was wondering if a phial of deuterium oxide poured into a reservoir would poison anyone who drank from that source, understandably unaware that for a brief period he had been in the company of some of those instrumental in leading the world into the atomic age.

From a window in the ivy-clad wall some twelve feet above his head a familiar voice asked, 'Does all your family suffer from insanity, Bulstrode?' The question had been harshly put and Harding knew also that Captain Mansergh usually addressed his submarine commander's by their christian names. Harding stopped walking and heard his captain reply, 'I wouldn't say "suffer", sir. They quite enjoy it on the whole.'

'Bulstrode.'

'Sir?'

'It would be in your own best interests to subdue your inclination to indulge in repartee. Apparently you are not yet aware of the seriousness of your position, so let me warn you that one more remark like that and I'll have you placed under arrest.'

Bulstrode saying coldly, 'It won't happen again, sir, provided that you leave my family out of this,' and Mansergh replying, 'Yes, I was very much out of order there and I apologize. Now, if any explanation is possible, perhaps you would have the goodness to explain to me what induced you to hazard your ship by the futile bombardment of a small enemy barracks of virtually non-existent military value. Surely you have some slight conception of your true function in this war and . . .'

Harding had resumed walking, striding fast, and the words from the window no longer reached him, but concern about the effect the scene taking place in the flotilla commander's office would have on his captain's first-night-ashore drinking followed him like a cloud. Twenty yards further on he changed direction towards the main gate, left the base and booked a single room in Bulstrode's name at the nearest inn. That done he returned to keep his appointment with the paymasters.

At six, as he thought he would, Harding found Bulstrode at the wardroom bar staring thoughtfully at nothing in particular with a glass of gin resting in the breast pocket of his jacket. Except for the bar steward there was nobody else there.

'The other half, sir?'

'Thank you, Number One.' Bulstrode took the glass from his pocket, drained it and put it on the bar.

'Two gins please, steward,' Harding said, and to Bulstrode, 'I've booked that single room you wanted for tonight at "The Gordon Highlander", sir.'

Bulstrode didn't even blink. 'Oh, you remembered. Thanks.'

They talked generalities for an hour, drank two more gins, then, 'About tonight, sir.'

'What about tonight?'

'I'd like to come with you, sir.'

The bar was crowded now and Bulstrode's words were little above a whisper. 'I'm indebted to you for your initiative in reserving that hotel room, Number One, and I appreciate your concern. Having said that, I would be grateful in future if you would stay the hell out of my private life.'

He put his glass down, held Harding's gaze for a moment, then moved away through the throng of officers. Biting his lip

Harding watched him go, saw him hesitate, saw him turn and make his way back.

'I'm sorry I said that, Peter. I'd be glad of your company at "The Gordon Highlander" tonight. Shall we eat here first?'

'Good idea, sir,' Harding said.

Still fully dressed but for his uniform jacket which he had placed tidily on a hanger Bulstrode lay propped on pillows surveying the three inches of gin remaining in his bottle. Apparently satisfied by his inspection he poured half of the liquid into a tumbler and lowered the bottle carefully over the side of the bed to the floor. He didn't appear to be visibly drunk to Harding and that surprised him because the small man was no practiced drinker and no alcoholic. It surprised him the more as he knew that he was fast becoming inebriated himself and half his own bottle was untouched. Of that he was sure, but looked at it standing on the table beside his chair to make doubly so. Yes, over half still there. Nearer two thirds.

'Where was I?' Bulstrode asked.

'Getting the biggest bawling-out of your life from Captain Mansergh,' Harding said. He had given up calling his commanding officer 'sir'. It didn't seem appropriate under the present circumstances.

'So I was. He kept it up for half an hour and courts of enquiry were mentioned, probably leading to a court-martial. At one stage I was told wait outside while he discussed the whole thing with the Admiral on the blower.'

'But you got away with it.'

'Not entirely. I'm to be notified officially of the Admiral's displeasure. That should be quite a document. Inscribed on vellum probably. Never mind. I still have a command, thanks mainly to the brilliance of my own eloquence.'

'What form did that take? The sort of thing that makes our chief sonar operator break up?'

'Oh God no,' Bulstrode said. 'It was stirring stuff. Confounding the King's enemies. Proving to the Germans that they aren't safe from attack anywhere. The sort of thing these new commando troops are doing with their raiding parties. What the frigates did during the Napoleonic wars. I got quite lyrical about what we'd done for Norwegian morale locally. It was all a load of crap, but I think it persuaded Mansergh that an attempt at over-hauling my sense of proportion should be made instead of consigning me direct to a lunatic asylum.'

Harding picked up his glass of gin, looked at it and put it down again untasted before asking, 'Was it really a load of crap? Shooting those bastards up seemed a good idea at the time.'

Bulstrode's reply was oblique. 'A modern submarine is a formidable weapon, Peter. It's capable of sinking the most powerful battleship afloat. You don't risk squandering that capability for petty returns. Mansergh was right in everything he said to me. In his shoes I'd have had me shot'

'Then what made you do it?'

'Rage,' Bulstrode said quietly. 'Rage and hate. I didn't know I was capable of hating until I saw those seven bodies hanging there and I think I came apart at the hinges for a little while.' He finished his bottle by drinking straight from it, looked hopefully at Harding's, accepted it with a nod and added, 'I once warned you against getting excited. Learn from me and never get angry either. Anyway, enough of that. Did I tell you the most embarrassing part?' Without waiting for a reply, he went on, 'We opened fire under the Nazi flag. Only one round, thank God, before I remembered that we had been flying it when we dived for those destroyers. I pulled it down pretty quickly, believe me. Hope nobody noticed the bloody thing.'

A slurring of words had at last appeared in Bulstrode's speech Harding noticed. He watched him curiously, saw him drink from the bottle, heard him say, 'Hell, I hate this stuff. An armful of woman would be so much nicer.'

'That's what you said last time,' Harding told him.

'Did I? Well, it's all right for lofty characters like you. I bet you have them queuing up. Young Gascoigne even more so. How tall is he anyway? Eight foot six?'

'Six foot three I think.'

'Is that all? He looks eight foot six from where I stand and I bet he has them climbing all over him.' Bulstrode's eyes drooped shut, then opened again. 'You know something, Number One? Ever since I was about sixteen I've dreamed of being ensnared by attractive women with corrupt natures. And what happens? All I'm clutched by is nice old Norwegian grandmothers who get hanged.'

Harding nodded wisely and said, 'Not long ago I met a girl called Stephanie Empson who would meet your requirements perfectly. She . . .' He stopped talking abruptly, furious with himself for having drunk so much, for having mentioned something he was ashamed of. The glance he gave towards the bed was almost furtive.

It hadn't mattered. His captain was fast asleep, mouth open, beginning to snore.

Chapter 13

'What a beautiful looking vessel,' Lieutenant Unwin said.

Harding looked at the great ocean-going luxury yacht overhauling the idling *Shadow* to take station ahead of her for the passage around the north of Scotland and down the Irish Sea to Devonport. Whether or not she carried any significant armament he didn't know and, either way, it was unimportant as her sole function was to protect the submarine from the unwelcome attentions of friendly aircraft who invariably attacked first and asked questions afterwards when confronted by anything resembling a U-boat. He nodded and turned to the dead Tollafield's replacement.

'Yes, isn't she? Do you know her story?'

'No.'

'Used to belong to an American millionairess,' Harding told him, 'and she offered it to the Admiralty as a gift at the outbreak of war. The way I heard it told, the Admiralty consulted the Foreign Office who advised against acceptance because it could endanger American neutrality, so the Admiralty asked her if they could buy it and she agreed. Guess what she made them pay.'

'I haven't the remotest idea. How much was it?'

'One dollar,' Harding said. 'It's nice to have friends, isn't it?' He stooped to the voice-pipe then added, 'Half ahead together. Steer 010. Tell the Captain that I'm taking station astern of the escort and that there's no need for him to come on the bridge unless he wants to.' The orders were repeated back to him, *Shadow* picked up speed and her bows swung to steady exactly in the wake left by the big yacht. As if on cue, three Hurricane fighters scythed down out of the low cloud cover in echelon formation, pointed their noses at the submarine, then banked away at the sight of the accompanying surface ship.

'Do you think they're going to come in?' Unwin asked.

'Of course not,' Harding told him. 'That's what we're being escorted for, to keep them off.'

'No, I meant the Americans, Number One. Not the RAF.'

'Oh, I see. They will as soon as something happens to annoy them enough to persuade them to stop listening to all that isolationist drivel the Hearst newspapers churn out. The world has shrunk a lot since the last war. I bet you a quid they'll declare war before the end of the year.'

'Done,' Unwin said.

The Battle of Britain came and went, the *Luftwaffe* licked its wounds, London staggered under the night-time Blitz, *Shadow* carried out two long fruitless patrols in the Bay of Biscay and, with the giant across the Atlantic barely stirring in its sleep, Harding lost his bet.

For two weeks the third Biscay patrol followed the pattern of those which had preceded it with only the coast of France breaking the monotony of heaving empty horizons. The days passed in dragging hours of near-silence, with only the quietly spoken orders of the officer of the watch in the control room, the soft hydraulic hiss of the periscope going up and down, the whispering of the ventilation system and the bored talk coming from the crew's messes preventing it being total. It was a relief for everyone when darkness came, bringing with it violent wave-induced motion, the thunder of the diesels and the smell of the sea. But even that distraction, with the ship achieving nothing more than covering miles of empty ocean and recharging her batteries in preparation for the next torpid day, did little to dispel the general feeling of lack of purpose and wasted time. The captain worked the men hard in a repeated sequence of drills planned to counter any emergency. He was ingenious about it and so was Harding, but all too soon their ingenuity was exhausted and the unexpected became routine.

Towards the end of the second week quarrels broke out and, to his dismay, Harding found himself dealing with more defaulters than would have been the case in harbour when there were always drunks to contend with. When a mild form of influenza swept through the ship he was almost grateful to it for making everybody too ill to be quarrelsome.

'I don't understand it,' Bulstrode said. 'With France occupied the Germans have direct access to the Atlantic, but all they seem to be using the French ports for is U-boat bases. Why don't they run some convoys up and down the coast in a civilized fashion like everybody else?'

Harding pointed out that they were doing just that and that other submarines in the flotilla had intercepted and attacked enemy shipping on France's west coast.

'It is no part of your duties to acquaint me with unpalatable truths, Number One,' Bulstrode told him. 'You will all write down one hundred times "When the Captain wishes to be maudlin, we are required to maudle with him".'

1941 was fifteen days old and a thick sea mist had covered the surface of the water when the war returned to *Shadow*.

There was scarcely wind enough to cause ripples, but the swell created by the recent storms rolled remorselessly towards Europe. The submarine rose to each bank of water, crested it and slid down its far side with, Harding felt, a senseless obduracy as though, like King Canute, it had nothing better to do than show its contempt for the waves. Propped in one corner of the bridge, conscious of his throbbing head, the soreness of his throat, the coughing and sneezing of the four look-outs behind him, irritated by all those things and the ship's mindless soaring and dropping he was for two near-fatal minutes not longer an effective officer of the watch.

Able Seaman Amersham saved him. Able Seaman Amersham saved *Shadow*.

'Sir! Something big on the port bow! Bloody big it is, sir!'

And that, Harding's mind fogged by influenza and nearly four months of only manufactured activity told him, was about the least precise report he had ever heard. That irritated him too, but he scanned the sector from the bow to the port beam before delivering a reprimand. There was nothing to be seen but the mist.

'Listen, Amersham, when you make a . . .'

'There it is again, sir!'

Something showing briefly where only opaqueness had been, then vanishing again. Not big. Enormous! Reappearing, cliff-like, towering! Harding's mind clicking back into gear.

'Emergency full astern together! Collision stations!' It seemed superfluous to call for the captain to come to the bridge. His orders had been enough to ensure that Bulstrode would try to do that. *If* there was time.

Startled confirmation coming up the voice-pipe from the control room, the rumble of diesels cutting off abruptly because they were not designed to go astern. Only the electric motors could do that, but they couldn't do it until the engine clutches were disconnected, and that took seconds. Harding learning how long seconds could be with the huge ship bearing down on them, thrusting the curtain of mist and night aside. Vibration setting up with the propellors biting in reverse. The voice-pipe saying, 'Both motors full astern emergency, sir,' and Harding thanking it automatically.

'How very inconvenient.' Bulstrode's voice from beside him, light and taut at the same time.

Shadow slowing, stopping, gathering sternway.

'There was no time to turn, sir.'

'I believe you, Number One.'

Harding glancing around him as though seeking more company from the look-outs. All of them, their sectors forgotten, staring transfixed at the advancing colossus. No reprimand for that. It would be asking too much of any man to ignore his own death rushing at him.

The surge of the bow wave clearly audible, growing louder, a hissing roar as though the sluice gates of a dam had been opened, tons of white water cascading, surging over *Shadow*'s forward casing, swirling around the 3-inch gun, a vast black wall sliding by within five yards of her stem, the thrashing of propellors as the swell lifted them partly clear of the surface, the liner receding, vanishing as the mist closed around her.

'Stop both. In both engine clutches,' Bulstrode said to the voice-pipe. 'Secure from collision stations. Hands to diving stations. Stand by all tubes. Bow caps to remain shut. Stand by gun action. Machine – gunners to the bridge.' Then to Harding, 'That was well done, Number One.'

'It was Amersham, not me, sir.'

'Nevertheless, you took the right action. Well done, Amersham. You have quite a knack for spotting things just in time. Like that jetty in Norway. I'll see that your conduct is reported.'

'Oh. Yes, sir. Thank you, sir.'

'Engine clutches in, sir,' the voice-pipe said.

'Full ahead together. Starboard thirty. Steer 090. Ask the Engineer Officer to work up to best possible speed as quickly as he can.'

Diesel exhausts coughing, spluttering, rumbling. *Shadow* moving ahead, swinging towards the coast of France, steadying on east.

'That was a bit hairy, Number One.'

'Yes, sir. Permission to faint, sir?'

'You wait your turn,' Bulstrode said.

Vibration building up again, the wind of motion in their faces, the bow knifing through the smooth swell.

'Heading for Bordeaux of course. What speed do you think she was making?'

Harding thought for a moment before saying, 'Not more than ten knots at a guess, sir. There was a lot of weed along her water-line. Could be one of those ships which have been holed up in the Dutch West Indies or somewhere since the outbreak of war.'

'Yes. I'm going below for a look at the chart.'

'Aye aye, sir.'

Bulstrode was back on the bridge within two minutes.

'We're fifty-seven miles from the mouth of the Gironde, Number One. That's five hours to find her in if your "guesstimate" of her speed is correct and it'll still be dark then. This may not be easy.'

'No, sir. Do you want me to go to my diving station, or stay here?'

'Stay here.'

Shadow running fast, running blind through the fog, visibility varying between one and two hundred yards, the coughing and sneezing of the people on the bridge less now that they had something else to think about, Harding's sore throat and headache almost forgotten.

'Permission to send two of the look-outs below, sir? The machine-gunners aren't doing anything.'

'Yes, of course, Number One. Stupid of me. Prentiss, Mungo, leave your guns on their mountings and take over from the after look-outs.'

Murmured acknowledgements, the shuffling of shoe leather and the hiss of air as two bodies impeded its progress down the conning tower, then only the throb of the diesels.

'Do you think there was any chance of their having seen us, Number One?'

'Doubt it, sir. We're very low in the water, the visibility's lousy and they passed so close to us that I'm sure we'd have heard yelling from the bridge if they had.'

'That's what I think too and that being the case it's reasonable to assume that they've maintained their course, so why aren't we coming up on them?' Without waiting for a reply Bulstrode stooped to the voice-pipe. 'Control room, how long since we went full ahead on main engines?'

'Sixteen minutes, sir.'

'Sod it!'

'What, sir?'

'Nothing,' Bulstrode said and turning to Harding. 'We must have got her course wrong. We're diverging. It means losing ground, but I think we must stop and listen. There's no point in charging about sightless. Alert Topham and then stop the engines so he can hear. I'm going up onto the periscope standards. It may be clearer up there.'

Thirty seconds later the coxswain's voice coming from the control room. 'Sonar reports hydrophone effect bearin' Red 140, sir. Sounds like reciprocatin' engines.'

'Half ahead together. Port twenty. Steer 320,' Harding told him, then called up to the captain on top of the periscope standards, 'Got her, sir. We've overshot and I'm turning to intercept.'

Bulstrode clambered down, stood beside him and spoke to the control room. 'Man the gun and load with high explosive.' When the order had been passed he went on, 'As soon as we're steady on 320 tell Topham to transmit fine on the port bow and give me a range every fifteen seconds.'

The clang of the gun tower hatches opening, the subdued talk of men on the platform forward of the conning tower, the click of a shell being loaded and the thud of the breech closing.

'Guns.'

'Sir?' Gascoigne's voice coming from the darkness.

'The target is a large ship which should be on the port bow when you sight her. Range point-blank in this visibility. Point of aim the water-line. As soon as you see her open fire without any further orders from me.'

'Aye aye, sir.'

'Prentiss, Mungo, whenever your machine-guns bear, fire into her wheel-house unless there is any answering fire. If there is, shoot at that.'

They acknowledged their instruction almost in unison.

'Bridge, sir.'

'Yes?'

'Ship steady on 320 and sonar reports range nine hundred yards and closin'. Bearin' Red 5.'

'I see. Come to starboard onto 035.'

Shadow swinging to close her quarry at an angle of forty-five degrees, rolling uncomfortably with the swell on her port quarter, the mist thickening in patches to become fog which occasionally obscured even the bows from sight.

'Sod it!' Bulstrode said for the second time.

'Would it be worthwhile trying a torpedo attack by sonar, sir?' Harding asked him.

'I don't think so, Number One. We know so little about their course and speed we'd almost certainly miss at any distance and if we got close enough to make sure there wouldn't be time for the torpedoes to run off their safety range and arm themselves. We'll try it as a last resort, but I'd rather knock them to bits with the three-inch if we can.'

The range down to five hundred yards now, five hundred yards and closing, the bearing constant which meant that the two ships were on a collision course.

'Steer 050,' Bulstrode said.

Eery, very eery, Harding thought, this boxing in the dark, this blindman's buff. Range three hundred, the bearing moving slightly ahead. Soon, he knew, the sonar transmission and its echo would come so close together that no distance could be calculated from it. That meant partial deafness as well as blindness for *Shadow*. The memory of the stalking of the submerged U-boat came to him and he felt the prickle of nerve-ends across the skin of his back.

'Sonar reports instant echo, sir, bearin' Red 10,' the voice-pipe announced.

Nothing, nothing but the darkness and the mist which simultaneously made the darkness lighter and more opaque.

'Steer 070,' Bulstrode said, then went on, 'I wish we had that radio direction finding gadget they used in the Battle of Britain. RDF they call it. Some ships are being fitted with it now and . . .'

'Broken water ahead, sir!'

A soft sigh from Bulstrode then the words, 'Good for you, Amersham. We're in their wake. Increase speed by twenty revolutions, Number One.'

Before Harding could relay the order, 'Fuckin' hell!' Amersham shouted. 'Look up there, sir!' and ridiculously, Harding's mind recorded the fact that the able seaman had made another non-regulation report, but he looked up for all that. So did Bulstrode.

The stern of the liner like the side of a house, looming massively less than *Shadow*'s own length away and a few degrees to port. Two clipped statements from the direction of the gun – 'Trainer on!' – 'Layer on!' – Gascoigne's single order 'Shoot!' and the slamming detonation of the propellant charge. A flash where the shell struck home, but with the range so short the sound of it merging, losing itself in the roar of the cordite which had sent it on its way.

Gascoigne saying, 'Continuous fire!' Bulstrode ordering the speed reduced for fear of running into the target vessel. Harding reading *'Van Haren* – Rotterdam' painted on the stern, the letters briefly illuminated by the second flash from the muzzle of the 3-inch.

'Try to smash her rudder, Guns!' Bulstrode's shout and Gascoigne's answering 'Aye aye, sir!'

The big ship starting to alter course, *Shadow* altering with it to stay directly astern, maintaining the same absurdly short range so that the barrel of the big gun almost certainly mounted on the after deck could not be depressed sufficiently to engage them. Harding's ears ringing from the repeated concussions, his head aching again and his throat sore from the combined assault of influenza and the gun-smoke drifting incessantly past. About eight hits now he thought, but was not sure that he had counted correctly.

A ripple of flashes from the guard-rail around the liner's stern and the whine of bullets ricocheting from the side of the conning tower. The stuttering snarl of Mungo's machine-gun close behind Harding's head, making him jump more than the banging of the 3-inch did. A dimly seen body falling slowly seaward as though its descent was impeded by the stream of .303 ammunition lancing up at it. Bulstrode saying, 'Good shooting, Mungo!'

A thicker bank of fog and the target fading, vanishing, but leaving a Cheshire cat's grin of flame still visible through the holes torn in its plating. Gascoigne's gunners using that as their point of aim. The fog becoming only mist again, the ship reappearing and a voice calling, 'Please to stop your shooting! We have English and Dutch prisoners!'

'Cease fire,' Bulstrode said, then cupped his hands to his mouth and shouted, 'I've heard that one before! Heave to and abandon ship! You've got exactly five minutes before I put a torpedo into you! *Funf minuten*, you understand?'

'But is true! We have prisoners!'

'Then heave to and send them up on deck where I can see them!'

The fire at the stern burning fiercely now, like glowing coals seen through the side of a workman's brazier. *Shadow* moving cautiously out onto the port quarter of the slowing liner, watchful in case the move exposed her to guns placed further forward, but Bulstrode knowing that it was unreasonable to expect men, prisoners or anyone else, to stand directly above the conflagration his shells had started. The enemy vessel lying dead in the water, a small group of men assembling by the rail, others clambering into life-boats.

'Let's have an Aldis lamp up here,' Bulstrode said. When he was given it he pressed its trigger, aiming the beam at the group, illuminating it with radiance made hazy by the mist. 'Are you people English?' he called and one replied, 'Ahm no fockin' English. Ahm fockin' Scots.'

'And the others?'

'Dutchies. Can ye no hurry and get us off? The Jerries have set demolition charges.'

'Be my guest,' Bulstrode said. 'It's a long drop, but only a short swim.'

'I canna swim.'

'Then you'd better learn bloody quickly.' Untypical irritability in Bulstrode's voice. 'I'm getting out of here any moment now.' He turned to Harding. 'Number One, get some men onto the casing and . . .'

'They're on their way, sir,' Harding broke in. 'Six with heaving-lines and life-belts. I told them to go up through the gun tower.'

The Dutchmen jumped one by one. With obvious reluctance the Scot followed, sending up a mighty splash, then floundering until two of the others took him in tow. Less than a minute later ten shivering, dripping men were being hustled along the casing and down below.

Shadow backed slowly away and within seconds darkness had swallowed the doomed ship, only the fire raging aft a beacon marking where she lay.

'Secure the gun,' Bulstrode said.

'Torpedo tubes are still standing by, sir,' Harding reminded him.

I know. Leave them. If the scuttling charges don't go off soon I shall put a fish into her.'

Four separate explosions shook the *Van Haren* as he finished speaking, but for a minute the beacon continued to glow. Then it blinked out.

'Secure the torpedo tubes, Number One,' Bulstrode said. 'The men may now go back to enjoying the flu again.'

Chapter 14

Bulstrode wrote, 'Cross-examination of the released prisoners of war elicited the fact that the ship purporting to be', groaned and struck the words through.

'Something wrong, sir?'

'Only my literary style, Pilot. It has succumbed to the repeated assaults on the English language my bank manager directs at me for my financial enlightenment.'

'I know what you mean, sir,' Lieutenant Unwin said. He didn't know what his captain meant and privately considered him to be slightly insane.

Sticking his tongue out as an aid to concentration, Bulstrode began again. 'The ex-prisoners tell me that the ship calling itself the *Van Haren* of Rotterdam was in fact the 19,000 ton Norddeutscher-Lloyd liner *Neustrelitz* of Bremerhaven which had been sheltering at Maracaibo, Venezuela, since the beginning of hostilities. They were transferred to it at sea from a German armed merchant raider which had sunk their . . .'

At the sound of Gascoigne's raised voice calling, 'Captain sir?' from the periscope he put down his pencil and tilted his chair back so that his head and shoulders were in the passage-way outside the wardroom.

'Yes, Guns?'

'Would you come and take a look, sir? I think I can see one of the life-boats. Visibility's much better, but whatever it is it's up sun from us and I can't be sure. Also, I thought I caught a glimpse of a plane just now, but I can't swear to that either. It could have been a flock of gulls dodging in and out of the overcast.'

Bulstrode was at his side before he had finished speaking and Gascoigne relinquished the periscope to him. Automatically, the operator lowered the periscope a foot so that the much shorter man could see through it and that placed the upper lens too low to clear even the now flattening swell.

'Come up to thirty-three feet,' Bulstrode said.

When he could see he turned through a full circle, sighted nothing but clouds and water, then settled on the bearing Gascoigne had been looking along.

'See anything, sir?'

'No.'

'It might have been just a floating crate or . . .'

'Aha!'

Gascoigne fell silent at the exclamation, watching Bulstrode's face and the refracted light from above the surface of the sea striking at his eye-balls.

'Down periscope,' Bulstrode said, watched it sink into its well, then looked up at Gascoigne with a puzzled frown.

'You were right, Guns. It is a life-boat and it's full of people sitting watching a Heinkel 115 seaplane giving an intrepid birdman show. Now why, I ask myself, is it doing that?' He paused before adding, 'Myself apparently having nothing to offer by way of a reply I think we had better go and take a closer look. Sixty feet. Group up. Full ahead together. Steer 115.' Shadow went deep and fast, her hull humming with vibration.

When the crew were ordered to their stations Harding appeared in the control room rubbing sleep from his eyes.

''Morning, Number One.'

'Good morning, sir. From the feel of things we're going somewhere in a hurry. What's up?'

'Not sure. You know the reason for hanging around near the scene of last night's sinking was based on the certainty that they got off an SOS and in the faint hope that they might send out a destroyer to collect the survivors from the life-boats. Well, all would have been jollity and mirth if we could have torpedoed that, but they seem to have sent a seaplane instead and nobody taught me how to torpedo one of those.'

Harding looked sleepily bemused and Bulstrode went on, 'Gascoigne sighted a life-boat with a Heinkel 115 in attendance. It looked to me as though it was making practice runs at landing across the swell. Now, how many people can you stuff into an He 115?'

'I don't know, sir. Two? Three? It isn't very big.'

'Exactly, and there are about twenty people in that life-boat which is only some thirty miles from France. What's the panic? If the engine has broken down they could sail it, or even row it there quite quickly. It occurs to me that there might have been somebody aboard that liner they want to make absolutely sure of getting home and getting home fast.'

'Ah,' Harding said and Bulstrode replied, 'Quite. So, accepting that as a working hypothesis, I'm hoping to frustrate the attempt. Group down. Slow ahead together. Periscope depth. Ryan, ask Mr Menzies to come here, please.'

With the situation explained to him, the Scot stood waiting while Bulstrode carried out another rapid all-round search, then took his place at the periscope. The life-boat was within a hundred yards now.

'Aye, that's them.'

'You're sure that's one of the boats from the *Neustrelitz*?'

'Ahm certain. Ah can see the first mate sitting in the stern.'

'Thank you, Mr Menzies.'

Two periscope observations later, 'stand by to surface. Machine-gunners man the tower,' Bulstrode said and added,

'Your target is a seaplane on the far side of a life-boat, taxying towards it. Bearing straight ahead. On no account hit the boat.' His gaze flicked to Harding then back to the binocular eye-pieces. 'He must have landed while we were deep, Number One, and I couldn't see him because he was screened by the boat. Come up fast when I give the word.'

'Aye aye, sir. Do you want look-outs and Unwin on the bridge with you?'

'No. Too much of a crowd if they have fighter cover and we have to dive quickly. You and Unwin take a periscope each and cover the for'ard and after sectors respectively. Issue four men with .45s and heaving-lines. They wait here. Surface.'

Listening to the raving of Prentiss's and Mungo's guns, traversing the forward periscope across the bows from port to starboard, Harding never did see the life-boat. High above the sea as it was, he would have had to angle the upper lens downward to do so, but his job was to watch for hostile fighters. Being further away the seaplane did appear at the bottom of his field of view and he saw its transformation into a brilliant orange fire-ball, a ball which flung streamers of flaming debris up and away from itself. When he traversed back in the opposite direction all that was left was patches of oil burning on the surface of the water.

Chief Petty Officer Ryland at the steering wheel acknow-ledging the manoeuvring orders coming from the voice-pipe, shouting, 'All right, you four! Up on the casing through the gun tower and stand by to receive German prisoners!' The tele-graphs tinkling their instructions to the motor room. A slight bump as, Harding supposed, submarine and life-boat touched. Silence for a moment, then a brief burst of machine-gun fire and the sound of distant cries of alarm.

The clattering of feet on the steel casing. Figures seen by peripheral vision lurching from the wardroom, where the gun tower was, to be hustled forward by members of *Shadow*'s crew. Petty Officer Proctor saying, 'Get the whole bloody shower lying on their faces in the torpedo stowage compartment.' The gun tower hatches thudding shut. Harding and Unwin main-taining their constant sweep of horizon and sky through the two periscopes until the double snarl of the klaxon relieved them of the necessity of doing so.

Shadow slid under faster than usual with Harding giving orders for a ton and a half of ballast water to be pumped outboard to compensate for the weight of prisoners. Back at periscope depth, 'What was that firing about after the seaplane had been destroyed, sir?' he asked.

'The Jerries didn't seem to want to leave the life-boat,' Bulstrode told him. 'Gave Nazi salutes and spat over the side. That sort of thing. Mungo thought that was rather uncivil so he rendered the life-boat a liability by blowing its bows off. They agreed to change transport rapidly enough after that. Can't say I blame them really. Mungo was looking awfully irritable.'

'It's his missing teeth, sir. I've given up thanking him for anything in case he smiles and scares the daylights out of me.'

'That must have been it,' Bulstrode said. 'Well, if you've got everything under control here I'll go and see what we've collected.'

It was two German-speaking Dutch officers who provisionally identified the odd-man-out. He had, they told Bulstrode, an educated Berlin accent and was certainly not a sailor. His papers proclaimed him to be Ernst Walzel of Spandau and his occupation that of mining engineer. When the ship surfaced for the night a ciphered signal was transmitted reporting the sinking of the *Neustrelitz*, the submarine's own badly over-crowded condition with twenty-nine extra people, nineteen of them German, aboard and the details of a set of circumstances which was puzzling her commander. The reply ordered her immediate return to harbour and contained the added instruction that no attempt was to be made to interrogate any of the prisoners.

Shadow turned north-west for the English Channel.

In a corner of the control room, the only sitting space he could find with the ship so full, Mungo wrote Edna a lurid account of his recent activities with a machine-gun and handed the letter in for censorship by an officer.

In the wardroom Gascoigne obliterated all fact in the letter, let fantasy stand and concluded correctly that the result would please Mungo's wife more than the original version would have done.

On the bridge Harding scanned the black horizon constantly with his powerful Barr and Stroud binoculars and contemplated the bizarre fact that there was nothing like dealing out death and destruction for turning a disgruntled, divided crew into a harmonious entity. It even seemed to be a cure of influenza, his own included.

In the torpedo stowage compartment Mr Menzies walked up to the German calling himself Ernst Walzel and drove a sailor's clasp knife under his ribs and into his right lung.

Shadow broke radio silence for the second time that night, then, in obedience to an almost immediate answer, altered course directly away from the coast of France and increased to full speed.

The Sunderland flying-boat came out of the west with its navigation lights burning just as dawn was breaking. It failed to sight the flashing Aldis beam directed at it and Bulstrode ordered the firing of a flare. Harding moved quickly to the after periscope standard, jerked the lanyard of the cylinder clipped to it and brilliant green light spread across the sea. The Sunderland banked at once and circled for a landing run. When at last the flare spluttered out Harding sighed with relief. Even with France two hundred miles astern the unnatural glare had made him feel nakedly exposed, vulnerable, but he forgot about it soon enough in the bustle of preparation for receiving visitors.

Rocking gently to the urging of the swell the Sunderland lay stopped twenty yards away, attached to the submarine by a manilla line. It disgorged a rubber dinghy and four duffel-coated figures climbed down into it. Harding walked to the bows to receive them as, one after another, Able Seamen Ryan and Amersham pulled them up onto the casing. Mr Menzies, wrists tied behind him, a bandage round his neck, a man gripping each of his arms and with Petty Officer Proctor's .45 in his back, waited near the 3-inch gun.

To the first arrival, 'Oh! Hello, sir,' Harding said.

The man with an interest in heavy water wasn't wearing his Homburg hat, but looked as though he would have done so had he remembered to bring it with him when he nodded and pushed past without a word. Harding was steadying the second dinghy passenger to be jerked aboard when from behind him he heard the voice he had once listened to at Rosyth saying, 'Helmut Maisch! I thought it might be you. Nice to know that the *Gestapo* internal liquidation squad is still trying to do our job for us.' He listened for a reply from 'Mr Menzies' but there was none.

The third person to arrive on board sounded breathless. 'Goodness me! Today really has been exciting! Fast cars, aeroplanes, little boats and now submarines! I wouldn't have believed it possible! Still, never mind that now. I must get to my patient.'

Harding stared in open astonishment at the short, tubby girl with the gentle eyes and mouth in a tired plain face, a head-scarf showing under the hood of her duffel coat.

'We weren't expecting a female nurse,' he said.

She smiled at him, a small bright smile. 'You haven't got one,' she replied. 'He's a man. I'm the surgeon. The other man is Doctor Castle. Apart from the chap from the Foreign Office, that is. Please show me where to go.'

With 'Mr Menzies' and seven other Germans transferred to the Sunderland, *Shadow* submerged. She was at periscope depth before the flying-boat lifted from the sea.

All that day she cruised silently to the north ninety feet below the swell so that not even the infinitesimal motion of periscope depth should disturb the steadiness of the surgeon's hands. All that day Sarah Allison and her medical team fought to save the life of an enemy alien called Ernst Walzel lying unconscious on the wardroom table. All that day Ernst Walzel slid closer to death. Half an hour after sunset he reached it. *Shadow* surfaced.

Harding had the watch. His captain stayed on the bridge with him as there was little comfort to be found below with the wardroom crowded again now that it was no longer an operating theatre and with an exhausted woman asleep in his bunk.

They had been strange hours. Meals taken with the coxswain and his mess mates. 'Be a privilege, sir, as you ain't got nowhere to sit,' Ryland had said, 'if the officers would consider themselves ordinary members of the chief and petty officers' mess.' Bulstrode had enjoyed 'ordinary', but accepted the formal invitation with due gravity. Little else to do but wonder about the stabbing by the man calling himself Menzies but who his second-in-command had heard addressed as Helmut Maisch and who, whatever his name was, had then attempted to cut his own throat. It had been quick of Petty Officer Proctor to knock him unconscious with the barrel of his .45 before he could complete that. There had also been the Admiralty's swift reaction to his signal to think about, the rendezvous with the flying-boat and the invasion by specialists of different kinds. When he wasn't thinking and wondering he had just listened to the high, clear tones coming from behind the wardroom curtains as the surgeon stated her requirements for what he now knew to have been a losing battle.

'Bridge?'

Harding bent to the voice-pipe. 'Yes?'

'Civilian gentleman wants to know if he can come on the bridge for a breath of fresh air, sir.'

Bulstrode spoke into the second voice-pipe. 'Yes, that's all right, but get somebody to lend him a couple of sweaters. It's cold up here. Mine won't do. He's too big.'

'Couple of sweaters. Aye aye, sir,' the voice-pipe answered.

A dark figure loomed up beside Bulstrode three minutes later and said, 'I'm very grateful to you, Commander.'

'Not at all. Just one thing though. If I say "clear the bridge" you'll have to nip down that ladder pretty quickly. Okay?'

'Yes, of course, but I hope you won't have to dive again before daylight.'

A pause, then, 'Are you claustrophobic?'

'Yes, very.'

'Oh Christ!' Bulstrode said. 'You must have been sweating buckets. What a job for them to send you on.'

'They don't know about it, Commander, and I'd be glad if you'd keep my secret. We aren't supposed to have limitations of that sort. Anyway, it's unlikely I shall find myself aboard a submarine again.'

'It's safe with us,' Bulstrode told him. 'Now, what I suggest you do is stay up here for the night and get yourself good and tired, then at dawn I'll ask the doctor or that nice surgeon lady to give you something to knock you out for tomorrow's dive.'

Harding, maintaining his near-constant watch on the empty night horizon, heard the man's almost comical exhalation of relief and listened to him saying, 'I really hadn't anticipated such understanding. You can't be a sufferer, surely?'

'No,' Bulstrode said, 'but put me on top of a twenty-foot wall and I'd freeze so solid the fire brigade would have to chip me off with their axes. We all have our little quirks. Harding here is a furloughphobe.'

'Oh? I don't think I know the word.'

'That's probably because I've only just invented it. He has a horror of going on leave. At least, I can never persuade him to take any.'

The nameless civilian laughed, relaxed now, and Harding admired him for having shown no sign of the extreme fear which must have had him in its grip throughout the long hours under water while he went quietly about his investigation, talking to Bulstrode, talking to the coxswain, talking to Petty Officer Proctor, talking to everybody who had had any contact with either the attacker or the attacked. He respected his captain too for the quick and casual way in which he had reassured the man and seen to it that he need not endure another day of terror.

The matter disposed of, Bulstrode changed the subject. 'Would I be out of order if I asked you what's going on?'

Surprise in his voice, 'No, of course not,' the man replied. 'It's all about your intuition. Nothing more, nothing less. You found it peculiar that an attempt should be made to airlift probably a single survivor from a life-boat. In fact, you found it so peculiar that you intervened, foiled the attempt, took prisoners and reported your suspicions by wireless. Almost immediately you were proved dramatically right in your assumption that something odd was in progress and you reported that too. My masters sent me and the medical team as a result so that I could question Walzel, if that's his name, if he recovered consciousness.' There was a shrug in the words when he added, 'He never did.'

'Yes,' Bulstrode said. 'I understand all that, but there are still several oddities. I . . .'

'You're asking yourself why Menzies teamed up with the Dutch and came aboard here instead of getting into the life-boats with the rest of the Germans. Right?'

'That, and how you know him to be Helmut Maisch. That really was a "Dr Livingstone, I presume" situation in the middle of the Bay of Biscay.'

'Well, let's take things one at a time,' the civilian said. 'On the first point, and I'm guessing now, it's likely that Maisch was Walzel's bodyguard. Guessing rather less, I'd say that he had orders to kill him if there was any likelihood of his falling into our hands. I can't think of any personal reason strong enough to make him choose a time and place which required his suicide.' The speaker fell silent then until Harding heard him murmur half to himself, 'Brave and dedicated chap, Maisch, even if he is the most frightful shit.'

A longer pause followed before the civilian went on, 'I would imagine that Maisch had his doubts, well founded ones as you have shown, about the ability of the *Neustrelitz* to break through our blockade, so he took out some insurance by presenting himself to the Dutch as a fellow prisoner and survivor from a British ship. The papers you took from him are genuine and obviously belonged to somebody called Menzies now dead or a prisoner of war. He probably picked a Scots name because although his English is fluent and colloquial it's also accented, but harsh Scottish sounds are very easy for the Germans to mimic and as they are also often incomprehensible to the English that would give him an added degree of protection. All of which brings us to the point of why he chose to come aboard here.'

Bulstrode and Harding, as well as the nearer lookouts who were certainly listening, stayed at that point while *Shadow*, diesels rumbling, crossed half a mile of sea, then the voice came out of the darkness again.

'My reading of his thought processes would be that on realizing that he was being shelled by a submarine, which is not a vessel famed for picking up enemy survivors because of space limitations if for no other reason, he reached two conclusions. First, that Walzel, with only a few miles left to make it to France in a well-found life-boat, could safely be left to his own devices without further molestation from you. Alternatively, he may have set up that air pick-up for him by wireless while you were shelling the *Neustrelitz*. Second, that you provided him with a golden, no-risk opportunity of a free ticket to England as a rescued Scottish seaman.'

The civilian laughed shortly before adding, 'Then you messed everything up for him by staying at the scene of the sinking instead of making yourself scarce as he might reasonably have expected you to do. Imagine his feelings when you asked him to identify that life-boat and he could see Walzel sitting in it. Oh dear me. He couldn't deny that it was from the *Neustrelitz* because you would almost certainly have established that it was and that would have pointed the finger straight at him.' He laughed again and said 'Oh dear me' for the second time.

It occurred to Harding that Maisch, now undergoing interrogation in England, wouldn't be finding life very amusing, then he chided himself for the criticism of the man from MI5, or whatever he was, implicit in the thought. Maisch was a killer and deserved everything he got. It did *not* occur to Harding that he was a killer himself, an accessory to legalized murder. Nor could he foresee that in due time he would be personally responsible for more deaths than a thousand men such as Maisch.

'I didn't know that the *Gestapo* was in the spying business,' Bulstrode said and the other replied, 'Oh, Maisch isn't *Gestapo*. I just said that to make him think I thought he was. He and his department were my special concern when I was attached to our Berlin embassy in the mid-thirties. I know what he is all right.'

Harding waited to hear what Maisch was, but the information was not forthcoming and the further thought came to him that the civilian had said a great deal without telling them anything they could not have worked out for themselves. Still sweeping the horizon through his binoculars he fell to wondering who Walzel had been and what had made him so important that he had had to be eliminated.

Quite correctly he assumed that he never would know and doubted if anyone in England would either, as it was apparently necessary to take the corpse home with them, instead of burying it at sea, in the vague hope that somebody might be able to identify it. He didn't like that. Not that he cared, but because the crew did, because all submarine crews did. They were superstitious about many things, but high on the list was the presence in their ship of either corpses or clergymen. Dead bodies were for sliding respectfully over the side at the earliest possible moment. The clergy, of whatever denomination, were for stopping at the gangway and being requested, equally respectfully, not to set foot on board.

It had, Harding told himself, been a very peculiar patrol and, whether or not he was a 'furloughphobe', he would be glad to be back in Devonport, rid of supernumaries dead or alive. For a few seconds he rested his eyes, letting the lids droop, then raised his binoculars again.

Chapter 15

After the first night in harbour when, as had become customary, he had kept Bulstrode company on what he called his 'alcoholiday', Harding saw little of his captain for several weeks. The main motors which had propelled *Shadow* for thousands of miles beneath the sea and the diesels which had driven her for many more across its surface required greater attention than the crew was equipped to give. In addition, other defects, both major and minor, were growing in number. Devonport dockyard took the submarine into its care for a refit of considerable proportions and a majority of her ship's company dispersed. Most went on leave, a few joined training courses or took examinations to improve their ratings from able seaman to leading seaman, from leading seaman to petty officer. One or two were transferred to fill vacancies in other boats in the flotilla. Harding and Wright immersed themselves in the work of preparing *Shadow* for her return to sea. Neither minded because neither had anything he would rather have been doing.

Winter became spring and, with its coming, air reconnaissance located the German battle-cruisers *Scharnhorst* and *Gneisenau* in the enemy-occupied French harbour of Brest. Immediately a submarine blockade was set up around the port. 'The Iron Ring' the press called it, but in the Submarine Service it was known as 'The Scrap-iron Ring', a name which suited it better because the heavy losses of the North Sea campaign had not yet been made good and submarines of astonishing antiquity were pressed into service to contain the powerful German warships.

Shadow lay unheeding, her sleep troubled only by the workmen swarming on and in her. During one of his periodic visits to check on the progress of the refit Bulstrode took Harding out to lunch.

'Wanted to ask you a favour, Peter.'

Except during an 'alcoholiday' it was rare for Bulstrode to address his second-in-command by his Christian name. Harding looked at him questioningly.

'Would you be my best man?'

Stupidly, 'What?' Harding said.

'You know, take me on the town the night before, try not to lose the ring and see that I get to the church on time the next day.'

'Are you serious?'

'Never more so.'

'Well I'm damned! Who is she?'

'Sarah Allison. Soon, poor child, to become Sarah de Vere

Charnley-Bulstrode unless my aunt has the grace to depart this world before the wedding. We could shorten it a lot if she did.'

'Oh I say! I really am most awfully pleased!' Harding said and raised his glass. 'Here's terrific happiness to both of you!'

He drank, choked and, with no warning, exploded into laughter. Bulstrode watched him for a moment, his expression puzzled, then annoyance grew in him when Harding's spasm showed no sign of abating.

'What's so bloody funny?'

For a few seconds Harding laughed on, then breathed in deeply and got control of himself. He spoke tremulously.

'I'm sorry, but do you remember what you said to me at Rosyth?'

'I don't know what you're talking about.'

'You said . . . You said that ever since you were sixteen you had had this dream of being ensnared by attractive women with corrupt natures. Oh boy! Have you slipped up? Sarah Allison is one of the nicest, gentlest women I've ever met and . . .'

Harding went off into another paroxysm of mirth and, mollified, Bulstrode stared smilingly at his plate, then, 'You haven't answered my question,' he said.

'What question was that?'

'If you would be my best man.'

'I most certainly would. Thank you for asking me. When is it to be?'

'Next Saturday.'

'In London?'

'No,' Bulstrode said. 'Plymouth. We thought that the crew might . . .' He let the rest of the sentence go, then added almost diffidently, 'We could hire a hall and get in a couple of barrels of beer. That sort of thing. Do you think they'd come?'

'Come? Of course they'll come! You couldn't keep them away. Just about everybody is back from leave now. I'll make all the arrangements. That's the best man's job anyway.'

'Well, if you could just book the hall and order the beer and some food that would be nice.'

'Oh, there's more than that,' Harding told him. 'There's a carriage to find for the crew to tow you both away from the church in. Then you must have an arch of swords and . . .'

'Swords? Nobody carries swords in a submarine, for goodness sake!'

'I'll borrow them from the officers at the barracks,' Harding said and Bulstrode looked absurdly pleased.

They were drinking indifferent coffee when he asked, 'What made you say earlier that she was a gentle person? As it happens you're absolutely right, but how would you know? You hardly spoke to her.'

Harding smiled. 'We talked for a couple of hours after I came off watch that night you let the mystery man stay on the bridge. First, she was so obviously concerned for him. She said another day under water could mark him for life, so she woke up Dr Castle and organized the sedation with him right away. If you remember, she hardly moved from Mr X's side all the next day until we surfaced in case he began to show signs of knowing where he was.'

'I remember,' Bulstrode said.

'Then, at some point, I told her I was sorry about her patient dying, but she said she wasn't, because all she could ever have done was keep him alive long enough for Mr X to interrogate and, as that would have been pretty ghastly for him, she was glad for him when he pipped it without regaining consciousness. To her he was a human being, not an enemy alien with a load of information locked in his skull waiting to be extracted. A most compassionate lady.'

It was Bulstrode's turn to smile. He did it shyly.

'What rhymes with "surgeon"?' Chief Petty Officer Ryland asked. 'And I don't want nobody tellin' me "virgin", as I'm not 'avin' no disgustin' innuendoes in this 'ere poem of mine for the bride and groom.'

'How about "urgin'"', 'Swain?'

'Well done, Proctor. That's more tasteful,' the coxswain said, licked the end of his pencil and began to write laboriously.

'One cake, large, iced, wedding guests for the consumption of. Four swords, ceremonial, officers for the forming of an arch with. Yes, we can manage that for you,' the commander of Devonport Barracks said.

'Thank you very much indeed, sir. We'd have made the cake on board, but the cooker isn't connected up yet. Would it be possible to let my leading cook help with it? He'd be a bit hurt if he was left out.'

'Of course. Send him along, but I'm afraid all this is going to cost you a gin.'

'I'm sorry, but I can't agree to that, sir. It'll have to be a double. That's my final offer.'

The commander smiled. 'You drive a hard bargain, Harding, but I accept your terms.'

'A brougham? Where on earth did you find that?' The captain of the dockyard sounded intrigued.

'Laid up at the back on one of the local garages, sir.' Harding said. 'It's in a rather ramshackle state, but our engine room artificers say they can make it sea-worthy if we can get it alongside the ship. Well, road-worthy I mean.'

'I see. Yes, of course you can bring it into the yard. I doubt there's been one of those in here since the Boer War. I'll warn the dockyard police. What fun!'

'Would you like to come down and look at it, sir?'

'I certainly would.'

'Then how about noon tomorrow, sir? We could give you a gin on board *Shadow* afterwards.'

'You're on,' the four-stripe captain said.

'It was such a strange way for a couple to meet that we thought we'd make them something to remember it by, sir,' the chief engine room artificer said. 'Would it be all right to present it to the bride at the reception? We thought of putting it on the cake, but that would need reinforcing or it'd be crushed.'

'I see what you mean,' Harding told him. 'It would flatten any cake, wouldn't it? We'll rule that out, but certainly present it to her. You people really must have worked on this. It's beautiful and she'll be absolutely enchanted. So will the Captain.'

The heavy object lying on the wardroom table was exactly the kind of thing he imagined a newly married woman could most do without, the non-functional dust-trap that it was. For all that, the workmanship was of a very high standard. The model of *Shadow*, of a Sunderland flying-boat, of a rubber dinghy between them resting on the thick base of the sea, all of them in gleaming metal, were extremely well done.

'Glad you think they'll like it, sir,' the chief engine room artificer said.

His borrowed sword crossed with Gascoigne's, with Wright and Unwin making up the rest of the short arch, Harding glanced sideways as the couple came out of the church. Bulstrode was smiling. His wife, eyes and mouth wide with delighted astonishment at the sight of the four-wheeled brougham, of Chief Petty Officer Ryland on the driver's seat raised above the closed carriage, of the long ropes held by forty sailors, twenty in front, twenty more behind to act as the brakes the engine room artificers had been unable to replace in time. There was a police car as well, its occupants grinning as broadly as *Shadow*'s crew and a growing crowd of local people. Then suddenly everyone was cheering.

She looked like royalty, Harding thought, sitting beside her husband in the great old-fashioned vehicle, hand raised, white veil thrown back, her small plain face alight with happiness and excitement.

'Slack off aft! Give way for'ard!' Chief Petty Officer Ryland roared and the swaying, jolting contraption rumbled off along the road preceded by its police escort.

None of the crew misbehaving at the reception, the chief and petty officers seeing to that. Mrs Bulstrode visibly touched, crying a little when the chief engine room artificer presented the model of the Biscay rendezvous. Able Seaman Mungo saying to Harding, 'Bloody marvellous show this, but then it would be from our ship, wouldn't it sir?' The coxswain deciding not to deliver his poem and Harding feeling relieved about it. Mrs Bulstrode kissing the cheek of each and every one of the forty-eight men present. Then it was time for the couple to leave for the railway station and their family reception in London.

'Thank you, Peter. Thank you for everything.'

'It was more than just a pleasure, sir.'

Harding felt content but tired. It had been an emotional day.

A fortnight later *Shadow* slipped her moorings and set course for Brest to add some steel to 'The Scrap-iron Ring'.

Chapter 16

Torpedo Mechanic Klaus Tanz removed the shaft of the detonating mechanism from the warhead of the torpedo from Number 3 tube, dismantled it, reassembled it, greased it and slid it back into place. The action made him think of the raven-haired Madelaine at the brothel no more than two hundred metres beyond the dockyard gates. It was his first port of call every time his ship returned from the Atlantic and Madelaine was his favourite girl.

Tanz was educated beyond the station the war had placed him in and he was able to put words to his train of thought. 'Very Freudian,' he said to himself and grinned happily both at his own erudition and his memories of the hours he had spent with her. Mentally reliving some of the more imaginative manoeuvres she was capable of, he replaced the streamlined fairing surrounding the impeller designed to drive the detonator into the priming charge as the torpedo sped through the water without noticing that the impeller was the wrong way round.

'Ready for loading,' he said to the petty officer in charge of the torpedo room, slapped the warhead with the palm of his hand and made his way up the access hatch ladder to the upper deck. There he stood, wiping grease from his fingers with a piece of rag, looking around him at the port of Brest, at the other UA–VIIC-class U-boats moored near-by and at the fires still burning after the air raid of the night before. English Halifax bombers again he had been told. Not that they had achieved much except mess up the town some more. The port itself had very heavy anti-aircraft defences and seemed untouched. Just as well with the *Scharnhorst* and *Gneisenau* in harbour in addition to four U-boats. For all that, he thought, life would be a lot more comfortable when they had finished building the big submarine pens. Then, with the battle cruisers back at sea, the English could bomb all they liked provided the authorities moved Madelaine and her brothel into the pens with the U-boats.

Tanz grinned again and decided to try for another shore pass before the ship sailed for patrol the next day.

At exactly one minute to midnight twenty miles to the west of Ushant Harding took over the watch from Gascoigne on *Shadow*'s bridge.

'Course 090, Number One. Revolutions for ten knots and we have a running battery charge on the starboard engine. The zig-zag pattern is 'D' and we make a ninety degree base alteration in course to port at twenty-two minutes past and eight minutes to each hour.'

Harding glanced around him at the sharply etched line of the night horizon, at the broken wave-tops glinting silver every time the seemingly scudding moon broke clear of the patchy overcast, at the compass repeater and at the four silent figures of the look-outs.

'Thank you, Guns, I've got her,' he said.

At exactly five minutes past midnight nineteen miles to the west of Ushant the torpedo hit *Shadow*.

Staring aft through his binoculars the sudden thudding clang from the direction of the bows spun Harding round in time to watch the great cylindrical shape, foreshortened by perspective, leap dolphin-like from the sea at a point close to the port forward hydroplane. Moonlight revealed its full gleaming length as it flashed past the conning tower, arcing down to strike the ballast tanks a glancing blow before smashing into the water astern. Spray soared skyward. For countable seconds he stood as though paralysed by the memory of what he had witnessed, the insane screaming of an engine and propellors out of their natural element still, in his imagination, beating at his ear-drums, then the upper half of his body jack-knifed down to the voice-pipe.

Pain stabbed at his face, but he ignored it, shouted 'Dive! Dive! Dive!' and, as though they might not have heard the order, pushed the two forward look-outs towards the conning tower hatch. The fourth look-out was disappearing into the tower by the time he had shut the two heavy voice-pipe cocks. He followed the man quickly, closed the hatch above his head, clipped it in place and scrambled rapidly down the vertical brass ladder to the control room.

'What the hell's going on, Number One?'

Harding ignored the question. 'Go deep, sir,' he said. 'Whatever you do, don't stop at periscope depth!'

The urgency in his voice was clear. Bulstrode nodded and said, 'One hundred feet, Cox'n.'

'One 'undred feet, sir. Aye aye.'

The diving angle increasing now. Five degrees. Ten degrees. Fifteen. Harding clutched the control room ladder for support, shaking his head slowly from side to side like a wounded bull, trying to clear it of mist. The first thing his eyes registered was the front of his duffel coat. In the dim red control room lighting it appeared to have turned black and he wondered why that was.

'You don't look too good, Number One. Can you manage to tell me what we hit?'

'Hit, sir?'

Bulstrode's hand on his shoulder, shaking it. 'Yes, two bloody great thumps, one for'ard, one near the engine room. A floating wreck perhaps?'

'Oh,' Harding said. 'We didn't hit anything. A torpedo hit us. Near the bows first, then it took off, went past the bridge like a Zeppelin and landed on the saddle-tanks aft somewhere.' He hesitated before adding in a wondering voice, 'It didn't explode, sir.'

Somebody pushing a chair behind him, forcing him down onto it, a warm cloth dabbing at his face. Mungo saying, 'Keep still, sir, while I tidy you up. Your nose had taken a right hammering it has. Did that torpedo hit it on the way by?' That made Harding giggle and the mist cleared from his brain.

'I just banged it on the voice-pipe I think. Thanks. That's enough. Leave me the cloth, please.' He stood unsteadily upright and faced Bulstrode. 'There's a U-boat out there somewhere on the port bow, sir.'

Bulstrode calling for a torch, shining it into first one then the other of Harding's eyes, nodding, satisfied.

'Yes, we worked that out while you were doing your impersonation of a broken ketchup bottle. We're at two hundred feet and silent routine, but Topham can't hear anything on the sonar. Why don't you go and change your clothes? You look like Dracula two hours into overtime.'

For the rest of that night and all the next day *Shadow* remained submerged, gliding soundlessly away from the French coast and the point at which she had been attacked and, but for the malfunction of a torpedo warhead, would certainly have been sunk. Lieutenant Wright reported that there was no damage to the pressure hull, but could say nothing about the condition of the main ballast tanks until the ship surfaced. Topham, promoted from leading seaman to acting petty officer now, and his assistants on sonar watch, heard only the sounds of the sea. Bulstrode held an enquiry which established nothing beyond the facts that an excellent periscope attack assisted by the bright moon had been carried out on them and that nobody had been aware that it was in progress until the faulty torpedo had erupted from the water.

'We seem to have been just a little bit lucky,' Bulstrode had said and Gascoigne had replied, 'Probably your sainted aunt Agatha de Vere Charnley watching over us, sir.'

'Unfortunately for my bank balance she's still in the land of the living, so she's not in a position to do that yet,' Bulstrode had told him, but he had done so without smiling. Nobody felt much like smiling. *Shadow* had suffered a theoretical defeat and even had her officers known that they had a black-haired French prostitute called Madelaine to thank for its not being an actual one they would have felt no better. They had been out-thought, out-fought and saved only by chance.

The defeat had its practical side too because, temporarily at least, *Shadow* had been driven off station by an unseen enemy which might still be in contact with her. A gap had been left in the ring, a gap big enough for the two battle-cruisers to slip through. That it would be filled soon after *Shadow* had surfaced, recharged her batteries and replaced the stale air inside the hull was small consolation, for by then it might be too late.

'In view of this incident', Bulstrode wrote in his patrol report notes, 'I believe that consideration should be given to the advisability of submarines withdrawing further to seaward to charge their batteries in conditions of high night-time visibility. This will, of course, increase the length of the arc they have to cover, but this effect will be cancelled out by the greater distance over which bright moonlight will enable them to observe the movements of enemy shipping. In my opinion the distance of withdrawal should be greater than that which a U-boat can cover submerged from Brest between sunset and sunrise'.

Bulstrode need not have felt concern about his brief absence from his assigned position. It was to be nearly a year before the battle-cruisers, with the light cruiser *Prinz Eugen*, made their successful bid to break free of the submarine blockade, but there was no way in which he could have known that.

The nineteen hours under water were a bad time for Harding, his thoughts constantly returning to the tracking and sinking of the submerged U-boat in the North Sea when Cheaver had had command, his imagination picturing the situation in reverse now with German sonar locked on some sound or other which *Shadow* should not have been making. Telling himself that there had been no such unacceptable noises recorded by the test sound-range *Shadow* had repeatedly crossed after her refit did not help him.

Self-doubt had taken hold of him too, his wasted seconds of frozen immobility after the torpedo had hurtled past the bridge preying on his mind. He saw that as debilitating fear crippling his reflexes rather tham a simple matter of stunned incredulity and that made him question his own courage. Then there had been his apparent inability to give his captain a prompt and precise report of what had occurred and he found no excuse for that in his collision with the voice-pipe, seeing it as trivial and something he should have been calm enough to avoid. Harding, alone in the wardroom, breathing stale air through his mouth because his nostrils were still clogged with dried blood, stared sombrely at the table with eyes swollen to slits.

'You bear a strong resemblance to Cyrano de Bergerac after a month on the booze, Number One.'

He looked up to see the captain standing at the curtained entrance.

'I expect I do, sir.'

Bulstrode sat down opposite him, then appeared to admire his own finger-nails for a moment before saying, 'You know, Peter, you don't get seven yards of infuriated torpedo whistling round your ears every day of the week. In fact the occurrence is so rare that no mention of it appears in the liturgy for survival they grind into us. Something tells me that you find the omission offensive.'

Harding almost smiled, failed to do so and said, 'It really is rather spooky the way you read my mind, sir. This isn't the first time by a long way either.'

The captain shook his head. 'There's nothing spooky about it. I don't read your mind any better than you read the rest of the crew's and mine too probably. We both simply observe, reflect and conclude. You know that. You also know that we can only push our conclusions so far without help, so suppose you help me by telling me where you got that hair shirt you're wearing. I don't think I've seen it before.'

With hardly any hesitation Harding told him.

When he had finished, 'Well, I hope you feel better now you've sicked that lot up all over the carpet,' Bulstrode said. 'God, how I hate perfectionists. They're the most limited people I know. Don't you dare turn into one. You got the ship under water with commendable alacrity and told me not to hang around at periscope depth. Admittedly you neglected to inform me of your reason, which was that further torpedoes might follow, but in view of your savage assault on your own proboscis and the fact that you had just been startled out of your skull, I find that less than remarkable.'

Bulstrode stood up and added, 'Now, as our American friends might say, if you're all through moping I'd like to get this show on the surface and head back east.'

The night was identical to the one before, patchy cloud hastening towards the land-mass below the horizon ahead, the sea choppy, visibility extreme, but now every broken moon-lit wave-top was a porpoising torpedo targeted on *Shadow*. Harding cursed himself silently, savagely, for allowing his imagination to run riot, but that did nothing to ease the tautness of his neck muscles as his imagination no longer appeared to require his permission for the form of activity it undertook. He swore again, not so silently.

'What, sir?'

He glanced at the starboard forward look-out. 'Forgot to bring any lens tissue on watch with me, Ryan. You got any spare?'

'Yessir. Here y'are.'

'Thanks.' And you keep your stupid mouth shut, Peter Harding. What's got into you? It's obvious now that that U-boat lost contact with us as soon as we dived last night and the Chief says there's nothing wrong with the ballast tanks except for a long scour-mark for'ard and a bloody great dent aft. Not even a slow leak in them, for God's sake! Pull yourself together!

It took him three days to do that. Three days of soul-searching which left him mentally and physically tired but steady again, steady enough to make him wonder what the prolonged nervous spasm had really been about. During that time, his ability to disguise his feelings improved markedly and that was to stand him in good stead, but his distrust of moonlight persisted long after the incident of the air-borne torpedo had faded in his memory.

Harding's introspective probings reminded him that he had been extremely nervous before on a number occasions, but that the tenseness had left him with the ending of whatever the event had been which had caused it. Never before had he felt himself rendered directionless, like a toppled gyroscope. Never before had there been the need to apply rigid self-discipline to restabilize himself. The knowledge that such a need would recur with increasing frequency would have caused him grave concern but, fortunately for his present peace of mind, the future was as closed to him as it was to anyone else and, content with what he failed to recognize as a plastering of cracks in himself, he got on with his job.

Furious at his own stupidity, his lack of insight, even what he now believed to have been the selfishness of his courtship and marriage, Bulstrode watched him do it. He had been mildly amused when he had coined the word 'furloughphobe' in relation to Harding in an attempt to divert the man from Intelligence locked in claustrophobic torment, but now it stood as a condemnation of his behaviour as a commander. Reference to the records, and to his own memory of what Harding had told him of his service in cruisers, gave him the number of days of official leave his second-in-command had had in a year and a half of war. The realization that he needed only his thumbs to count them on shocked him.

So willing a horse had required no flogging and the road he had set it on had been paved with the best of intentions, intentions born of the necessity to show his complete faith in a very young officer in a highly responsible position, but now the evidence of where that road led was before him. At first as a demonstration of trust, and later by complying with Harding's genuine preference for work over relaxation, he had reduced him to a state bordering on mental, physical and nervous exhaustion. *Shadow*'s encounters with the enemy had been few and Bulstrode found himself guilty of badly underestimating the cumulative effect of the draining weeks of tension between them when nothing had happened but could, as the encounter with the unseen U-boat proved, have done so at any second of any minute of any hour. Then there had been the long refit over which he had held no more than a watching brief when he should have ordered his first lieutenant to go away and rest whether he wanted to or not. But Harding had been so anxious to gain the additional experience and there was Sarah . . .

Bulstrode was very angry with himself indeed.

The tramp steamer *Döbeln* displaced 3,200 tons and had done so for thirty-six years which made her exactly half the age of her master. It had been in June of 1940 when she had loaded a full cargo of coal at Osaka for delivery to the Southern Oriental Trading Company of Macao and that being precisely the freight required to fire the boilers which provided steam for her ancient reciprocating engine Friedrich Stohrer ordered course set for the Indian Ocean and Germany, taking the property of the Southern Oriental Trading Company with him.

He didn't seriously expect to reach Germany, but there was news that France would soon be in German hands and as that country might be a little easier to reach and because he knew that the Reich would be glad of the coal, possibly even of his old ship as well, he was going to try.

The cards stacked against him he knew to be formidable and in descending order of importance he listed them as the British navy, the decrepit state of his ship, the necessity to provision and water her during the voyage with so few places open to him, the weather and his own age. But he tried and spent ten months doing it.

Only twice had he been seriously alarmed. The first time had been when a Walrus flying boat had circled the *Döbeln* two hundred miles south of Capetown. The plane, was, he knew, of the type launched by catapult from British cruisers and, as he feared it must, the cruiser duly appeared an hour later, her brilliant signal lamp ordering him to stop instantly. He had done so and stood in total dejection watching the rakish pale grey shape grow in size until he seemed to be staring down the barrels of the twelve 6-inch guns trained on him. Then, inexplicably, the warship had turned away. It was only when the sound of gunfire reached his ears from beyond the eastern horizon that he was able to assume, and assume correctly, that the flying-boat had located bigger game for the cruiser to destroy. Darkness had followed quickly and a great wave of relief had swept over him at the knowledge that it would be almost impossible for the enemy to find him again in the vastness of the ocean when the next day dawned.

His second fright came when, just north of the equator, a submarine had surfaced within half a mile of him, but that turned out to be a U-boat which, his identity established, sent him on his way with cheers, good wishes and congratulations on what he had achieved.

On 28th March 1941 Cape Finisterre at the north-west corner of Spain was sighted from the *Döbeln*'s mast-head. She had circumnavigated half the globe, her voyage was nearly done and for the first time in almost a year her master broke radio silence and asked for an escort to see him safely to harbour.

Gascoigne read out the numbers written on the pink signal form in groups of five, Unwin looked for the corresponding words in the code book and Wright wrote down what Unwin said they were.

When they had finished, 'Well I'll be damned. Where's the Skipper?' Unwin said.

'Oh the bridge with Number One,' Gascoigne told him.

A moment later, 'Bridge. Captain please,' Unwin called up the voice-pipe.

'Captain here.'

'Signal for us, sir. We're to proceed immediately to Gibraltar for . . .'

'Starboard 20, steer 210,' Bulstrode's voice said and, when the order had been acknowledged, went on, 'All right, Unwin. Read it to me.'

'Yes, sir. It says "Proceed at once to Gibraltar at best possible speed diving by day for purpose providing UK-bound convoy with protection against enemy heavy units known to be at sea. Acknowledge". That's all, sir.'

'Very well. Acknowledge it.'

Shadow, already turning onto approximately the correct course, raced to the west of south leaving the 'Scrap-iron Ring' to its own devices.

Unwin watched the big plane and was beginning to wonder why it was flying in a wide circle when he thought he saw a puff of smoke beneath it. He called Bulstrode to the periscope.

'It looks like one of those long-range jobs, sir. I think it's called a Condor. Probably spelt with a "K", being German.'

'Probably,' Bulstrode said. He wasn't interested in how it was spelt, or much in it, only in why it was there off the north coast of Spain.

'I thought I saw smoke in that direction a moment ago, sir, but I can't be sure.'

'Did you indeed?' Bulstrode said and turned the periscope in a slow sweep of the horizon before settling on the sector off the port bow. High overcast, grey sea, short steep waves with broken tops, low swell. Perfect submarine weather. The chances of the airmen seeing *Shadow*'s shape beneath the surface were negligible.

Had that been another trace of smoke living for a second before the gusting wind dissipated it? Difficult to be sure with spume repeatedly misting the periscope's upper lens.

'Come up to thirty feet.'

'Thirty feet, aye aye sir.'

He could see much better now, but it was still half a minute before he could say, 'You saw smoke all right, Unwin.'

So slow was the approach of the target that an hour and thirty-seven minutes had passed before Bulstrode ordered the crew to their stations. By then the old-fashioned freighter with its tall thin funnel belching black smoke was in full view, its course and speed established at 060 degrees and five knots. There was no zig-zag.

Bulstrode put into effect a decision he had taken twenty minutes earlier by saying, 'It's all yours, Number One.'

Harding looked at him questioningly. 'What, sir?'

'Let me put it another way,' Bulstrode said. 'As I am told they used to say in the days of sail, "Sink me that ship, Master Gunner".' He moved to the first lieutenant's normal position and added, 'I've got the trim.'

For a moment Harding stood, blinking rapidly at him, then he muttered, 'Good Lord,' and turned to the periscope. It slid upwards at his gesture and he felt idiotically suprised at that because he couldn't bring himself to believe that anybody would pay any attention to what a usurper said or did. They paid attention. They acknowledged his orders and acted on them. They gave him the information he needed when he asked for it. *Shadow* made a slight alteration in course at his command. The merchantman grew bigger in the periscope lens. The plane continued to circle, unseeing.

He glanced over his shoulder at his captain. 'A salvo of two fish enough, sir?'

Staring intently at the hydroplane indicators, ignoring him, 'Are we a little heavy aft, Cox'n?' Bulstrode asked. 'I'm rather out of practice at this.'

Chief Petty Officer Ryland shook his head. 'No, sir. We're just right. The new skipper shouldn't 'ave no trouble.'

Harding grinned, relaxed now. 'Stand by numbers 1 and 2 tubes. Open bow caps,' he said.

Somebody reaching over his shoulder, wiping his forehead with a rag, the first realization that his face was running with sweat. Thanking him. Not moving his eyes from the binocular viewer. Asking for the Director Angle. Being told it. Saying 'Put me on that'. Hands covering his from behind, inching the periscope round. 'You're on Green 3, sir.' The blunt bows of the old ship creeping into the right-hand side of his field of view, moving with agonizing slowness towards the hair-line at the centre of the lens, reaching, passing it.

'Fire 1!'

The familiar slight jolt and the pressure of air on his ear-drums. The bridge bisected by the hair-line, then the funnel.

'Fire 2! Down periscope,' Harding said.

The explosion lifted the master of the *Döbeln* and hurled him against the side of the wheel-house breaking his right shoulder and wrist. A hurtling shard of glass from a shattered window had laid his left cheek open to the bone, but he didn't notice that. Wincing, he staggered upright on a deck already beginning to slope, supporting himself with his good arm.

With quiet resignation, 'Well, we tried,' he said to his second officer. 'Abandon ship.'

The list increased lurchingly, sending him across the bridge to the port life-boat in an uncontrollable rush. The pain was savage when his shoulder struck it, but he began at once to release the life-boat's securing lines.

Friedrich Stohrer was still trying when Harding's second torpedo struck within eight feet of him.

Chapter 17

The north-westerly storm struck *Shadow* before Portugal was abeam and kept her company all the way south to Cape St Vincent. It was a cold, wet and uncomfortable time with the submarine cork-screwing wildly in the following sea. Once she was pooped, sliding like a giant surf-board before a huge swell, the great wall of water rising, covering the after casing, engulfing the conning tower and pouring into the control room before the officer of the watch could fight his way to the upper hatch and force it shut from outside. Some of the water found its way into Number 2 battery tank and chlorine gas set the crew coughing, choking, before the mess was cleared up and the sumps pumped dry. The experience alarmed everyone aboard.

Submerged at a depth of ninety feet throughout the hours of daylight all was peaceful, a time to change into dry clothes, a time to eat and sleep, but everyone aboard was to be alarmed again when the ship surfaced for the night, wallowing, listing further and further to port, then staying there at an angle of fifty-five degrees.

The control room deck quickly wet, slippery from the spray pattering down the conning tower, making footholds difficult to find, treacherous in the extreme angle. The sound of startled cries from forward and aft, the crash of crockery, people grasping whatever they could for support. Harding wrapping his arms round the vertical ladder and giving rapid orders, surprised to hear himself doing it calmly when he was convinced that *Shadow* must capsize with such a list in such a sea.

With the starboard high pressure blowing valves shut, air roared only into the port tanks, obliterating the sounds of the storm, making Bulstrode's orders from the bridge inaudible to him, but he did hear the coxswain shout up the voice-pipe, 'The First Lieutenant already done that, sir!'

Slowly, slowly, almost reluctantly it seemed to Harding, the angle came off and the blowing stopped.

'Cap'n says to tell you "nice work", sir,' Ryland said.

Harding nodded, found to his embarrassment that he was still clutching the ladder, released it and gave the orders which would bring the ship to full buoyancy with the low pressure blower then said, 'Start the compressor. We must have used up a lot of HP air then.'

His legs felt wobbly and he moved to the chart table, leant on it pretending to examine the chart.

'Sir?'

'Yes, Cox'n?'

'What happened, sir? That felt a bit dicey to me, that did.'

'It's a thing called metacentric height, Cox'n. Or the lack of it.'

'What's that then, sir?'

Wishing that the coxswain had chosen some other time to ask questions Harding picked up a pencil and drew a circle on a sheet of paper.

'That's a cross-section of *Shadow*'s hull,' he said. 'That's the centre of buoyancy and that's the centre of gravity.' He put a dot near the top of the circle, another near its bottom and added, 'The distance between those marks is the metacentric height.'

'Yes, sir?'

'Well, the centre of buoyancy must be above the centre of gravity or the ship will roll over, and when our main ballast tanks are half flooded the two centres move very close together. That means that there is no righting moment, so if a big wave pushes us over at an angle we just stay there. It only ever happens in rough weather and it only happens to a submarine.' Harding paused for a moment before going on, 'Or a sinking ship of course, but that's what a submarine is, isn't it? A ship that sinks.'

'Gotcher, sir,' Chief Petty Officer Ryland said, but Harding didn't believe that he had understood either what he had just been told or how 'dicey' the incident had been. He checked that all was now in order and walked forward to the wardroom, a little troubled that Bulstrode had paid him a public compliment, not realizing that the captain was as prone to anxiety as he and had every right to express satisfaction when the need for anxiety was past.

Unobtrusively, Bulstrode continued to watch Harding and was pleased with what he saw. Harding had come down off the high plateau of elation he had reached on sinking his first ship to more level ground between it and the lowland of bewilderment he had inhabited following the attack by the U-boat. But, for all that, Bulstrode knew that his first lieutenant was no less tired and he hoped very much that they would be permitted a few days at Gibraltar before sailing with the convoy because he had plans for him there, plans made possible by *Shadow*'s fortuitous detachment from the 'Scrap-iron Ring'.

In his patrol report notes Bulstrode wrote, 'I instructed my first lieutenant to carry out the closing stages of the attack on this old ship, closely supervized by me, for reasons of training'. He looked at the written lie thoughtfully then, feeling the need to cover himself for his unprecedented action, added, 'It was virtually impossible for him to miss such a slow-moving target but, had he done so, it could readily have been overtaken and attacked again without surfacing'. He typed that section of the final report himself.

The storm forgotten, *Shadow* sailed through the Straits of Gibraltar into summer.

Enjoying the warmth of the sun on his back Harding stood for a moment on the quay watching the dockyard workmen filing aboard *Shadow* to repair the small damage to the main ballast tanks the defective torpedo had caused. It had been decided that that could be achieved without putting the ship into dock. That, he told himself, was Wright's problem anyway and looked down at the long list of things to be done he had recorded on the piece of paper he was holding. A hand reached from behind his shoulder and took it from him.

'You're relieved of all duties, Number One.'

He turned and faced Bulstrode.'

'What did you say, sir?'

'Oh, don't look so alarmed,' Bulstrode said. 'I've just been checking the leave records and you're way behind everybody. The convoy won't start to assemble for another three days yet they tell me, so I want you to push off until I send for you and don't give me that line about having nowhere to go. There's a room reserved for you at The Rock Hotel and bear in mind that in peace time people pay a lot of money to come to the Mediterranean, so be grateful for a free ticket. One more thing. If you say 'But, sir' I'll have you flogged round the Fleet.'

Harding pointed at the paper. 'There's a lot to be done, sir.'

'As long as it isn't technical and you haven't used any long words I can probably manage,' Bulstrode told him.

Ten minutes later, carrying a small suitcase and wearing his shore-going uniform Harding climbed the fore hatch ladder onto the casing.

'Going ashore, sir?'

He looked at the able seaman. 'If you've no objection, Mungo.'

'I do have one, sir. Look at your shoes.'

Harding looked at them. They were badly scratched and the black leather showed patchy white stains of salt.

Still puzzled and a little worried at being so abruptly sent off on leave he said irritably, 'Well, it's your job to clean the damn things.'

'How can I when you're always wearing them, sir? You was even sleeping in them during the storm. You're the only officer I ever met what's only got one pair of shoes.'

'Oh. Yes, I threw the others away, didn't I? The salt had rotted them.'

Mungo nodded and said, 'You sit down on the capstan and take 'em off, sir. I'll have 'em shone up in a jiffy.'

Obediently Harding did so, feeling silly sitting there in his socks with members of the crew grinning at him, but the incident had lightened his mood.

Shadow looked very small indeed to Harding from the window of the hotel bedroom, the little figures moving about on the casing unrecognizable. Forbidden by Bulstrode to put a foot inside the dockyard gate he was wondering what to do with so much spare time to which he had become totally unaccustomed when the telephone bell rang.

'Aha, I'm needed,' he said aloud. 'Too technical and too many long words.' Harding laughed and lifted the receiver.

'There's a Miss Bulstrode here to see you, sir,' it told him.

'I'll be right down,' he replied, paused, frowned and asked, 'Did you say *Miss* Bulstrode?' but the connection had already been cut.

She was tiny, with an eager, animated, elfin face. Pretty? Yes, but better than just pretty. Fun. The laughing eyes said so.

'Bill asked me to look after you.'

'Bill?'

'Bill Bulstrode. Your captain. Who else?'

'That's very kind. Very kind of you both.'

A flick of her fingers disclaimed kindness and she said, 'But looking after you doesn't include getting into your bed. I thought it would be best to make that clear so that . . . Oh, I'm sorry. I didn't meant to make you blush. Buy me a drink? Please?'

Harding walked with her to the bar, still blushing.

'What would you like, Miss Bulstrode?'

'Gin and ginger ale, please, and call me Agatha, or Aggie if you prefer.'

'Agatha?'

'That's right. Awful name, isn't it?'

'Not at all. I suppose you were named after his aunt.'

'No I wasn't,' she said. 'I *am* his aunt.'

Lack of expression in the small face contradicted by the laughing eyes. Harding gaping at her foolishly.

'But you're very old and very rich and . . . I mean she's very old and . . .'

'Go on.'

'I don't think I will,' Harding said. 'I'm a little confused, so I'll just order the drinks.'

When they were placed in front of them, 'The rotten bastard sort of invented me,' Agatha Bulstrode told him, grinned happily and clapped her hands together.

It was impossible not to grin back at her despite his now complete confusion, so he grinned and listened to her saying, 'He simply can't stand our silly name, all that de Vere Charnley stuff, so he made up this story about me cutting him out of my will if he didn't use it. I'll out-live the wretched man if it's the last thing I do and that shouldn't be difficult because I'm not much older than he is. Even if I don't, all he'll inherit will be my overdraft.' She nodded her head, her face a study in grim satisfaction, then went on, 'If you're puzzled about the "aunt" bit it's because I was an after-thought or a mistake, I've never been sure which, born twenty-one years after my brother who is Bill's father. All clear?'

'I'm just thinking it through.'

'Take your time. Now, what would you like to do this evening? The Admiral is throwing a cocktail party I could take you to if you'd like that. Say, "No, thank you very much".'

'No, thank you very much.'

'Hooray!' she said. 'We'll throw our own cocktail party for two and take it from there.'

She was a civilian something or other on the staff of the Governor. Harding never did find out what, but she gave him the happiest three days he could remember because everything they did together was fun, funny or both, all of it carried out at a breathless pace. From one hour to the next Harding was unable to forecast what, at her urging, he would be doing. As much of the great fortress of the Rock was explored as the military regulations permitted, Harding, clever with a pencil, sketched the famous apes for her, a boat was borrowed, houses opened their doors to her and to him because he was with her, people welcomed them into their groups, she made herself attractive for him, but never flirted, then, like Cinderella, at midnight she left him.

It took the sight from his bedroom window of the first ships of the convoy assembling in the harbour below to bring home to Harding the extent to which she had diverted his attention away from his job. A sense of pleasurable shock took hold of him with the realization that for the first time since he had originally stepped aboard at Rosyth all those many months ago he hadn't given *Shadow* a thought.

Of his feeling of physical desire for Agatha Bulstrode there was no question, and he knew himself to be at least a little in love with her, but neither condition worried him unduly. She had laid down the ground-rules within ten seconds of their meeting and it had never occurred to him to attempt to transgress them. That she was ten years older than he made her fascinatingly mysterious, but placed her beyond any practical reach.

Apart from the dance floor, and being dragged through tunnels in the Rock by the hand on some apparently urgent mission to the other side, there had been no physical contact between them. That made the gentle kiss on the mouth she gave him when he had to return to his ship something special to remember.

His attempt to thank her was cut off by the words, 'Look after Bill for me. You're so right for him.' Not entirely sure what she meant by that it still made him rather proud.

'Hello, Number One. You're looking fit.'

Harding saluted. 'Yes, sir, I feel it, and – er – thank you, sir. Thank you very much indeed.'

'She would even have cheered up Diogenes, wouldn't she?'

'She certainly would.'

'Number One, would it be asking too much . . .'

'Don't worry, sir,' Harding broke in, 'Your slanders are safe with me.'

Over lunch in the wardroom, 'We hear you've met the Captain's aunt, Number One,' Gascoigne said. 'What's she *really* like?'

'She's a very nice old lady,' Harding told him. 'One of the last of the *grande dames*. She liked me pushing her around in her wheel-chair.'

'Really? The piece I saw you with yesterday looked more likely to put *you* in a wheel-chair inside a week. You were laughing too much at something to notice me across the street.'

'Oh yes,' Harding said. 'That's Felicity, her companion. She's nice too.'

Bulstrode smiled faintly, but didn't speak.

Chapter 18

There were nineteen masters of merchant ships and nearly the same number of naval officers at the convoy conference. Harding was sitting next to Bulstrode in the back row.

The commander who was operations staff officer to Flag Officer Gibraltar said, 'I think that about wraps it up, gentlemen. Any more questions?'

Bulstrode stood up. 'I don't have any questions, sir, but I'd like to make a suggestion. Two, in fact.'

'Fire away, Bill.'

'If, sir,' Bulstrode said, 'the convoy scatters at the first sight of an enemy heavy unit as it has been ordered to do, that will make my presence pretty useless as there is no way of telling which part of it the enemy will decide to attack. I haven't got the speed to chase thirty-knot cruisers around the Atlantic.'

'So what do you suggest?'

'That I dive where I am and that the convoy turns stern on to the enemy and runs for it, still in formation at first, then gradually beginning to disperse. That should draw the enemy right over my position. I'm talking of daytime of course.'

'Bloody hell, man,' one of the merchant captains said, 'you'd be making them a present of the whole damned convoy!'

'Not if I sink the thing I wouldn't,' Bulstrode answered and conversation buzzed throughout the big room, one voice rising above it saying, 'Our job is to transport war materials, not act as bait for the bloody Navy, for God's sake!'

The hubbub subsided slowly when a tall elderly man rose from the front row and turned to face the gathering. He was a vice-admiral who had come out of retirement to offer his services in the much more junior capacity of convoy commodore.

'I think the submarine commander is right,' he said. 'Unless

183

we can provide him with the opportunity of taking successful offensive action there is little point in his accompanying us. In fact, he would be placing his own ship at risk to no purpose by doing so.'

'Then let the bugger stay behind!'

'We've got the destroyers to look after us.'

'Yes, who needs the thing? I can't tell the difference between it and a U-boat and my gunners won't stop to ask questions!'

Voices from various parts of the room.

'Gentlemen, please!' the commodore said and waited until he had their attention before going on, 'We aren't the only convoy, you know. We are simply one that is privileged to have with it a weapon powerful enough to destroy a German capital ship. I think we owe it to all the other convoys to give the weapon a chance to do just that.'

Eventually it was agreed, but the feeling of hostility emanating from the civilian sailors towards Bulstrode and Harding was a tangible thing.

'You had another suggestion, Bill.'

'Yes, sir,' Bulstrode said the operations officer. 'I assume that the harbour here is under observation by German agents in Algeciras across the bay. If that's so it would be showing our hand if I were to sail with the convoy. I'd rather leave at once and rendezvous with it out of sight of land.'

The other nodded and replied, 'Your assumption is correct and the matter had been taken care of in your written orders. I have them here for you. Thank you, gentlemen. That's all.'

Harding hated it and, watching his captain look gloomily round at the mass of lumbering surface ships, so, he thought, did Bulstrode.

'God, how I hate this, Number One,' Bulstrode said and that made Harding smile.

'So do I, sir. They don't want us here, we don't want to be here and it feels all wrong anyway. I wish we were off on our own somewhere.'

'Like the Mediterranean where it's all happening,' Bulstrode agreed.

The triple column of ships with its screen of destroyers and smaller anti-submarine escorts moved ponderously north with *Shadow*, the centre ship of the centre column, hemmed in as no submarine was meant to be. In the darkness, station-keeping by the merchantmen was poor, bringing with it the risk of being rammed from either side, from astern or of running into the ship ahead when, as happened twice, its engine failed. Each dawn escort vessels sped about like sheep-dogs urging stragglers to regain their correct positions in the flock. Throughout the hours of daylight the signal most often directed by the commodore at one culprit after another was 'Make less smoke'. More often than not the culprits couldn't do much about the black plumes streaming from their funnels. They did not possess the equipment which enabled the destroyers so finely to balance the mixture of air and oil fed to their boilers that only a haze of heat appeared above their smoke-stacks. But the commodore had to force them to try because the smoke was a banner proclaiming the convoy's position.

No surface raiders sighted the tell-tale clouds of combustion products, but the U-boats did and, on the fourth night, they struck with vicious efficiency.

It began at seventeen minutes past one in the morning. Harding was on watch.

'Faint flash of light starboard beam, sir,' Able Seaman Ryan said and before he could train his binoculars on the bearing the boom of an explosion reached Harding's ears across the water.

'Cap'n to the bridge sound the alarm,' Harding told the voice-pipe. It came out as one sentence.

Another detonation from the starboard quarter and a third from somewhere to port. Ryan saying, 'Ship burning starboard beam, sir.' Bulstrode arriving at Harding's side panting slightly after his rapid ascent of the conning tower ladder. Harding telling him, 'Two ships hit to starboard and one to port, sir, I think.' Bulstrode replying, 'I see.'

The ship on the starboard beam beginning to burn brightly now, illuminating those near it. The deep-throated bellow of the commodore's siren ordering an emergency turn to port. Harding supposing that he had done that either to get away from the light from the burning ship, or on the assumption that on a two to one basis the main attack was coming from the convoy's starboard side. Intense alarm blotting out further conjecture with the ship immediately ahead erupting into flame. Bulstrode giving rapid manoeuvring orders. A big freighter turning the wrong way narrowly avoided, its side towering above *Shadow* like a factory wall. A brilliant necklace of star-shells from a destroyer's guns high above, banishing the night, for concealment was no longer a factor to be considered and it would help to drive the surfaced U-boats under water. One of them briefly sighted submerging with columns of water thrown skyward by 4.7-inch shells all round it.

'I think he's got the right idea,' Bulstrode said. 'Clear the bridge. Dive, dive, dive.'

Harding had never heard the sea so alive with the sound of ships. It required no assistance from Topham's sonar earphones to listen to the propellers of the convoy churning overhead.

'Sorry, sir, can't tell you nothing definite,' Topham said. 'Loud hydrophone effect all round. It's swamping out everything. Reciprocating engines they are.'

Bulstrode nodded. 'Keep listening and let me know at once if you identify turbines, or hear sonar transmissions.'

The depth-charging started then. It was not directed at *Shadow*, but the concussions made her hull quiver and hum.

'Three hundred feet, sir,' Harding told Bulstrode.

'Very well. That'll do for now. Hand me that microphone.' Bulstrode took it and spoke into it. 'This is the Captain speaking. I'm sorry for having placed you in the position of possibly being depth-charged by our own side, but it was getting a bit hairy up there and I prefer that risk to being torpedoed, shelled or rammed by any of the people milling around up top in an excitable condition. With any luck most of the escorts will stick close to the convoy, so we may not have any trouble from them. Now, I want complete silence throughout the boat and we'll try to make ourselves scarce until they've sorted themselves out. That's all.'

'Hydrophone effect all to port of us now, sir. Mostly reciprocating, some fast turbine. About eight sonar transmission sources, all of them sweeping, sir. No contact with us.'

'Thank you, Topham.'

Fifteen cracking explosions in three patterns of five, not close. Five more two minutes later, then the depth-charging becoming desultory, receding.

'Can't 'old 'er at this depth, sir,' Chief Petty Officer Ryland said.

Harding had been aware for some minutes that the upward thrust of the hydroplanes set at full rise was insufficient to counteract *Shadow*'s increased weight. It had intrigued him when he had first learned that a submarine became smaller as it went deeper below the surface. The decrease in size was barely measurable, almost microscopic, but taken over its entire surface it was sufficient to reduce its displacement and therefore make it relatively heavier than the surrounding water. It took a lot of pressure to do that but, at 300 feet, there *was* a lot of pressure, ten atmospheres of it. He looked at the captain.

'I'll either have to pump or speed up, sir.'

'Pump,' Bulstrode told him. 'We may be down here all night.'

At such a depth it took time for the ballast pump to expel enough water to give *Shadow* neutral buoyancy again, quite enough time for the destroyer lying stopped and listening on the surface far above to register the sound by sonar and take a bearing on it.

Acting Petty Officer Topham got a bearing too. 'Sonar transmissions and slow hydrophone effect on Red 125, sir,' he said. 'Turbine, I think. Yes, turbine and speeding up.'

'Is he in contact?' Bulstrode asked.

'No, sir, but he knows roughly where we are. Sweeping over a narrow arc to either side of us he is.'

Bulstrode muttered, 'Crafty bastard lying doggo like that.' Then he raised his voice. 'If he goes over to a passive listening watch, Topham, transmit "*Shadow* to destroyer – kindly fuck off". Don't check with me, just send that message the first chance you get.'

'Aye aye, sir,' Topham said and grinned.

But there was nothing amusing about the period that followed. The quarter of an hour seemed an eternity to Harding, an eternity of being locked in a dark room with a blind man who might or might not be a homicidal maniac, who might or might not pause to differentiate between friend and foe. The blind man appeared to be partially deaf too, not hearing sufficiently well to enable him to strike out at *Shadow*, but hearing well enough to keep him close, very close, groping constantly with electronic fingers, stopping, starting again, turning this way and that, following wherever the submarine went in the black cavern of the night sea.

Twice the destroyer passed directly overhead, the thrashing of its screws clearly audible to everyone aboard *Shadow*. The first time it did it slowly, too slowly to presage an attack because its charges would have exploded almost directly under it. But the second run was fast and, although there had been no firm sonar contact, Harding was conscious of the tenseness of the figures around him, aware of the rigidity of his own muscles as imagination followed the big grey cylinders down through the water to their points of detonation. There were no cylinders, no detonations. He glanced at Bulstrode.

'Do you suppose they've got gremlins in their sonar set, sir?'

Bulstrode shrugged. 'I doubt it, Number One. It's more likely that there are water temperature variations around here distorting their echoes and, anyway, they must be unsure whether we're us or a U-boat.'

Again the noise of propellers above their heads, again the waiting, again nothing happened.

'Almost be a relief if they dropped a depth-charge or two, sir.'

Turning to face the speaker Bulstrode said, 'Don't be obscene, Gascoigne. I've had occasion to remark before on the extreme discomfort such activities induce in my sinuses. Is it too much to expect a little charity from . . .?'

188

He stopped talking at the sudden clicking of Topham's transmitter key, watching him intently.

'Message acknowledged, sir. He went over to listening watch, so I transmitted like you said. He gave me an "R" in reply.'

'Well done, Topham. Listen out for what happens next.'

For two hours Topham listened and reported on the destroyer's movements. Immediately on receipt of *Shadow*'s signal it had retired at high speed, the sound of its progress diminishing on the starboard beam. There, some distance away, it had set up a new search pattern, its sonar probing in a constant all-round sweep. Then, as though in a gesture of defiance, it released a pattern of three depth-charges before withdrawing rapidly to the north in pursuit of the convoy.

When its presence was no longer to be heard Bulstrode nodded as if satisfied about something, but when Harding asked him if they should prepare to surface he had shaken his head and it was not until day was close that *Shadow* began to glide slowly upwards.

The periscope showed them the life-boats in the half-light of early dawn, two of them with about twenty men in each.

'Are you going to take them aboard, sir?' Harding asked.

'No,' the captain said. He seemed withdrawn, preoccupied. Harding looked at him and away again, wondering why the small, gentle man should so casually deny his own countrymen their best chance of life. It was not, he knew, because the presence of the survivors would make the submarine almost impossibly crowded. Three minutes later the reason was clear to him.

'Loud noise bearing Red 170, sir!' Topham announced, his voice sharp. 'Sounds like a submarine blowing main ballast!'

Bulstrode jerked the periscope round onto the bearing.

'Still blowing, Topham?'

'Yes, sir! No, sir! Stopped this second Wait! There it goes again!'

Later Bulstrode was to say to Harding. 'They looked like three rubber ducks popping out of the bath water, Number One. Then at the second look the resemblance was more to three loping wolves, so I had obviously gone into one of my poetic phases.' But that *was* later. Now there was no levity, only a heightened concentration. It was visible to Harding in the set of the shoulders of the coxswain and his second coxswain at the hydroplane controls and Mungo's at the steering wheel, in Gascoigne's stance by the 'Fruit Machine' and Unwin's at the chart table readying his pencils, dividers and parallel ruler. He could see it, too, in the whiteness of the knuckles of Bulstrode's fingers gripping the periscope handles and feel it in himself with every tiny fluctuation of the depth-gauge needles something to be regarded with grave suspicion because not for an instant must he unsight his captain by allowing the periscope's upper lens to dip under water.

Suddenly, 'Stand by all tubes,' Bulstrode said. 'Port 20. Steer 270. Set masthead height as for a U-boat conning tower. Start the attack. Bearing is that. Range is that. I am 40 degrees on their starboard bow. Down periscope.'

Quiet voices answering him, acknowledging his orders, relaying the information he had given, Gascoigne saying, 'Range 3,700 yards, sir, and distance off track 3,400,' Bulstrode ordering *Shadow* deep at full speed, the hull beginning to tremble at the urging of the propellers, the depth-gauge pointers moving slowly round the dial, Harding's excitement growing at the captain's next words.

'It worked, Number One. There are three of them up there in line abreast, trailing the convoy on the surface ready for tonight. At least I can't imagine what else they're doing. That's why I've been hanging around back here, waiting for them to regroup. They haven't suspected our presence as part of the escort.' Bulstrode frowned before adding, 'Or it will have worked if I can hit one of the bastards.'

Shadow surging upwards, slowing before she reached periscope depth, Bulstrode giving more bearings, more ranges, more estimates of angles on the bow which indicated the enemy's course, the picture growing clearer as the minutes passed. The U-boats were idling, little more than matching their speed to the plodding advance of the ships beyond the horizon, not wanting to get too close to a target they had savaged the night before until later in the day, knowing that the convoy's smoke would be in sight before darkness fell leaving ample time to close in for their second assault. Because of their slow rate of advance the nearest U-boat was within eight hundred yards when Bulstrode fired the first of six torpedoes.

Hands clasped behind his back Harding stood, eyes constantly moving from depth-gauge to hydroplane indicator to inclinometer, alert for the first sign that the loss of the weight of the torpedoes might cause *Shadow* to rise and reveal her presence to the enemy, his lips ready-formed to give the order 'Flood Q'.

The downward thrust the flooding of the emergency quick-diving tank would have given was not needed, but so intense was Harding's concentration on maintaining the ship's stability that the few seconds it took a torpedo travelling at close to fifty miles an hour to cover the short distance to its objective passed unnoticed by him. The slamming concussion of the exploding torpedo warhead caught him so much by surprise that he jerked visibly, then glanced at Bulstrode in rueful embarrassment, but the captain had eyes only for the periscope rising out of its well. Crouching low, he was staring through the binocular viewer almost as soon as it lifted above deck-level.

'Write down time and add "First U-boat struck amidships and sinking in two halves",' he said. ' "Both bow and stern pointing skywards".' Then he murmured, 'Looks like Churchill giving the V sign.'

Able Seaman Ryan keeping the record of the attack, wrote it all down including the bit about Churchill.

' "Second and third U-boats turning away",' Bulstrode went on. ' "They have . . ." '

Shadow jolted and shuddered as the shock wave hit her, sending men reeling, cannoning into each other, clutching for support. Harding grasped the ladder leading up to the conning tower. Gascoigne measured his full length on the control room deck, then staggered upright cursing softly, massaging an arm. Bulstrode used his sleeve to wipe blood from a small cut where his forehead had hit the periscope before returning his attention to the eye pieces and his commentary.

'Note time and add "Second U-boat disintegrated. Presume struck in bow causing sympathetic detonation of its own torpedoes. Third U-boat submerging steering roughly west". That's all.' He turned to Harding. 'All right, Number One, let's surface and get the hell out of here.'

Shadow surfaced and raced north, her diesels thundering at maximum revolutions, spray from her curling bow wave lifted by the wind and hurled across the bridge like a horizontal rain-storm. By noon the convoy's pall of smoke was visible ahead, two hours later a forest of masts could be distinguished by eyes slitted against the air's watery assault then, at last, the ships were hull up above the horizon and within signal lamp range.

To the signalman Bulstrode said, 'Make as I speak, "To Commodore from *Shadow* . . . two U-boats torpedoed and sunk at dawn . . . in area of last night's attack . . . Third U-boat undamaged and will presumably resume pursuit . . . Two life-boats with some forty survivors . . . in same position . . . Message ends".'

Beside him the Aldis lamp ceased its staccato clatter only seconds after he had finished talking and less than a minute passed before a light began blinking again from the bridge of the commodore's ship.

'Reply from Commodore, sir,' the signalman said. ' "Well done indeed and welcome back. We thought we had lost you. Am requesting senior officer of escort to despatch corvette to pick up survivors".'

Bulstrode had read it himself, but thanked him anyway.

There was a lot of cheering, waving and blowing of sirens when *Shadow* ran between the starboard and centre columns of ships, shorter columns now, to resume her station in the middle of the convoy.

Harding grinned at Bulstrode. 'They seem to have changed their minds about us, sir.'

'Yes,' Bulstrode said, 'but you mustn't blame them for their original attitude. They have a rotten, thankless, dangerous task with no glamour attached to it at all and to them we symbolize everything that makes their task a rotten dangerous one. I didn't enjoy last night's ten minute experience of what they have to put up with month after month after month and I'm not exactly looking forward to tonight either.'

But no U-boat attacked that night or on the succeeding ones and when the convoy moved within range of RAF air cover *Shadow* was instructed to return to her position in the 'Scrap-iron Ring' around Brest where the German battle-cruisers still lay.

Nobody on board was sorry about that. Not at the time.

Chapter 19

Ushant, Douarnanez, Le Conquet, Chaussée de Sein. Harding came to loathe the names, the racking boredom they represented, the unremitting vigilance they demanded, the chances of worthwhile positive action they utterly failed to provide. The battle-cruisers remained static in Brest and the knowledge that it was the presence of *Shadow* and others like her which kept them there immobilized, impotent, through endlessly dragging weeks was small consolation to him.

Devonport, where they spent the periods between patrols, held little for him either except for the first bath on returning ashore. That was a thing beyond price, an hour of wallowing, of scrubbing dead skin, untouched either by soap and water or the sun for so long, from his body. Nearly as valuable was the knowledge that he could sleep a whole night through without being called to relieve Gascoigne on watch, but that pleasure was lessened for him by land sounds to which his ears were no longer attuned transmitting some imagined emergency to his brain and jerking him awake.

The news from the Mediterranean where, despite heavy losses, British submarines were wreaking havoc upon enemy shipping, only served to increase his frustration. Given the best of all possible worlds Harding would have elected to go there, with a call at Gibraltar to see his captain's captivating aunt again.

During the months it had taken to turn summer into autumn and autumn into winter he found only four events memorable. The torpedoing of a ship flying the Spanish flag which was on the 'wanted' list as a German blockade runner, a heavy depth-charging by a destroyer in the confined waters of the Iroise, the destruction by gun-fire of an anti-submarine trawler which had tried to emulate it off Cap de la Chèvre on the following patrol, and Edna Mungo's pregnancy.

On an October day in Devonport Chief Petty Officer Ryland had come to him.

'Able Seaman Mungo requests to see you privately, sir.'

'Oh, does he? Well, he can't see me privately in this crowd, Cox'n,' Harding had said and looked at his watch. 'Tell him I'll be on the jetty in ten minutes from now.'

'Aye aye, sir.'

He had found Mungo standing rigidly to attention at the end of the gangway and returned his salute.

'Able Seaman Mungo reporting, sir!'

'All right, Mungo. This isn't a parade ground and I didn't send for you. *You* wanted to see *me.*'

'Yessir!'

'Fine, well relax and . . . Oh look, let's stroll along here while you tell me what's on your mind.'

They had gone several paces before Mungo said, 'Edna and me's going to have a baby, sir,' and flushed as though admitting to something improper.

Genuinely pleased Harding had told him so and shaken him by the hand.

'Thank you, sir. Sir?'

'Yes?'

'We was wondering, sir . . . we was wondering if you would be a godfather, sir.'

'Me? Why me, Mungo?'

'Because, sir,' Mungo had told him in a firm voice, 'If it weren't for you there wouldn't be no baby and there wouldn't be no marriage.'

194

Harding had felt that that left him with no option but to accept the responsibility.

Another month went by before the longed for news arrived and *Shadow* left the area off Brest for the last time. 'Proceed Portsmouth for refit and leave prior departure Mediterranean theatre' the deciphered signal read. Morale soared.

In the wardroom mess at Fort Blockhouse near the mouth of Portsmouth Harbour Bulstrode said, 'There's to be no non-sense about leave from you, Number One. You're to go with the first batch. Understood?'

Harding nodded, smiling. 'Don't worry, sir. I've already told my parents we're back and they're expecting me. After I've taken the ship across to the dockyard tomorrow I'll push straight off to London.'

'Good. By the way, Sarah's down here. We're staying at the Queens. Would you care to dine with us this evening?'

'Yes, I certainly would, sir. Thank you.'

'Excellent. Make your own way there about seven, would you? I've got to see Captain Submarines outside my union hours, but I shouldn't be more than forty-five minutes behind you.'

It was very pleasant, Harding thought, to see the tubby smiling lady again, to take both her hands in his and stoop to kiss her cheek.

'Hello, Peter dear.'

'Hello, Sarah. I'm afraid I'm here under false pretences. The Captain . . . I mean Bill won't be along until about quarter to eight.'

'I know. He telephoned. Let's go to the bar and get a flying start on him.'

Peering suspiciously at the little pools of liquid in the two glasses set before them Harding said, 'War or no war this is ridiculous,' pushed the drinks back across the bar and added to the barman, 'The lady wishes to get a flying start on her husband. It would take her all night to get air-borne at all at that rate. Make those doubles, please.'

Beside him Sarah Bulstrode chuckled. 'Wouldn't be much help on an "alcoholiday", would they?'

He looked at her. 'You know about those?'

'Of course. And your part in them. Married couples do tell each other things, for goodness sake.'

'Oh dear,' said Harding.

'No "Oh dear" about it. You took care of him beautifully. I'm as grateful as Bill was.'

Harding shrugged. 'It was like magic after you arrived on the scene. Regardless of where you were it never happened again.'

'I know,' she said, 'but it's sweet of you to put it that way.'

Vaguely troubled by the course the conversation had taken Harding felt himself stiffen when she went on, 'Talking of married couples telling each other things, would you tell me something he won't? Or can't?'

Not prepared to commit himself, wondering what in the world was coming, he raised his eyebrows enquiringly, not speaking.

Sarah Bulstrode noted his guarded reaction, touched his hand with her finger-tips, and spoke quickly. 'Oh, Peter, it's nothing awful. It's just that I'm wondering why they haven't given him a medal. Why they haven't given *you* a medal. I know there are lots more glamorous submarines, but *Shadow* hasn't done badly when you add it all up, has she? I would have thought *some* recognition was merited.'

Harding relaxed a little and said, 'The same thing has occurred to me and I think I know the answer. I think he's being punished.'

'Punished? What on earth for?'

'Something that happened in Norway.'

'Oh, Peter. What happened in Norway?' A small, anxious voice.

His expression grave Harding said, 'He got angry, lost his temper and his sense of proportion with the result that he placed the ship at risk for a trifling return. One of the basic rules of submarining is that you never allow yourself to get excited or lose your temper, and he broke it. There was talk of a court of enquiry and even a court-martial, but they decided to let him off with an official reprimand. Actually, he should have been shot.'

Unable to look at her Harding sipped his drink and heard her say in a fiercely cold tone, 'I never imagined that you could be so contemptible as to sit in judgement on your betters. Now, if you'll excuse me, I . . .'

Harding snorted, spraying the bar surface with fine droplets of gin, the sound so explosive that heads turned in their direction. He groped for a handkerchief, choked and blew his nose before saying tremulously, 'I'm quoting *him*, Sarah. They're your husband's words I'm making you a gift of. Don't blame me.' Laughter shook him and it was several seconds before he sobered and said, 'Oh dear me. I enjoyed that. Still, to be serious, I gather they were a bit annoyed with him and are probably making him wait. But don't worry. He'll get his medal. They can't just ignore the sinking of two U-boats and all the rest. Let's have another drink. I did the nose trick with most of mine.'

'Peter Harding!'

'Yes, Sarah Bulstrode?'

'If you don't tell me at once what happened in Norway, I shall remove your vital organs one after the other without benefit of anaesthetic!'

She listened, unmoving, while he told her of the mission, of the landing of the Norwegian men and the elderly Norwegian woman, of the hangings and of Bulstrode's reaction to them, of the retribution he had exacted and the Viking's funeral he had engineered.

When he had finished, 'I'd like that drink now, Peter,' she said.

'Hello, you two. What have you been talking about?'

They turned to Bulstrode.

'Organs, sir, and their removal. All of them,' Harding said.

Bulstrode looked at his wife. 'Has he been drinking?'

'Strangely enough, no,' she said. 'He seems to prefer pouring it into his mouth and expelling it through the nostrils. If you'll buy another round I'm sure he'll show you how he does it.'

Harding saw their fingers entwine and the look of gentle pride in Sarah Bulstrode's eyes. He looked away, knowing that, for a moment, his existence was forgotten, content that it should be so.

Chapter 20

The wave of humanity cascading from the Portsmouth train carried Harding with it into the sea already present on platform number whatever it was at Waterloo Station in London. Clutching his suitcase he began to work his way towards the ticket barrier, not minding the throng. For the next few days he had nothing to do but be spoiled by his parents, nothing he had to hurry for, nothing he had to organize or plan. It was a pleasant prospect. Not exciting, but pleasant, and one that he had faced hardly at all in more than two years of war. Slowly he moved forward through a crowd made faceless by the black-out.

Near the bottle-neck of the barrier, ' ''Ello, sir. Take station astern of me. I'll act as ice-breaker through this lot.'

Harding laughed. 'Full ahead, Cox'n.'

'Full ahead it is, sir,' Chief Petty Officer Ryland said.

Progress was faster after that.

There was more space on the long forecourt fronting the platforms and a group of *Shadow*'s people had formed.

'Hello, Amersham. Hello Lloyd. Ryan. Dunsmore. Prentiss. Hello Mungo.'

'Hello, sir,' they all replied, grinning, delighted to be in the big city with its abundance of women and beer.

'Ah, Petty Officer Proctor too. The Ryland-Proctor combination. What are you and the Coxswain aiming to do?'

'Straight across the river to the nearest boozer, sir. Not much fun south of the Thames.'

'Good for you,' Harding said. 'I'm going to the Regent's Park area. Anybody want a lift in that direction?'

Mungo did. 'Edna and my mum was bombed out at Bethnal Green and moved to Euston,' he told Harding.

The 'alert' sounded as their taxi was crossing Waterloo Bridge, a solitary siren wailing its slow oscillating dirge away to the east of them. A second, a third, a fourth, picking up its message, proclaiming it to the dome of the night and the teaming millions below. Others followed until from horizon to horizon the air trembled to their lament. He had heard it often enough before, but to Harding the sound was the eeriest, most stirring he was ever likely to listen to.

''Ere we go again,' the taxi-driver said.

The first searchlight reached above the buildings as they approached the Strand and another leapt to meet it like a swordsman engaging another's blade. Then the sky was full of them, swaying, steadying, focussing on individual points. The bark of anti-aircraft guns, distant yet, and shell-bursts living briefly like fire-flies near the intersection of the beams. The gunfire coming closer, the taxi quivering in sympathy with the shuddering earth. When they were driving fast along Tottenham Court Road the guns fell abruptly silent.

Knowledgeably, 'They've put up night-fighters,' the taxi-driver said and, as if to bear him out, an invisible plane became visible as an expanding ball of flame, a ball which tossed parts of itself earthwards in glowing streamers before it faded into nothingness.

The bombs came then and Harding guessed that they were aimed at the main-line railway stations of King's Cross, St Pancras and Euston, but didn't say so for Mungo's sake.

Warren Street tube station was to their left when the blast of hot gas hit them, slewing the taxi through sixty degrees, stopping it thirty yards short of a gaping crater in the road, a crater which, seconds before, hadn't existed.

'Fuckin' 'ell!' the taxi driver said and Harding heard himself say, 'Out! Everybody out and get down the stairs to the tube!'

He was running fast, avoiding the crater, sprinting across the Euston Road towards Regent's Park and the street in which his parents lived, where he knew they were now because he had spoken to them on the telephone from Waterloo before he and Mungo had found the vacant taxi. Something was impeding him, bumping repeatedly against the side of his leg, and that couldn't be allowed to continue. The bomb which had halted the taxi had been the first of a stick of them and he had seen the direction which the rest had taken. Angrily he looked down to see what was hitting his leg, realized that he was still carrying his suitcase and threw it from him with a curse. After that he ran faster, but didn't hear the footsteps pounding behind him, matching his own.

The guns started again then and he supposed that the nightfighters had made their run, made their solitary kill, and passed on to new targets. Beneath his driving feet the ground resumed its shuddering, drifting smoke thickened around him irritating his already bursting lungs, making him choke, gasp. He ran on, the night ahead turning bright orange. When he reached it it was as though he had known from the beginning that it was his parent's street, his street, which had been hit. There was no surprise in him at the sight of the fiercely burning row of broken houses, just a cold rage.

They had been quick, the ambulances, the firemen, the figures in shiny black coats with yellow markings wielding picks and crowbars, the heavy-rescue vehicles ploughing their way forward through and over piles of rubble. Harding swerving round groups, dodging individuals, jumping over hoses that twisted and writhed like scotched snakes, still unaware of the man at his heels.

Ahead a hastily erected barrier bearing the message 'Danger UXB!' and a policeman beside it shouting at him, waving his arms. Harding checking his stride to vault the obstruction and crashing to the ground under the policeman's flying rugby tackle.

'What are you trying to do, you bloody young fool? There's an unexploded bomb there! Can't you read?'

'My parents . . .'

'There's nobody alive in those buildings! Not a hope! You just . . .'

The sentence cut short, a sailor with an arm round the policeman's neck dragging him off Harding. Mungo, panting harshly, saying, 'If my officer wants to go through there, that's where he's fucking going!' The policeman hurled aside. Both of them running, the barrier splintering at their charge.

'Which house, sir?'

'That one!'

The night split open by thunder beyond hearing. A gale lifting him, dropping him. A wall leaning, falling.

'*Mungo!*'

Harding stood slowly upright, brushing absently at the white dust covering his uniform, unaware that it was drifting in the air all about him, resettling as he brushed. He was only dimly conscious of the flame-lit street, the noise, and of the heat from the fires. Then a hand clamped down on his shoulder, spinning him around, the angry face of a steel-helmeted policeman thrust within inches of his own, a face he had last seen with it's eyes bulging from the pressure of Mungo's neck-lock.

'Ah! so it *is* you, sir. Right! Let's be having that sailor of yours for a start. We're taking him in charge!'

There was a second, younger policeman behind the man's left shoulder. Harding's gaze rested on him without interest for a moment, then focussed on the jets of water arcing from the fire appliances to play on his parent's funeral pyre. Much of the water seemed to be vaporizing before it reached its destination.

Without looking at the speaker, 'Yes,' he said. 'Well, some-body better.' He shook off the restraining hand, gestured towards the section of demolished wall resting on the crushed body of Able Seaman Mungo and added. 'You know some-thing? He never did get his teeth fixed.'

The policemen watched him go, then looked at each other.

'Shall I follow him for a bit, Jim? I think he's in shock.'

'Yes,' the older man replied. 'If necessary take him across to one of the ambulances and – No, it's all right. He's been taken in tow already.'

Harding was crying. Whether he was doing it for his parents, for Mungo, for Edna Mungo and her unborn child, or for himself he didn't know. He was just crying.

'Hey, easy, sailor. Take it easy, you hear?' A quiet, slightly nasal voice and a hand on his arm. Girl. Pretty too. That was obvious despite the dirt-streaked face, torn white raincoat and dusty tangled hair. He walked on with tears tracing paths through the grime on his cheeks. The ground trembling under his feet again from the concussion of the anti-aircraft guns not recorded.

'Listen, I think you'd better come home with mama.'

Words registered. *Fury.* 'Who the bloody hell are you? The proverbial golden-hearted tart?'

'If you say so. Just come, that's all. In case you hadn't noticed, it's raining shrapnel all over.'

The snap, click and clatter of metal dropping about them. Heard that. Heard too the growing screaming wail of more falling bombs. Reaction instinctive. Thrust girl to ground. Cover her body with his own. The heavy crump – crump – crump – crump of bombs exploding a street or two away. The rumble of collapsing masonry.

'I never knew you British were so passionate.'

'Oh don't be so *damned* stupid!' Harding shouted then, suddenly, he was back inside himself, the rigidity flowing from him, aware that his face was buried in the side of her neck, held there by her fingers interlaced behind his head.

She must have felt the relaxation of his muscles. 'That's better,' she told him. 'Thanks for the protection, but we should get away from here before they arrest us for indecent behaviour. Anyway I prefer watching battles from a distance.'

Harding levered himself off her, pulled her upright and they ran, hand in hand, until they found a public air raid shelter. He didn't look back at the burning street where his parents and Mungo had died.

It was crowded, the shelter, but Harding found a narrow space on a bench against a wall, forced himself into it and drew the girl down onto his knees.

'I'm Peter Harding,' he said.

'Lee Lawrence.'

'American?'

'Yes.'

'I'm very grateful to you for pulling me together out there.'

'My pleasure. What happened?'

'It's a bit difficult to explain. I wouldn't know where to start.'

'Then start at the beginning,' Lee Lawrence said. 'That usually makes it easier, even if it is a cliché.'

Harding didn't start at the beginning, but he told her what he thought to be the salient points ending with the deaths which had occurred a few minutes before they had met. It was nice telling her, nice to share the load. It was nicer still when she half turned on his lap, put her arms around him and whispered, 'Oh baby.'

They sat like that for a long time, feeling the shelter tremble beneath the blast of high-explosives, hearing the overly cheerful talk of the people and the frightened whimperings of a child. Harding's legs had gone dead under the girl's weight, but he didn't mind that with her finger-tips kneading the nape of his neck and her breath playing softly on his ear.

A stunning explosion, the bench beneath them jumping and the shelter plunged into darkness. Another, and pieces of ceiling dropping about them. People crying out in fear and children screaming. The girl gasping and jerking round, sitting with her back to him as though she were facing some adversary and he were a wall. He putting a protective arm around her, his hand settling on her left breast, having his wrist grasped and drawn aside. Hearing himself murmur 'Sorry,' and her fiercely whispered reply, 'Don't go apologetic on me! This is getting really *scary* and *I* need some comforting now!' Then his hand being guided inside her raincoat, inside her dress, back to her breast. His other wrist sought, found and crossed over the first.

'Oh hell,' Harding said. He thought he had only breathed the words, but heard her say, 'That's what war is, buster. If I've given you such a tough assignment just grit your teeth and hold me until the RAF gets around to driving those Krauts off. Maybe you'll get a medal for it.'

Excited, disturbed, he held her while the bombardment

waned, kept doing it when her head fell back onto his shoulder and she slept, was still doing it when, just before dawn, the monotone banshee wail of the sirens announced the 'all clear'.

There were several big fires to look at when they left the shelter together, walking slowly, listening to everybody telling everybody else that it had been the worst raid since the main blitz of the winter before.

Shy now that they could see each other again by the light of the burning buildings, 'Shall we try to find some breakfast somewhere, Miss Lawrence?' Harding asked.

She looked at him wide-eyed and said, 'Oh my God! It's all true! Only the British could fondle a girl's tits all night and call her "Miss Lawrence" in the morning. Wait till I tell them that one back home.' Then she gave him a lop-sided grin and added, 'I'll take a rain check on breakfast. I have to get to work. There's copy to file and a deadline to meet.'

'Copy? Are you a journalist?'

'Yes, a war correspondent working for AP. I do a bit of moonlighting for *The New Yorker* magazine as well, but I can be free by tonight if you want. Or do you have to go back to your ship?'

'No, I don't. I was going on leave when . . . Where shall I meet you for dinner?'

For a long moment she watched his face in the flickering light of the fires, then took a notebook from her bag, scribbled an address in it, tore out the page and gave it to him.

'There,' she said. 'I'll cook it for you. Come at seven.'

He watched her walk away, torn raincoat flapping, dirty hair blowing in the morning breeze. Even like that she looked completely self-possessed, almost arrogant, all traces of her sudden panic in the air raid shelter gone. Harding decided that, physically attractive as she was, he really didn't like her at all and that made him feel guilty because she had very effectively come to his aid when he most needed it.

Chapter 21

'Certainly we can help, sir,' the assistant manager said. 'We can't have the Senior Service walking around looking like that. Noisy night, wasn't it?'

Harding agreed that it had been a noisy night, then leaned tiredly against the reception desk of the hotel while the assistant manager selected a vacant room from a list and summoned a page.

'Take this officer to 152 and see to his requirements.'

'Thank you very much indeed,' Harding said to the man and followed the boy.

They gave him a towelling dressing-gown to wear and took his uniform away to brush and press. He bathed quickly, then slumped in a chair and at once emotions flooded over him, confusing him with their variety. Sadness vied with resentment that such a triple shock should so suddenly have come to him. Contempt for his own bull-headedness mingled with a spurt of anger against Mungo for racing after him like a crazed dog, the last thought drowning itself in a surge of self-disgust at his own unspeakable ingratitude. The girl swam in and out of his mind too, inducing more emotive thoughts in him. Gratefulness for her gentle concern, resentment of her quick, tough sarcasm but, strongest of all, the tactile memory of her breasts lingering still in the palms of his hands. His feeling of dislike for so attractive a creature he was too inexperienced to recognize as a sign of his vulnerability to her.

'Your uniform, sir. I don't think the military police will run you in now.'

The assistant manager had brought it back himself.

'You've been very kind. What do I owe you for the use of the room?'

'One bath towel used? I think the Company can just about bear the cost of that, sir.'

Strange, Harding mused, how war produced a friendliness between strangers that would never flourish in times of peace. The man refused money for himself, but accepted a note to be shared by the valet and the page, then departed.

Nearly ready now to face the unpleasant day ahead, Harding dressed, had himself shaved by the hotel's barber and ate breakfast thinking miserably about what had to be done. There was the fate of his parents to be reported to whoever one reported the fate of parents to. The ship to be telephoned so that he could establish the address at which Edna Mungo was living with her mother-in-law and to set in train the arrangements for a naval funeral for her husband. The mortuary Mungo would have been taken to to be located and the body identified. Then the news had to be broken to the two women, and that he was dreading.

In an attempt to get his mind off such a painful duty he searched it for other things he should do, but could think only of replacing the personal belongings he had lost when he had cast his suitcase aside and that he deleted from his mental list. They had been mostly civilian clothes and he had no use for them now as there was no point in taking leave.

The hours that followed were as unhappy as he had expected them to be, the unhappiest the one he spent with the new widow. When her hysteria had subsided sufficiently he had left her in charge of a neighbour because her mother-in-law was visiting relatives somewhere in Lancashire and could not be immediately contacted.

'Yes,' he had said, 'Yes of course I'll come back and see you tomorrow. Now try to rest if only for the sake of my godchild.'

Eventually he had done all that he had to do and it was nearly time to join Lee Lawrence. His body aching with tiredness, eyes gritty from lack of sleep, Harding walked towards the nearest tube station.

The building at the address she had written on the piece of paper was imposing, not at all what he had expected, although why that should be he didn't know. The door of the apartment was imposing too and he pressed the bell-push diffidently as if that might make it ring less loudly. It shrilled, startling him. Much more faintly her voice reached him through the heavy wood.

'Peter?'

'Yes.'

'Come in. It isn't locked.'

In the hall-way a gilt console table with a vase of flowers on it and a matching mirror above. Thick pale blue carpeting and a portrait of somebody's ancestor on the wall at the far end.

'I'm in here. First to your left.'

A dining-room with a long mahogany table, the surface reflecting the candles glowing on it. Two places set, one at either end, far apart. Silver serving-dishes with silver covers, a salad bowl, a bottle of wine in a cooler, on a sideboard. Quiet elegance, subdued luxury all around him, and she so much the focus of it that he found it difficult to associate her with the bedraggled girl of the air raid. Hair piled high on her head, a backless full-length evening dress showing a glimpse of slender-heeled sandals, gloves reaching almost to her shoulders. All of them golden. Turned away from him, she was busying herself with something steaming over a small methylated spirit lamp.

Trying to think of something to say he remembered the habitual American remark 'Nice place you have here', said it and immediately felt foolish.

'It isn't mine. It belongs to a man at our embassy. He's in Washington for a couple of months, so he lent it to me.' She straightened, faced him and added in an expressionless voice, 'There's a couple of whisky sours in the ice-box through there. Go get 'em, will you?'

'Whisky sours coming up,' Harding said and was both pleased and relieved by the steadiness of his voice as though he had contrived an emotionless acknowledgement of one of Bulstrode's orders during a particularly devastating depth-charge attack. His progress towards the kitchen was a determined march and he was unconscious of her amused regard on his retreating back.

Harding stood by the refrigerator trying to gather his wits. Such glossily presented semi-nudity had never occurred to him and he was cursing himself for his failure to say something clever like, 'They look as pretty as they felt last night,' but he should have said that as soon as he saw that what he had thought to be a strap around her neck supporting the bodice of her dress was a choker collar supporting nothing. It was too late now after his quickly averted gaze and her calm regard which had acknowledged nothing out of the ordinary. A glass in each hand he went back to the dining-room.

At times throughout the exhausting day the thought of the possibility of sleeping with Lee Lawrence had recurred to him and he had viewed the prospect with a mixture of excitement and alarm and the fervent but undefined hope that it would somehow be different to being with Stephanie Empson. Now that the outcome of the night ahead had been immediately and dramatically placed beyond question alarm surged into the ascendant.

As the meal progressed the strain on him increased. He had no recollection of drinking his cocktail and was not aware of what it was he was forcing himself to eat, his whole focus of attention on answering her questions about himself and keeping his eyes from the beguiling movements of her breasts. One of them had brushed his cheek when she had stooped to put something on his plate and he knew that he should have turned his head and kissed its silken skin instead of sitting frozen.

A little after that he heard himself say, 'I can't take any more of this,' and her reply, 'Leave it. I always was a lousy cook.'

'I didn't mean that.' Voice no longer steady.

'I know you didn't, Peter. I guess such an unsubtle attempted seduction hasn't come your way too often before.' For the very first time she smiled, an open friendly smile, and the room seemed to light up. 'Which are you going to do?' Lee asked him. 'Scream for help, or take a representative of the colonial press to bed?'

It was so very good, the softly yielding pressure of her against his bare chest in the darkness, the slow caress of long fingers on his hair.

'Something bad happened to you the last time, didn't it honey?'

'Not really bad, but it – it . . .'

'Threw you?'

'Yes.'

'Was it the first time?'

'Yes.'

'It figures. Go to sleep. Nobody around here's going to throw you anyplace.'

Sleeping, waking, loving, then repeating the sequence. Waking finally in daylight and alone, a piece of paper pinned to the pillow beside him. 'Don't go away. Gone to buy you a tooth-brush.' It was all very wonderful. Not like Stephanie Empson. Not like Stephanie Empson in the least. Happiness washed over Harding in a wave so warm that not even the memory of his parents and Mungo could chill it.

Lee returned with the promised tooth-brush, a razor, blades, underwear, and uniform socks and shirt. The clothes bore the label of Gieves, the naval tailors.

Touched, 'I hope you put these on my account,' he said.

She looked at him pityingly. 'Oh sure. They make a habit of handing out merchandize to any floozy who walks in and says to charge it to some officer.'

'Yes, that wasn't very bright of me. What do I owe you?'

'Forget it,' she told him. 'It's just that I couldn't have you take me to lunch looking like a shipwreck survivor. A girl has her pride to consider.'

'I can't take you to lunch, Lee. I promised Mrs Mungo I'd go and see her again today. She may want to talk if she's over the first shock.'

Disappointment was clear in his words and she looked down at him gravely for a moment before saying, 'I like you, Peter Harding. You don't do things by halves. What do you say I come with you? She could maybe use a woman's shoulder to cry on too.'

'Would you really do that?'

'Sure,' she said. 'It's no big deal. Now get out of that sack, hog. The day's a'wasting.'

Edna Mungo said, 'Oh sir,' twice to Harding in a quavering voice, then flung herself past him and at Lee Lawrence. The American girl held her close, jerked her head at Harding and mouthed the word 'Scram'. He let himself quietly out of the little house, feeling guiltily glad that Mungo's mother was away, that there was only one distressed woman to deal with.

There was a pub diagonally across the road. He bought himself a pint of beer there, then stood by the window watching the house he had just left. Seventy minutes later he was still standing there and saw Lee as soon as she opened the front door. Harding left the pub at once and crossed the road to join her.

'She wants to thank you, Peter. Go and get yourself kissed.'

In his turn he found himself holding Edna Mungo, being more nuzzled than kissed, listening to almost incoherent expressions of gratitude, feeling strangely affected by the outburst of this very ordinary woman who seemed to think so much of him for having done what was no more than his job. At last he disengaged himself, patted her awkwardly on the shoulder, told her that the Navy was making all the necessary arrangements and left the house again.

'I expect you'd like a drink about now,' he said to Lee.

She shook her head, took keys from her bag and handed them to him.

'No, darling. If you want to make yourself useful go back to the apartment, pack an over-night bag for me and bring it here. Don't come in. Just leave it inside the front door. Her mother-in-law arrives around nine in the morning. I'll see you shortly after that.

'You don't do things by halves either, do you? Where shall I meet you tomorrow?'

Her hand touched his cheek briefly and she said, 'At the

apartment, of course. You aren't aiming to sleep anywhere else for a while, are you?'

Three days had gone by and they were talking quietly, Lee Lawrence and Peter Harding, in the little room Mrs Mungo Senior called her front parlour, when Bulstrode came in.

'Good morning, sir,' Harding said. 'Darling, this is my Captain, Lieutenant-Commander Bulstrode. Sir, this is Miss Lawrence from New York. We're sort of engaged.'

Bulstrode smiled up at her, taking her hand in his. 'At first sight I can't imagine anyone I'd rather my First Lieutenant was sort of engaged to, Miss Lawrence.'

'Lee. Just Lee, Commander.'

'Fine. I'm Bill. Thank you for cheering up this not very happy occasion by your presence. Peter here will tell you that my chief preoccupation in life is decorative women.'

She returned his smile, watched him turn away and look at the coffin, heard his whispered 'Hello, Charlie Mungo. Bad luck, old chap. We'll miss you and your machine-gun.'

As though that completed the formalities Bulstrode stripped off his raincoat, threw it across the arm of a chair and faced them again. He had opened his mouth to speak when Harding noticed the blue and red ribbon of the DSO on his jacket and said, 'Congratulation, sir. It's about time they gave you that.'

'What? Oh. Thanks. Yes. Wait.' The monosyllables shot out of Bulstrode while he rummaged in his pocket, produced an envelope and gave it to Harding. It contained a six-inch length of blue and white ribbon. Harding blinked, the astonishment on his face clear to see.

'So you didn't know.'

'Hadn't the remotest idea, sir.'

'Ah well,' Bulstrode said. 'What with one thing and another I don't imagine you two have been reading *The Times* recently. It was announced yesterday. Same day as mine. Well done anyway. I picked that up at Gieves for you on the way here.'

'Aren't those the colours of the Distinguished Service Cross?' Lee asked. Bulstrode told her they were and she nodded. 'I thought so. The same as in the States. Give me your jacket, Peter.'

Harding was thinking that the practice of picking things up for him at Gieves seemed to be spreading and he didn't hear her last sentence.

'Off with it, Peter.'

'Off with what?'

'Your jacket, for heaven's sake! I want to stitch a bit of that ribbon onto it.'

'Oh, don't bother. It can wait.'

'No it can't, dummy,' Lee said. 'I'm not doing it for you. I'm doing it for Edna Mungo. She'll be so proud.'

They said good-bye to Charlie Mungo in the big cemetery near his mother's home. A very small officer gave orders to four friends of Mungo's from *Shadow*. They raised their rifles in obedience and fired three volleys at the December sky, the sound lost immediately in the desolate place. A pretty American girl stood a few yards from the group telling herself that war correspondents did not cry. Edna Mungo, flanked by her mother-in-law and Harding, clutched his sleeve and was proud.

Chapter 22

'Please let go of me, Peter.'

Harding was holding her as he had in the air raid shelter, but with happy familiarity now.

'Request denied,' he said.

'No, seriously. There's something I've got to say to you and I want to look at you while I'm saying it.'

She sounded serious too, Harding thought, released her reluctantly, watched her sit upright, swing her legs over the side of the bed and turn to face him. Naked and without make-up she looked about nineteen to him, much too young to be a war correspondent.

'You don't seem old enough to be second-in-command of a submarine,' she said.

He smiled, feeling renewed delight over the coincidence of shared thinking which had grown between them during their few days together.

'You didn't have to look at me to say that, unless you're checking to see if I've aged in the last ten minutes.'

His smile wasn't returned. 'I'm frightened that you're going to be angry with me, Peter. You see, I've been using you.'

'I know,' he told her, 'and I'm practically all used up. Not that I'm complaining.'

Lee stood then, still unsmiling, wrapped a dressing gown round herself, and walked to her desk. When she came back she had a brown cardboard folder clutched to her stomach. She held it there, staring down at him with a worried frown on her face for several seconds before saying, 'You must believe one thing. None of this occurred to me until after I had made my play for you. In fact until after the funeral. I would be terribly miserable if you thought I had been using anybody else.'

Vaguely uneasy, 'What is it, Lee?' Harding asked.

'An article. A short story really. I wanted your permission to send it off to the States.'

'*My* permission? What on earth do you need that for?'

'Because it's about you,' she said, placed the folder carefully beside him and hurried out of the room.

'A British sailor and his loves' the title of the typescript read, with a pencilled note beside it saying 'Yuck. Think up something better than this'.

'Oh no,' Harding whispered to himself and began to read in an agony of embarrassment, but that fell from him before he was halfway down the first page to be replaced by a dawning enchantment. It wasn't about him, not directly about him, nor was he or anybody named, but the characters were immediately recognizable. It was twenty minutes before he closed the folder and looked up to find that Lee, hands clasped in front of her, lower lip caught between her teeth, was standing in the doorway watching him.

Speaking with quiet deliberation, 'It's the prettiest thing I ever read,' he told her, saw her shoulders relax, her lip released, then added, 'I understand about the ship and Edna, but it's a bit strong about me, isn't it?'

She shook her head. 'It grew all the time until, at the end, although he didn't know what you were doing, he died trying to help you do it. Nothing comes stronger than that. It rates more than an epitaph, but that's all I have to give Charlie Mungo.'

'I love you, Lee.'

'Still?'

'More.'

'I'm glad we think so much alike,' she said. 'I thought we did, but now I'm sure. Are you going to take me on the town for your last night?'

'Only if you insist.'

At last she smiled back at him and again there was radiance everywhere. Slipping the dressing gown from her shoulders, 'I'm not insisting,' she said.

'It was a solitary Me110 with a 500-pound bomb slung underneath,' Bulstrode said. 'You know, what the press calls a "sneak raider" when it's German and an "intruder fighter" when it's one of ours.'

Harding nodded. 'When did it happen, sir?'

'Yesterday afternoon. There didn't seem much point in bothering you as you were due back today. Anyway, there was bugger-all you could have done about it.'

They reached the side of the dry-dock and stood, looking at *Shadow* lying on her port side at the bottom of it like a broken toy discarded by a child. It occurred to Harding that the ship had been his home for the best part of two years and that it was the second he had lost within a week. To his surprise he experienced confusion more than sadness, a loss of direction rather than of surroundings which had become familiar to him.

'Anybody hurt, sir?'

'Not seriously. We were incredibly lucky there. Hardly anybody aboard. The Cox'n has a broken leg and half a dozen have cuts and bruises.'

'I see. What happens now? Can she be repaired?'

'Oh yes,' Bulstrode said. 'But it'll take months, so she's nothing to do with us anymore. They're giving me a brand-new T-boat, unnamed as yet. Think of the luxury! Think of the power! A cabin all to myself, a bloody great 4-inch gun and seventeen torpedoes! I'm almost grateful to that Messerschmitt pilot.'

Harding sighed softly, contendedly, his sense of direction coming back to him. 'Well done, sir. When do we join?'

'You don't, Number One. I'm not taking you with me.'

It was like being cut in the street by an old friend. His face rigid Harding turned his head slowly to look at his captain. Bulstrode was grinning.

'They've decided it's time you contributed something more to the war effort, Peter. You join the next Commanding Officer's Qualifying Course.'

'Who? Me, sir?'

'Yes. You, sir.'

'Good God!'

'The Padre assures me that He is just that. Come on. I'll buy you a drink before you go back to London.'

Stupidly, 'Back to London?' Harding echoed.

'Well, your course doesn't start for a fortnight,' Bulstrode said, 'and I thought you might want to be with that American girl you're "sort of" engaged to, but if you would prefer a temporary job running the mail room at the barracks I'll put in a good word for you.'

'Do I have to decide at once, sir?'

'Procrastination is the thief of time,' Bulstrode told him. 'I once had to write that down a thousand times at school as a punishment.'

'What had you done?'

'Failed to decide within the allotted time whether George Washington or Disraeli was the more alike,' Bulstrode said.

Talking nonsense they walked out of Portsmouth Dockyard and along the Hard to the Keppels Head hotel. Wright and Gascoigne were waiting for them in the bar. Harding told them what he wanted to drink, went to the telephone and came back glowing at the memory of the excited, astonished pleasure in her voice when he told her of his imminent return.

'Congratulations, Number One,' Wright said. 'The Captain tells us you're engaged.'

'Thanks. Yes, I am.'

'What's she like? Dishy?' Gascoigne wanted to know.

'Not bad.'

Gascoigne groaned theatrically and appealed to Bulstrode. 'You've met her, sir. You tell us.'

With complete seriousness Bulstrode said, 'A most attractive lady at all times, but when she smiles she's so pretty you want to stand up and applaud.'

Even had Harding disliked Bulstrode before, he would have worshipped him then and found it necessary to stare fixedly at his drink until the wave of pleased emotion engendered by his ex-captain's words had subsided.

He got a little drunk after that, then made his good-byes and went to see Chief Petty Officer Ryland in Haslar Hospital. The coxswain was lying in bed with his broken leg under traction.

'Hello, Cox'n. Tripping over things again?'

''Ello, sir. Yes, always was clumsy on me feet. Nice of you to drop by.'

'Self-interest,' Harding said.

''Ow's that then, sir?'

'They're sending me on my command course, Cox'n.'

''Bout time, sir.'

Harding looked around the big ward with its rows of beds before saying, 'If I pass the bloody thing it'll be months before I'm given an operational command, but if I do get one I was wondering if you'd consider joining me as coxswain. I'll have a completely strange crew to handle you see. I hope you don't mind my asking.'

'I'd 'ave been right pissed off if you 'adn't, sir. I've been with you longer than any other officer in submarines. Course I'll come. You pick yourself a good first lieutenant and the three of us'll lick the crew into shape in no time flat.'

All was very well with Harding when he boarded the train for London and remained so right up to the imposing front door of the apartment. There his world fell apart.

Ashen-faced, Lee Lawrence stood before him in the hall-way beside a pile of luggage. Her eyes were red from crying and there was no vestige on her face of the smile which inspired applause.

'Lee, darling. Whatever's the matter?'

'It's all over for us, Peter,' she said in a coldly controlled voice. 'I'm sailing for the States from Liverpool tomorrow. Leaving London tonight.'

It was as if the words had been a physical blow to the head deflecting his line of sight and he found himself meeting the supercilious regard of the portrait of somebody's ancestor on the far wall over her right shoulder. For a moment he held its painted gaze, waiting for the words 'I'm only kidding', knowing that they would not be spoken, then looked back at her.

'America is hardly at the end of the world. You'll be back.' It took an immense effort to speak as levelly as she had done and to hide his bitter disappointment.

She shook her head. 'I don't think so, my dear. I'll be going further than the States when – when it's possible. Much further.'

Harding put his hands on her shoulders and said, 'Are you going to tell me what this is all about?'

Suddenly she was in his arms, her own holding him so fiercely that his breathing was restricted. Her breath played on his ear as once it had in an air raid shelter, but gustily now as disjointed sentences tumbled out of her mouth. ' . . . telephoned me half an hour ago . . . It'll be on the news broadcasts soon . . . so awful . . . hundreds, thousands killed . . . I don't know how many great ships . . .'

The door-bell shrilled. Slowly Harding disengaged himself, turned and jerked the door open. A man in an old raincoat and a cloth cap was standing outside.

'Yes?'

'Taxi for somebody called Lawrence. That you?'

'No,' Harding told him, 'but Miss Lawrence will be down in a minute.'

The interruption had steadied the girl and with the door closed again she spoke slowly, clearly. 'The Japanese have bombed Pearl Harbor.'

As in the case of Dunkirk, Harding added to his vocabulary another place-name he had never heard of before, another place-name which was to go down in history. It was, he supposed, a port on the Pearl River.

'So what?' he said. 'The Japs have been bombing somewhere in China ever since the early thirties.'

Instant anger on her face changing to confusion, then to understanding. 'No, Peter. Not Canton,' she whispered. 'It's a big American Navy base on Hawaii. Most of the US Pacific Fleet has been destroyed.'

A growing recognition of the inevitability of personal loss left little room in Harding for dismay at the naval defeat suffered by Britain's best friend and mightiest supporter, what little shock he did register swiftly subdued by the realization that, again, good could come from evil. The thought turned itself into words.

'I'm so sorry, Lee, but it isn't all bad you know. With you people in it we can really start winning this war.'

She gave him a small, wan smile, no more than a contraction of the muscles of one cheek before saying, 'You British always have been an eminently practical race, but I doubt if my own folk are going to see it quite the way you do.'

For a moment she stood as though considering the statement, then tossed her head and added, 'Ah, the hell with it! You keep right on being practical and help me with these bags to the cab.'

The weight of the two suitcases she herself carried made her appear almost childishly unsteady on her high-heeled brown leather shoes as she preceded him down the stairs but, despite it, she seemed older to Harding, almost old enough to be a war correspondent. Shock, he supposed. That and her carefully composed features, the golden hair drawn severely back, fastened at the nape of her neck and lying in a loose knot on the collar of the new military-style raincoat she had bought to replace the one torn during the air raid. He picked up the remaining four bags, one under each arm, one in each hand, and followed, still unwilling to believe that she was walking out of his life.

'At least let me come to Liverpool with you,' he said.

The loop of hair swung in a series of negative arcs across her shoulders.

'That would only make it worse, Peter darling. Better to get it over with. Better for both of us.'

He considered the statement calmly all the way to the taxi, kept on considering it while he helped the driver with the luggage then, suddenly, everything was too much for him. His parents and Mungo dead, his ship gone, taking with it a crew he liked almost to a man and a captain he idolized, all within a few days. Now this.

'But we can still be engaged, can't we?' he asked.

It was as though she had read the catalogue of loss in his eyes, heard it in the tautness of his voice when, as once before, she murmured, 'Oh baby,' and took his face in her hands.

'Please, Lee. Even if we will be half a world apart.'

'All right. We'll be engaged. Sort of. Just as you described it to Bill Bulstrode,' Lee Lawrence said and slid her arms around Harding's neck.

The taxi driver shifted the match-stick he was chewing to the other side of his mouth, propped his back against the cab and watched them without interest. It made no difference to him how long they stood there holding each other. The meter was ticking.

Antony Trew

His novels of action and danger, at sea and on land, have been highly praised. A Royal Navy Commander during World War II, Antony Trew served in the Mediterranean and the Western Approaches, and was awarded the DSC.

His books include

TWO HOURS TO DARKNESS   £1.25
THE WHITE SCHOONER   £1.25
DEATH OF A SUPERTANKER   £1.25
THE ANTONOV PROJECT   £1.25
SEA FEVER   £1.50

FONTANA PAPERBACKS

Herman Wouk

One of the mosted talented novelists writing in America
today. All his novels have been high praised bestsellers,
and *The Caine Mutiny* won the Pulitzer Prize.

His books include

WAR AND REMEMBRANCE   £3.50
THE WINDS OF WAR   £2.95
DON'T STOP THE CARNIVAL   £1.95
MARJORIE MORNINGSTAR   £1.50

FONTANA PAPERBACKS

Richard Sharpe

bold, professional and ruthless
is the creation of

Bernard Cornwell

A series of high adventure stories told in the grand tradition
of Hornblower and set in the time of the Napoleonic wars,
Bernard Cornwell's stories are firmly based on the actual
events.

Sharpe's Eagle £1.35
Richard Sharpe and the Talavera Campaign, July 1809

Sharpe's Gold £1.50
Richard Sharpe and the Destruction of Almeida, 1810

Sharpe's Company £1.50
Richard Sharpe and the Siege of Badajoz, 1812

Sharpe's Sword £1.75
Richard Sharpe and the Salamanca Campaign,
June and July, 1812

'The best thing to happen to military heroes since
Hornblower.' *Daily Express*

FONTANA PAPERBACKS

Jon Cleary

'A noble gift for storytelling' *New York Times*

'If escapism is what you are looking for, seek no further.'
Irish Times

Jon Cleary's novels are renowned for their wide-ranging
subjects — adventure . . . family sagas . . . suspense . . .

FONTANA PAPERBACKS

Dudley Pope

'Takes over the helm from Hornblower . . . Dudley Pope knows all about sea and can get the surge of it into his writing.' *Daily Mirror*

'An author who really knows the ropes of Nelson's navy.' *Observer*

'The best of the Hornblower successors.' *Sunday Times*

RAMAGE   £1.75
RAMAGE AND THE DRUM BEAT   £1.75
RAMAGE AND THE FREEBOOTERS   £1.75
GOVERNOR RAMAGE R.N.   £1.95
RAMAGE'S PRIZE   £1.75
RAMAGE AND THE GUILLOTINE   £1.50
RAMAGE'S DIAMOND   £1.75
RAMAGE'S MUTINY   £1.75
RAMAGE AND THE REBELS   £1.75
THE RAMAGE TOUCH   £1.75
RAMAGE'S SIGNAL   £1.50
RAMAGE AND THE RENEGADES   £1.50
RAMAGE'S DEVIL   £1.75

FONTANA PAPERBACKS

Fontana Paperbacks: Fiction

Fontana is a leading paperback publisher of both non-fiction, popular and academic, and fiction. Below are some recent fiction titles.

- ☐ THE SERVANTS OF TWILIGHT Leigh Nichols £1.95
- ☐ A SEASON OF MISTS Sarah Woodhouse £1.95
- ☐ DOUBLE YOKE Buchi Emecheta £1.50
- ☐ IN HONOUR BOUND Gerald Seymour £1.95
- ☐ IN SAFE HANDS Jane Sandford £1.95
- ☐ SHARPE'S ENEMY Bernard Cornwell £1.95
- ☐ A WOMAN OF IRON Sheila Holland £1.75
- ☐ FAIR FRIDAY Peter Turnbull £1.50
- ☐ THREE WOMEN OF LIVERPOOL Helen Forrester £1.95
- ☐ FRIENDS OF THE OPPOSITE SEX Sara Davidson £1.95
- ☐ KNAVE OF HEARTS Philippa Carr £1.95
- ☐ THE SECOND SALADIN Stephen Hunter £1.95
- ☐ ECHOES OF WAR Joan Dial £1.95
- ☐ MAKING WAVES Liz Allen £1.95
- ☐ GLIDEN-FIRE Stephen Donaldson £1.25

You can buy Fontana paperbacks at your local bookshop or newsagent. Or you can order them from Fontana Paperbacks, Cash Sales Department, Box 29, Douglas, Isle of Man. Please send a cheque, postal or money order (not currency) worth the purchase price plus 15p per book for postage (maximum postage is £3.00 for orders within the UK).

NAME (Block letters) _____

ADDRESS _____

_____

While every effort is made to keep prices low, it is sometimes necessary to increase them at short notice. Fontana Paperbacks reserve the right to show new retail prices on covers which may differ from those previously advertised in the text or elsewhere.